SEDUCTIVELY UNDEAD IN DARK RIVER

DARK RIVER DAYS
BOOK FOUR

GRACE MCGINTY

ALSO BY GRACE MCGINTY

Hell's Redemption Series: The Redeemable/The
Unrepentant/The Fallen

Damnation MC Duet: Serendipity/Providence

The Azar Nazemi Trilogy : Smoke and Smolder/Burn and
Blaze/Rage and Ruin

Dark River Days Series: Newly Undead In Dark
River/Happily Undead In Dark River/Pleasantly Undead in
Dark River

Black Mountain Mates: Hunting Isla

Eden Academy Series: The Lost and the Hunted
(Prequel)/Heart of the Hounded (Prequel)/ Rebels and
Runaways (Book 1)/Sweethearts and Savages (Book 2)

Shadow Bred Series: Manix/Frenzy/Feral

Stand Alone Novels and Novellas: Bright Lights From A
Hurricane/The Last Note/ Inside The Maelstrom Part 1
and 2

Omega Lottery: Tryst In The Dark

For my favorite Canadians:

Gillian Geller,
*X thanks you for having his back about the *need* for an
Orgy. Thank you for being the ultimate Smut Queen and a
loyal supporter.*

Skye Cooper,
*Without your support right back at the beginning of my
Dark River journey, this series wouldn't be as popular as it
is. Thank you for pushing me to be better.*

SEDUCTIVELY UNDEAD IN DARK RIVER

FOREWORD

This book is set over fifteen years after the last Dark River novel. A lot of life has happened between the ending of Pleasantly Undead in Dark River, and the beginning of this book.

Including the pups going off to Eden Academy and the rediscovery of the Manix.

You don't have to read either of those series to appreciate coming back to Dark River. Just know, there will be vague references to the events of those books and characters.

If you've read any of my other books, you'll know this is par for the course. Just call me the easter bunny, because I'm dropping easter eggs all over the place.

CHAPTER
ONE

"The Convocation acknowledges Member Raine Baxter, for Endangered Preternatural Creatures."

I raised my hand, giving my best spirit fingers to the stuffy Voice, who was basically here to keep us all in line. "Present," I sang, drawing out the word into at least six syllables.

"May I remind Member Baxter that she does not have to respond," the Voice huffed, and I tried to hide my smirk. Badly, apparently.

"You can remind her until you're blue in the face, Aquarius, but she's still going to do it because she likes to annoy you. It's been twenty fucking years. Get over it," Wilde grumbled, scrawling something in the margins of a book that looked centuries old and made of someone's face. You could still see the ear.

Witches were gross.

I tipped my imaginary hat at Aquarius. He was a witch—not quite as powerful as Wilde, Member for the witches, but not far off. His position as the mediator for the Convocation got him a nice little power boost, so maybe he could probably take Wilde if he wanted. He wouldn't though; Aquarius was a chickenshit.

I waved a hand at all the people in the room. "You know the solution. Promote someone else. Maybe the pretty new Manix Alpha General. He looks like he'd be a good match for the dick-swinging club."

The Convocation had been testosterone-heavy ever since the female Member for the Fae got overthrown by an Unseelie princeling. Aurelius was cute, but he was a douche.

"Could he beat you in a fight?" the Member for the shifters asked.

I speared Alexander—motherfucking dragon and the closest thing I had to a father-in-law—with a scathing expression. "Probably. I bake cakes for a living. I'm not out there rending heads."

The old bastard lifted an eyebrow at me. "We both know he couldn't, Raine, so you're stuck with the position. Time to accept your fate."

"Accept this." I gave him the middle finger, which made the Voice gasp. Alexander just laughed, and I looked around the rest of the room. "Honestly, guys, you've all been around since Alexandria was giving out library cards. Surely one of you knows at least *one person* who could take this over?"

I looked imploringly at Titus, who was the Member for the vampires. And my brother-in-law. Yeah, it was a bit like a hillbilly family reunion when we had these meetings—just six people and a whole lot of incestuousness.

There was a seventh seat, set aside for deities. Lucifer—as in the freaking actual *Devil*—had turned up to watch us play house once. He said he had "a bit of skin in the game now," as did other celestial beings, so they'd switch it up and attend when they felt like it.

Personally, I hoped beyond hope that Lucifer never came to one of these meetings again. He scared the living shit out of me.

Titus shrugged. "I like it when you come to these things. You're at least a hundred years younger than the rest of us, and give the group a modern perspective. And you bring cake."

Honestly, baked goods were the only thing that kept Convocation meetings tolerable. "I'm going to start spitting in the frosting."

Alexander threw his feet up on the table in front of him. No one said anything, obviously, because he was a fucking dragon. "Ha, jokes on you, because he likes that shit."

"Member Alexander!" the Voice gasped.

3

I slammed my hands over my ears. "Ew, too much information."

"Seconded," said Aurelius, the Member for the Fae. "Can we get on with the meeting, or do we have to do this slapstick show every time we meet before we can get to the actual issues?"

I slumped down into the highback chair, which was insanely uncomfortable, and listened to them talk around me. It wasn't very often that one of the problems mentioned in these meetings had anything to do with me or my charges. With the exception of the rediscovery of the Manix. That had been all me.

I was a catch-all, really. A person to gather up all the strays and find them homes, like the supernatural ASPCA. It was rewarding, don't get me wrong. But it had been twenty years, and I still had no fucking idea what I was doing. I was fumbling around, pretending to know what I was doing, like this was prom night of 2016 all over again.

"Are we ready to pass a motion?" the Voice called, and I froze.

Ah shit, I'd zoned out again. I subtly looked around at the people who I'd come to rely on in this insane world of powerful beings and political espionage.

Alexander rolled his eyes. "On the motion on the selective breeding of failing supernatural species," he repeated slowly for my benefit, "I am firmly against."

Jesus fucking Christ, whose idea was that one?

Aurelius gave me a disdainful look. It was like he had his pretty sword of power wedged all the way up his ass. "I vote for. There are more than a few houses of the Fae that are at risk of dying out, and we need them for certain day-to-day industries."

Yeah, that didn't sound like he was breeding House Elves at all. Aurelius gave Dobby a lifetime of servitude. Dobby is a chained elf.

I glared at him. "Obviously, one thousand percent against. For fuck's sake, this isn't the goddamn Dark Ages. Get a grip." Apparently, I wasn't tactful either.

"I'm not inclined to impose on the balance of nature, no matter how tempting," Wilde added, still scrawling notes. Was he writing his opus? Smutty love poems?

Titus shook his head. "Against."

"That's a majority. Motion denied," the Voice announced.

The Djinn Member, who was a particularly gross old guy, scowled at me. "I'm with the girl. She needs to go. We need to break the chokehold that Alexander's *family*"—he spat the word like it started with f and rhymed with duckers—"has on this Convocation. I'm sure I can find someone suitable."

Yeah, no way was I going to get advice on possible replacements from feet-licker Magoo over there. I mean, I drank blood, but I'd once seen him lapping at a girl's foot like she was a never-ending gobstopper.

"I'll take it into consideration." My fake smile suggested that would be when Hell froze over. "Is there anything else?"

The Voice shook his head. "That's all."

I blinked at him. "You guys dragged me all the way to Toronto to discuss whether we should use people as broodmares? Get the hell out of here. I have a life to get back to, kids who are giving me gray hairs, and a business to run." I stood and gathered all my cupcakes, still muttering to myself.

Titus pouted until I finally thrust the box of baked goods at him.

"You should come for dinner," Alexander said, walking beside me as we left the warded conference room.

I shook my head. "Next time. I brought Nico with me, and I promised him we'd hit up the midnight showing of The Rocky Horror Picture Show. It's one of those audience participation ones. He's going to love it." Nico sucked up cheesy pop culture like a sponge.

"And you are taking your security detail?" Titus asked around a mouthful of pink buttercream. He had a lot in common with his brothers; he had Nico's love of all things sweet, and Lucius's love of rending heads. Balance, you know?

I rolled my eyes in his direction. "Buddy is coming, and I'm sure he'll bring guards to watch the exits. No one is trying to wipe me out, because no one wants to take my damn place. They wouldn't even have to murder me to do it. I'd give them the golden key with a smile on my face."

"No, you wouldn't," Wilde called from behind us, though now he'd replaced his weird skin book for a smartphone. Witches. So versatile.

"I so would."

"You wouldn't check them out first? What if it was someone like Asher, or maybe like Aurelius, who wanted to breed certain species back into existence? Would you just hand over your spot then, that golden key?"

I huffed out an angry breath. "You know I wouldn't."

I spun to face them. They weren't my friends, the three men in front of me. If I'd met them in a bar back when I'd first been turned, I would have run as fast as I could in the other direction, until my Converses melted to my feet. But over the years on the Convocation, they'd become equal parts mentors, confidants, and... okay, friends. Family, maybe.

"I'm tired. I'm not made for this. I don't want to jostle for power, or be responsible for the welfare of hundreds of people. I want to lie down in my bed and sleep, rather than think about coups, or the trafficking of supes, or where to put the new preternatural kid who can melt shit with his eyes, so he can't hurt himself or others but can still live a fulfilling life. I don't *want* to make life-and-death decisions for people who are scared and need someone to cling to. I'm too fucking soft, and even after all this time, I have no idea what I'm doing."

"It's why you're perfect for the job—you actually care," Alexander said, roughing up my hair sympathetically.

"Surely, there must be *someone*?" I implored one last time.

Titus shook his head. "You're in a strange position, Raine Baxter. You have the strength of the vampires but the lure of the succubi. You can take what you want by force, or by guile. It would be hard to top that without falling under the purview of a different class like the shifters, or perhaps the witches for your more human subjects."

I screwed up my nose. "Let's not call them subjects, okay?"

Titus rolled his eyes at me, a bizarrely youthful expression on the face of a being I knew to be thousands and thousands of years old. "If you wish. Look, the only being I could think of who would be able to exceed your natural abilities would be the Night Demon, and as far as I'm aware, the last one disappeared hundreds of years ago."

Wilde nodded. "It was in Amsterdam, but I haven't heard a word of it since the late eighteenth century."

Alexander slapped me on the back, and if I'd still

been human, I probably would have flown across the room. "Sorry, kid. But you're doing an amazing job, even if you don't feel like it. We're all just making decisions and hoping they're right; we just have more experience faking it."

I dragged a hand down my face. "I appreciate your words. I'll just keep tossing balls in the air and hoping I catch them, but be warned, if I find someone even remotely suitable, I'm out."

Titus smiled, all fang. "Duly noted, Member Baxter." He stuffed another cupcake in his mouth. "Give my regards to my baby brother." His words were muffled.

Even after all this time, excitement buzzed in my stomach at the thought of Nico waiting for me at the hotel. With one last wave, I was out of there and off to meet the man of my dreams.

Well, one of them anyway.

CHAPTER
TWO

I had confetti in my hair, and Nico was beside me blowing on his party whistle as a naked guy in a gold lamé speedo ran around looking confused on the big screen in front of us, while an alien in drag and a lab coat sang about making him a man. A guy in the row in front of us was fully decked out in a corset and fishnets, along with heels so tall they gave me vertigo just looking at them.

Nico had a huge smile on his face, and I thought my heart would burst. I snuggled into his side as we watched the movie, throwing toast and toilet paper for some obscure reason, surrounded by people who, not that long ago, I probably would have eaten alive.

Literally.

It felt normal now to acknowledge the amount of humans in the room and then forget about it. Mostly because I always had dirty, dirty sex with Brody and Tex before I came to the city, so as far as bloodlust went, I was stuffed. But partially because I had better control over the predator that lived inside me.

After the movie finished, we walked down the quiet streets of the city. I imagined that we must look like two teens on a date, Nico having been turned when he was barely eighteen, and I'd been nineteen when I woke up undead in a ditch. Really, if Nico had been alive, he'd be dust by now, and I'd be pushing forty.

Even now, when I was out with our adopted kids, people assumed we were siblings, because they were now the same age as I'd been when I was turned.

It was weird to think that Nico had seen the rise of the Americas. He'd seen the fall of the Roman Empire. He'd forgotten more things than most people could ever comprehend in their whole lifetime.

Sometimes, the sheer amount of time that Nico and Lucius had been alive gave me existential angst.

"What do you think I'd look like in a corset?"

A direct question, though he didn't mean it that way. Still, I was compelled to answer truthfully. It was Nico's vampire ability, being a walking truth serum, and it was a blessing and a curse.

I grinned, because I had no reason to be untruthful. "Like a wet dream."

"We should have a Rocky Horror night at The Immortal Cupcake. I'll bake."

Nearly two decades was a long time to master the craft of baking, and having Nico with me made it easy. Over the past ten years, we'd only gotten three new vampire members to Dark River, so Nico's work as counselor/interrogator was sparse. He spent more time baking cakes and licking frosting off my body than anything else these days.

He still sat on the Town Council, but things churned along, every year much the same as the last. I wasn't complaining, though. My first years as a vampire were more than eventful enough for a lifetime.

We took a shortcut down an alley that would lead almost directly to our hotel. The small corridor was littered with trash and human life, both casually discarded by society. Someone uncurled from behind a dumpster, and I knew they were human. Their heart was fluttering way too fast to be anything but prey.

"You took the wrong turn, kids," the dirty stranger grunted, pulling a knife.

Damn. There went all my good feelings.

I gave him a sad smile, because I could appreciate the struggle of humanity now more than ever. "You don't want to do this."

His eyes were wild, and spit was pooling at the corners of his lips. He stank of sweat and chemicals, likely drugs, so I didn't think reasoning with him would help. But I had to try, right?

"Just give me all your belongings and fucking leave," he screeched, his voice rising an octave.

I probably would have; I didn't need the money, and he very obviously did. But he made the stupid error of thrusting the knife in my direction, and Nico was in front of him in an instant, snapping his wrist until the knife fell to the ground.

His screams were like a dog whistle for my security. They melted from the surroundings like ghosts, and the guy's eyes wildly bounced around the five men who now circled him.

Ah crap. "Don't kill him."

Buddy and my security weren't bound by Dark River's covenants. They abided by them while in town, but when they went off shift, they did whatever they liked, including eating and killing humans.

Buddy, being the head of my security, just shrugged. He made no promises, and I couldn't compel him. I was his boss, but not his ruler. If I left and he came back to finish the guy off, I had no recourse. We both knew that.

"I mean it. Just leave him. He'll make better choices in life now, won't you?"

The guy was gasping in fear, like a fish out of water, his chest heaving out foul-smelling air in my direction. "I swear, I swear!"

I raised an eyebrow that said *See?*

Nico cleared his throat. "Will you ever try to rob a person with the threat of violence again?"

I appreciated he just didn't leave it at "rob a person again." You couldn't expect miracles.

"Yes."

Ah, damn.

"Sorry, man. I tried," I told the guy, and continued down the alleyway, Nico at my back. Security usually hung back when I was with Nico or Lucius. There wasn't a vampire alive—except maybe Titus—who could take either of them in a fight. But they still had a job, so they hovered around.

Nico wrapped an arm around my waist. "I'm sorry, Raine."

I hated to say I'd become desensitized to death, but it no longer affected me quite how it once did, back when I was still so close to my humanity. You couldn't live with men like Lucius and X and not become a little blasé about death. I mean, Lucius had wooed me with severed body parts.

"It's fine. Unfortunate, though. Let's run back to the hotel?" That way, no more dumb humans could appear and irritate the ancient vampire beside me.

He reached out, stroking his fingers down my cheek. "I know you just want to go home, but it is too close to dawn to run there without hurting you."

I sighed, because I knew that. It took us about four

hours to run from Toronto to Dark River, more if we took breaks along the way to feed. Which we had to. Expending that much energy was hell on the body. We'd taken our time getting here, sprinting short distances over two nights, and spending all day in bed, much to our security's disgruntlement.

I wrapped my fingers in his. "I know. Tomorrow is soon enough, but let's not go the long way?"

He kissed me softly, and I was still awed by the amount of love that shone in his eyes every time he looked at me. It hadn't dimmed even a little, despite the fact he'd once seen me vomit grape-purple frosting after having a cupcake-eating contest with X.

Apparently, forty-five was the limit, even for vampires.

He'd seen me crying, stressed, in every contorted sex position known to man or supernatural. And he still loved me.

"Whatever you wish, Sweetheart." We ran all the way back to the hotel, and once again, the Concierge gave us the side-eye. I got it, I really did.

We arrived early in the morning, after staying out all night. Nico was dressed like Rainbow Brite had sex with a discoball, in a pair of fluro orange parachute pants and a sequined jacket in a rainbow of colors. His t-shirt said *Fangs For The Memories* over a set of lips with bleeding vampire fangs. A bold fashion choice to be sure, given what we were. I was in a skintight faux-leather skirt and one of Tex's torn band t-shirts. Another reason why most of the Convocation Members hated me.

We slipped into the elevator, and Nico raised an eyebrow as my security detail stepped forward. "I am going to try and make my consort come in the time it takes to reach the penthouse. I suggest you catch the next one."

Buddy didn't even look surprised anymore. "We'll take the stairs," he said as the doors slowly closed between us.

I slapped Nico's chest. "That's embarrassing," I chastised.

"More embarrassing than when he caught you suspended from the ceiling in X's ropes?"

I closed my eyes at the horrifying memory. X was still tickled pink about how mortified I'd been, trussed up from the ceiling like a prized ham, while my security gaped in the doorway of the house.

Let's just say, no one forgot to knock anymore.

Nico hefted me into his arms and pressed me easily against the mirrored walls of the elevator. He had my skirt pushed up around my hips and my thighs pressed against his ears in the time it took me to say, "Oh shit."

"I made a promise," he purred against my pussy, and I squeezed his head gently with my thighs.

You know what the best thing was about being

with a man for twenty years? Especially horny-ass supernaturals? They knew how to make you come in the time it took to climb nine floors in an elevator.

It should be impossible. Nico just saw it as a challenge.

And as I came against his talented damn mouth, his fangs buried in my femoral artery, I acknowledged that impossible was just a state of mind.

CHAPTER
THREE

We went straight to The Immortal Cupcake because I'd left Lucius in charge, and honestly, I kind of expected the place to be strewn with dead bodies. He was getting better, able to go longer and longer without my presence keeping him sane, but still... he was Lucius.

The Immortal Cupcake was basically empty, only a few diehards sitting at the tables, all of them facing the kitchen. Tex was behind the counter and when he turned toward me, his smile bright—like I'd been gone a decade rather than two days—my heart melted. No one could do that to me the way Tex could, my beautiful mate.

"Raine, you're back," he breathed, moving around the counter. I met him halfway, kissing him softly as he wrapped his arms around me. I breathed his scent in deeply. The way I missed my shifter mates was always different to the way I missed the rest of my guys. It was the connection between us. Our bond burned deep in my chest and ached when I was away from them.

I looked up at Tex, who was finally losing the softness of youth. He looked like he was in his mid-twenties now, rather than the forty years he'd been walking the earth.

We didn't talk about what would happen when he got old. Didn't talk about what would happen when he died. He had decades and decades before that was an issue, and Brody said that seeing how Tex had an actual animal, he should live for almost as long as a regular shapeshifter.

He frowned down at me. "Why do you feel sad?"

I sucked in a shuddering breath. "I'm not sad. I just love you so much, that's all."

His jaw tensed, and he kissed me softly again. I wanted to turn him, but turning a shifter to a vampire didn't work well, apparently. They lost their animal and went mad. I'd be sentencing him to an eternity of blind madness. No matter how selfish I was, I couldn't do that to him.

I squeezed him tight and stepped away. "I thought you were in Nîso?"

He grinned. "Judge called. He and Lucius weren't

really… coping with the customer service side of the business."

I grimaced. Yeah, I could see that. Normally, one of the kids would be around to smooth things over, but they were out of school, living up their first year of adulthood. They didn't come home as much anymore, and that was okay. But I worried about them every single day.

Parenthood was a repeated loop of anxiety and joy. I was going to go back in time and kick Lucius's ass for gifting me a "puppy."

I cupped Tex's cheek. "Thanks for coming to the rescue. I better go and see if they've caused a massacre in the kitchen."

Tex winced, which was never a good sign. I smiled at the customers, slipping through the swinging doors and into the kitchen.

It looked like a warzone. There were cakes everywhere, some sunken in the center, some burned on the edges, and Judge was sitting on the bench beside the range hood, smoking directly into the vent.

"Judge, you can't smoke in the *kitchen!*" I hissed, quietly enough that no one in the dining room would hear.

"It was that or murder Lucius, and I figured you were attached to him now."

The ancient vampire in question looked at Judge. "You couldn't take me in a fight if I had one leg removed and you snuck up when I was buried deep in Raine." Then he looked back down at the cake in front of him. It was perfect. He frosted it carefully, spinning the board to get it evenly coated. Then he pressed too hard, and the spatula cut into the cake, making him growl. His fist came down on the cake, and buttercream flew everywhere.

Guess that explained the chunks of cake all over the benches.

"Lucius. Baby. What are you doing?"

"Making it perfect." He went and got more ingredients, and started making another cake.

I stared at him, then looked over at Judge, who shrugged. "You have a new thing on the menu. Deconstructed cake jars. Tex's idea. Lucius got it into his head that he was somehow less if he couldn't make the perfect cake, with edges so sharp you could slice an apple with them."

He stubbed out his cigarette and threw it in the trash, sauntering over to me. He leaned down to kiss me softly, and he tasted like Judge. Even though he'd cut down on the smoking when the pups came to live with us, he still snuck one in every now and then.

"You gotta stop letting him watch those baking shows. I tried to tell him that they didn't actually make that shit in six hours. There's a whole team of bakers out the back making the 'finished' cakes. He didn't believe me."

I stroked his wild hair back behind his ears, running my thumbs over his high cheekbones. "Thank you for watching the cafe for me. I know it's not easy."

He leaned down and ran his lips along my jaw, then kissed me softly again. "I know a way for you to make it up to me," he whispered against my lips, making my body pulse with need. Tex cleared his throat, and I saw him adjust his dick in my peripheral vision.

Judge nipped my lip until it bled a little, making Lucius's focus snap away from the bowl of ingredients in front of him. My sexy drifter winked and stepped away, going over to talk to Nico about our trip.

I focused on the predator looking at my bleeding lip with hungry eyes. "Lucius, what are you doing?"

"Baking the perfect cake. I'm a thousand years old. I saw the invention of refined sugar. Of chocolate. I should be able to bake a cake."

I stepped closer, until my body was pressed along his back, my arms around his waist. "What's the perfect cake look like?"

I didn't "manage" Lucius, like most people thought. The years of ennui, of the immortal madness, had done irreparable damage to him. But I accepted that. Loved him, regardless of the fact you never knew if you were going to wake up beside a cold-blooded murderer, or the man who'd taught the pups to defend themselves in the backyard, with sticks that were meant to represent knives. After an absence, I didn't know if I was going to get the guy who'd left me severed heads as courting gifts, or the man who made love to me like I was his last salvation.

No, people thought I was bringing out the good in Lucius, when really, I loved both versions of him. Deep down, they were just reflections of the man inside. The man who loved his twin, who loved our kids, who loved me in a way that was all-consuming.

"Three tiers, white buttercream so smooth that it looks like silk. Moist but with a defined crumb."

I hummed a non-committal noise. I slid to the side of him, so I could see his face. Moving my hand over his, I twined our fingers together. "You know what my perfect cake looks like?"

He was watching me with those dark eyes. I stroked his fingers through the remains of his previous cake, covering them in destroyed cake and butter-cream. I lifted his hand so it was between us, and then I sucked on his index finger, pulling it from my lips with an audible pop.

"Like this. And this..." I moved onto the next finger, swirling my tongue around the tip. Then the next, until his fingertips were clean again. "Mmm, perfect."

His eyes were on fire. I gasped as he grabbed a knife beside him and cut my shirt from my body, then my skirt, with supernatural precision. He physically tore my underwear from me with his bare hands.

That was how I found myself naked and laid across pieces of destroyed cake. He picked up a handful and smeared it down my body. It all happened so quickly that my head was spinning.

"If you throw in potato chips, pretty sure this is one of Rainy Day's greatest fantasies," Judge laughed from across the room.

I could vaguely hear Nico and Tex closing up the cafe early. God, I loved them.

Lucius's tongue ran up my body, eating the cake with gentle bites on my flesh, and I moaned.

"Fuck me. I'll leave you two to it," Judge growled, hotfooting it from the kitchen.

That was the secret to a long-lived polyamorous relationship. Knowing when a moment was something between two people or for the whole group. Especially with Lucius. Some of us just enjoyed sharing all the time, like Judge, Tex and X. There was always a "more dick, the better" policy with those three.

But I still tried to make one-on-one time with each of them. It wasn't easy, especially at the beginning, but I couldn't be happier. *We* couldn't be happier.

Lucius sucked on my clit, and I rocketed into a sitting position. "Fuck..." I breathed, and his eyes looked like pure mischief. He dragged me off the bench and spun me, bending me over the countertop as his cock pressed against my entrance. He licked the cake off my back as he thrust inside me, and my nails scraped on the steel countertop as I tried to hang on against his punishing pace.

The stroke of his tongue, combined with the pounding of his cock, had me screaming his name. He curled himself along my back until his lips touched the side of my neck, and then suddenly, his teeth were buried deep in my jugular, as he held my hips tightly so I couldn't move. He had me locked against his body, his movements short and sharp, hitting me in just the right spot to draw out my orgasm as my body convulsed from his bite.

Finally, his tongue licked over the bite in my neck, before he pulled back. He lowered me back to my feet, leaning down to kiss me. "You're my perfect cake too. Don't leave again."

Kissing a killer was always a funny thing. Vicious and soft. Dichotomous, almost.

"Never forever," I promised, like I did every time I came home.

CHAPTER
FOUR

I was sitting with Tex, Judge and X at our regular table in Bert and Beatrice's Diner the following morning when Walker strolled in, his new deputy on his heels. Hanna had turned up in Dark River about three years ago, a former New York City detective who'd had the unfortunate luck to stumble into a vampire nest late in the nineties. She'd been a rookie, barely more than twenty-four, and they'd eaten her alive. Not a euphemism.

One of the vampires, Josiah, had felt bad enough that he'd turned her, and had kept her sated and happy until she just couldn't deal with taking lives to feed anymore. Not when her own turning had been a crime against the natural order of things.

So when she and Josiah had petitioned to join Dark River, it had been an easy yes. It had been even easier to place her in the Sheriff's Department with Walker. With the increased interaction between the different species, especially coming from Eden and Nîso, Walker needed the help.

Judge, who was technically deputized, wasn't the type of law and order the town needed. Both he and X —and to a more extreme extent, Lucius—were kill-now-ask-questions-later type of guys.

Hanna went and sat with Josiah, who smiled at her like the sun rose and set with her. So sweet.

"Those two make me want to gag," Judge grumbled. He was not a romantic, even after all this time.

X had me on his lap, his hand gripping my thigh so high up, it was bordering on pornographic. The townspeople were used to it now, but I still nudged his hand further down. He huffed, but nibbled the back of my neck. "I have better ways to make you gag," he purred at Judge, thrusting up against my ass cheeks, and Judge rolled his eyes.

"Not with your tiny two inches," he snarked back, and my lips twitched. I knew what happened next.

"Two inches?" X's outrage was real. He lifted me off his lap and into Walker's arms, then grabbed the button of his pants. "This is a fucking bratwurst, not some kind of tiny chipolata—"

Walker immediately tossed me back at X, like I was some kind of football, but at least it kept his hands busy and his public nudity to a minimum.

"Put the girl down, Sassenach, she's got legs fer a reason," Beatrice grumbled, setting our food on the table.

"To go over my shoulders when we're nak—" I elbowed X in the gut, and he let out a loud, "*Oof!*" He was in fine form today.

Beatrice pointed a rolled-up set of cutlery at my English killer. "You be keeping that to yerself, otherwise Bert will be getting ideas, and I'm not as flexible as I once was."

Well... that was a mental image that I didn't need. I gave X a chastising look before he quipped back something terrible, and thanked Beatrice. The crafty old vampiress gave me a teasing wink as she bustled away.

Walker sat down beside me, leaning over to kiss my cheek, his hand stroking down my spine. "Good morning. Where's everyone else today?"

Craziest thing about having seven mates was how rarely we were all together in one room without a shit-load of planning, especially after I'd become a Convocation Member.

"Brody is still up at Nîso, but he said he was coming home for dinner tonight." That was actually around six a.m., but the day ran differently for the rest of us. Brody had taken to eating his meals in reverse, like the champion he was, so he could have dinners with us. When the pups were little, we'd tried to be more stereotypically human so their circadian rhythms wouldn't be screwed up for eternity, but now they were away at school and off on their own adventures, we'd swapped back. Tex didn't mind, but Brody sometimes struggled switching between his life in the light, and his love in the dark.

"Nico had to get an early start at the office and catch up on his paperwork before we open The Immortal Cupcake. Lucius is at home in bed."

Lucius didn't really enjoy coming to the diner, and the townspeople didn't enjoy it either. We didn't force it, so we usually only came to Bert and Beatrice's for breakfast. Lucius was a late sleeper so he didn't care, though given that he'd once led the most feared vampire military force, it was kind of surprising how much he enjoyed a good lie-in.

Walker leaned closer, brushing his lips over my temple like he couldn't help but touch me. "I missed you. How was the city?"

"Loud and filled with humans," I sighed, resting my head on his shoulder. "I prefer Dark River. People are too unpredictable." I kept thinking of the mugger in the alley. What a waste. "Anything exciting happen while I was away?"

His lips spread in a grin. Oh, this was going to be good. "Harriet cut off Arnold's dick when she caught him fucking a tree. She's convinced it was a dryad, and that he was cheating on her. But that's not why she cut it off," he said softly, so only my ears could hear. "She startled him so badly that he jerked wrong and got his dick stuck in the tree. She decided that cutting it off would be the best solution."

I winced. Not all vampires were created equal. I wasn't sure what hallucinogenic drugs Harriet and Arnold had been on before they were turned, but they'd made some serious Swiss cheese of their brains. That kinda stuff didn't manage to heal when they turned into vampires. So to say they were less than... reasonable in their responses, well, that was probably being kind.

"Hanna had to come out with the chainsaw and cut his dick out of the tree so X could reattach it."

I looked at X, who was vibrating with laughter around his porridge. "Poor bastard," he said with so much mirth, it was hard to take his words seriously. "I don't know who looked more pale, Arnold or Officer Hanna."

I would've thought that after twenty years, the people of Dark River would stop surprising me. But apparently, if you put a whole bunch of bloodthirsty vampires in a small area, make them go Vamp-Vegan, and then give them mundane lives, they were an endless sitcom of crazy shit.

I loved this town.

I'd just taken the first bite of my deep-fried banana and PB&J sandwich, moaning at the glory of it, when my phone rang. I groaned, swallowing. Fuck it.

I tugged it out of my boobs—because who needed a purse when you had a bra and no boob sweat once you're undead?—and hit the answer button. "Raine Baxter."

"Member Baxter, this is Helios from the Enforcers stationed in Los Angeles. There's a situation that needs your attention."

My breakfast turned to a lump in my stomach as I sighed. "I'll be there as soon as I can."

RUNNING ALL the way to LA would be ridiculous, but luckily, the Convocation kept a large fleet of private planes with great tinting on hand. Buddy and my bodyguards played poker at the back of the plane, and my unofficial bodyguards were with me. My blood-thirsty trio.

Lucius was spinning a ring around and around his finger, his body physically close to mine. He hated flying the most. He definitely would've preferred to run to LA. But we weren't all three thousand years old.

Judge and X sat opposite me. I really didn't need all three of them plus my guards, but Lucius had missed me, and honestly, I couldn't leave again so soon without taking him with me. At least, not without some seriously crazy consequences—no pun intended.

Judge had contacts in LA, plus it was his turn to accompany me. And X? He just had FOMO. We didn't really get out of town much for anything but Convocation meetings and the odd uprising, so he always wanted to come when the possibility of Convocation-sanctioned violence was to be had.

He was sharpening his knives, and the air hostess was looking gray. She was definitely a shifter of some kind—I wasn't sure which, without Brody here—and her hand shook as she put a cup of tea down in front of X.

"Did you put sugar in this?" he asked lightly.

"Yes, sir."

"Oh love, no one calls me sir unless they're wrapped in silk ropes and tied to my ceiling." He looked up at her, and his eyes glinted in a hard, deadly way. "I don't think you'd enjoy that, would you?" His voice was like the brush of his fangs along vulnerable flesh.

"No, s—" She cut herself off, shaking her head rapidly. "Uh, no. I wouldn't. No offense."

Just like that, the bubble of his menace popped. I knew for a fact it could be jarring. "No worries then. You're not my type, really. I like my martinis a little less shaken, if you know what I mean?"

Judge rolled his eyes. "No. No one knows what you mean." He looked at the hostess. "That'll be all."

The girl ran to the cockpit. Poor thing. I gave X a

stern look, but he just grinned at me. Fuck, that smile always got me. It always led me into making terrible decisions that somehow always resulted in an insane amount of pleasure.

I rolled my eyes at him and called Buddy down. When the guy appeared, I gave him a tight smile. "We should do a quick briefing."

"Sure thing, boss."

He knew I hated when he called me boss; he just did it to stir shit. Because I didn't have enough shit-stirrers in my life.

"Previously unknown nagini is being held by the Vamp Nation for trying to kill her lover, a vampire. Normally, they'd have just executed her, but they think she might be the last of her kind, so they called me in. I'm required to punish her for her transgressions, while ensuring she doesn't die and make yet another race extinct."

The pressure was fucking intense.

"A nagini?" Buddy asked, seemingly unfazed that there were still species roaming the earth that he didn't know after hundreds of years.

I sighed with relief that it wasn't just me. I had to Google this shit too, you know? "Snake woman. Not a two-natured one like Tex. She's apparently legitimately half woman, half snake. Though how she gets away with that in human society is a mystery to me."

Buddy snorted. "Not even close to the strangest thing you'd see in LA."

I'd never been to LA before becoming a vampire. Even now, I'd only ever gone to a Convocation meeting there and departed straight back to Dark River, but given Judge's snorted agreement, I'd take Buddy's word for it.

"Are we going to have trouble with the city's vampire nests?" I asked Lucius, and he looked at me like I was stupid. I guess it helped to have the biggest and baddest on your side after all. "Politically speaking, I mean. Do we need to ask permission?"

Politics wasn't Lucius's thing. Decapitation, yes. Diplomacy? Not so much.

"I was walking these lands before they were even turned. They should be asking *my* permission," he grumbled.

X rolled his eyes. "We know. You're so old, your pubes are gray." He turned to me. "Should be fine. We're there for a reason. In and out and done. Like Judge in bed."

There was a time that Judge would have brooded over this obvious camaraderie, with any signs of attachment—including friendship—met with distance and cool disdain. But now he just shot X the finger. Problem was X grabbed that finger and sucked it like a dick.

Buddy didn't even blink anymore. When he'd first

started, the very concept of the two most feared vampire assassins to ever walk the planet fucking like horny teens had seriously thrown him. Now, they wore their sexuality like a shield.

They loved each other. It had taken twenty fucking years, but they loved each other. And me. And Tex.

I fucking missed Tex.

"Member Baxter, we are beginning our descent into the city. We should land in twenty minutes," the Captain announced over the speaker.

I shook my head at the two men still eye-fucking each other. "Okay. We'll make it quick. But let's be alert. I don't want to fuck up anything; I just want to go home."

Famous last words.

CHAPTER
FIVE

The first sign that everything was about to go FUBAR was the fact we were met on the tarmac by at least ten vampires. Dark River vampires looked like extras from a sitcom most of the time, but these guys were taking the vampire stereotype and owning it. All black attire. Long hair. High collars. They looked like extras from a dinner theater company, where they'd reenact *Dracula* while you enjoyed either the chicken or the beef.

My bodyguards flared around me unobtrusively, but my guys, my lovers... well, there was nothing subtle about their movements. Judge faded into the darkness almost immediately, and honestly, he moved stealthily considering we were all supernatural creatures with superior senses.

X didn't do subtle. He pulled out his switchblade and started to clean his teeth with it. His eyes were hooded, his face seemingly relaxed. But I knew that flirtatious expression on his face. He was flirting with Lady Death, and she was his oldest mistress.

Lucius stepped off to the side, but a foot or so in front of me, ready. His hand flexed, and I knew that he was holding himself back from gutting them all. My blood had made him better... but what was better for a mass-murdering psychopath? An occasionally murdering serial killer?

I stepped closer to him and grabbed his hand, twining his fingers in mine. Maybe we should have joined the mile high club before we arrived. We both would have been more relaxed.

I gave the vampires in front of me a tight smile. "Gentlemen, and uh, one gentlewoman in the back there? Way to go. Undead equality, am I right?" I cleared my throat. "What can I do for you?"

The main guy—at least, I assumed he was, considering everyone was fanned around him—made a disbelieving noise. "I didn't believe it when I heard, but seeing is proof, is it not? The great Lucius, made soft by a girl. A mere fledgling."

Oh, he was going to be one of those. For fuck's sake. I really didn't have time for this bullshit.

"Let's cut the shit. Yes, I saved him with the power

of my magical vagina. No, it's not up for sale. And if your boy back there even thinks about flashing fang again, I'll have my security end him for threatening a Convocation Member."

The days after I'd become a Convocation Member for more than just the succubi had been hard. I was a previously unknown player, very young in my years as an immortal, now with a small but powerful group of preternaturals under my protection. Not everyone had taken it well, and the first few years had been all about bloody displays of power.

I wasn't an idiot. I knew people thought I coasted on Lucius and Nico's power to maintain my hold on the position, and honestly, they weren't wrong. By definition, as a succubi, I was a lover, not a fighter.

But man, I inspired some scary fuckers to fight in my stead, and they *enjoyed* it. They'd raze the world if anyone hurt me. Honestly, it still made my chest feel full thinking about the bloodbath Lucius, X and Judge would make of this vampire's nest if they harmed me.

Call me psycho, but it made me equal parts giddy with happiness and horny as hell.

"Of course, madam," the guy sneered. "We're here to escort you to our nest, at the request of our sire."

I raised a single eyebrow. "Please, thank your sire for me, but unfortunately, my schedule doesn't allow for visiting."

"If Rebus thought we were just going to walk into his home, you may need to think about your succession planning, because the old fuck is losing it," X said in a bored tone.

The fang-baring vamp lunged forward, but Judge was immediately behind him, breaking his neck. I hadn't even seen him move. Lucius was in front of me, blocking me from attack, and I could feel the rest of my guards spread out around my back.

X was still cleaning his teeth with his switchblade, even though everyone was hissing and snarling. "Calm your fucking panties. He'll be fine. Just twist that shit back and give him some blood." He gave me a look. "When did everyone get so dramatic?"

I grinned at him. "Everyone's always been this dramatic. You're just away from it now."

I had one hand on Lucius's spine, and I guess it probably looked like I was holding him for support, but in reality, I was stopping a damn bloodbath and we all knew it. One more act of aggression and I'd take my chances, though. The paperwork would be a bitch, but I found that in the supernatural world, the title only gave you so much. Sometimes you had to demand respect, or you had to take it by force.

It didn't matter if I hated every minute of it.

I gave the vampire in charge a smile, my eyelashes fluttering. "There's no need for this," I cooed, my now trained succubus powers spreading across the area around me. I still couldn't direct it at a single person if I used my powers intentionally like this, but I'd deal with that later. "Please, give your sire my gratitude, but we really must be off."

The older vampire in front was blinking rapidly, but he was also nodding. Win. He made a gesture with his hand, and they all loaded back up into their dark SUVs. They left the fang-happy vampire on the tarmac, and if I knew nothing about their nest, then that would have been enough.

I looked at Buddy, who sighed and walked over, twisting the dude's head back in the right direction and dragging him under a refueling tank where he'd be out of the way of the sun until his body healed him enough to move.

"What a bunch of fucking numpties," X grumbled. "Like we needed a fucking car transport to run a few miles. Does he think we're idiots?"

I shrugged, because in my experience, older vampires weren't idiots, but they were as vain as they were old. Whoever Rebus was, it probably didn't even occur to him that a "fledgling" vampire like myself would even consider defying his orders. If I hadn't had Lucius, X and Judge with me, he might have been correct. My bodyguards were good, but I preferred them alive-dead to dead-dead, especially when it was over some stupid power move.

We sprinted toward the Enforcer headquarters in LA, not as fast as we normally would because not all the security were vampires. However, most of them could still travel faster than human eyes could follow.

The Convocation headquarters in LA was a huge glass monstrosity with heavily tinted windows and at least thirty-six floors. In contrast, the Enforcer headquarters was a laundromat around the corner from the Convocation headquarters. Seventy percent of the washing machines had out-of-order signs, and the place looked like it hadn't been scrubbed in a decade. It was the kind of establishment where the homeless would sleep out of the cold. Which, I guess, kind of worked for the vampires.

Lucius led us back through a metal door that read *Staff Only*, and if the guy scrubbing his underpants in the sink thought that eight well-dressed people being in this scumhole was weird, he kept it to himself. He also didn't make eye contact.

Once you were through the heavy metal doors, you walked down a hallway lined with other doors, turning left into a completely random one, then down the hall, right through another, and so on, until you were completely turned around. Guess that stopped any curious humans making it anywhere they shouldn't until help arrived. And by help, I meant an Enforcer coming and making them a snack. And then dead.

The last door opened into a room filled with technology. I lifted an eyebrow at Lucius. He scowled around the room, especially when every Enforcer in there stopped dead.

Or stopped deader.

Shit, you'd think undead jokes would get old, but I could confirm with twenty years of anecdotal evidence that they really didn't.

"All this... technology," Lucius muttered with distaste. "This wasn't how I ran my branch."

There was a soft laugh from deeper in the room, and a beautiful ash-blonde woman stepped out from the darkness. "Lucius. Still disdainful of the twenty-first century, I see."

Ho-lee-fuck.

She was gorgeous. Like the love child of a Victoria's Secret model and some Russian princess. And she was looking at Lucius with the expression of a friend. And lover.

Ugh. Here it came. The burn of jealousy that ate at my gut every time I thought about my millennia-old consorts having other lovers, like they'd been monks during the fucking Dark Ages. Despite my brain knowing that, the succubus—okay, I couldn't blame it *all* on the succubus, but what was the point of being an almost extinct mythological creature if I didn't?—hated running into women, and men, who they'd fucked before. Worse still were the people they'd actually loved.

That definitely cut deeper.

"Ariana," Lucius grunted, barely even glancing at her as his eyes continued around the room. "I see you've doubled your force."

She shrugged. "With no boogeyman to keep them in line, the plebeians are bold. At least there had been some measure of control with the threat of the Judge, Jury and Executioner coming to murder them while they rested. Even after they were no longer a viable option, there'd still been the threat of the famous Lucius turning his all-seeing eye to them. Better to be murdered in your sleep, am I right? But now... Now they run wild because you three are up in Canada playing house."

There was censure in her tone that really, really rubbed me the wrong way. Still, I pasted a pleasant smile on my face. "Apologies. However, no one wants to be a monster for eternity, just because sires don't care enough to ensure their progeny don't turn into sociopathic murderers, am I right?" I stepped forward, holding out a hand. "We haven't been introduced. I am Raine Baxter, Convocation Member for Endangered Preternatural Creatures. Please, call me Raine." I used a touch of my power, and there was a low murmur of hushed groans around the room.

Ariana was forced to shake my hand. "An honor." Her tone was a little dismissive, so obviously she didn't swing my way. Oh well. One day, I'd get a bit of respect. Or I'd get some other schmuck to take over this role so I didn't have to do this posturing bullshit.

Lucius stepped up to my side, his blond brows pulled low over his eyes. "Apologies, my consort." He lifted my wrist to his lips, scraping his fangs across the pulse there in a way that was both intensely erotic and blatantly claiming.

Ariana's eyes narrowed on the caress with hunger now, then anger. Scorned lover, then. Man, not my fault she couldn't compete with the Xanny of my blood and my around-the-world trick in the bedroom.

Lucius dropped my hand, but stayed at my side, his hand possessively on my spine. Argh. I loved this man.

Ariana sucked in a sharp breath. "The prisoner is this way." She spun on her heel, her long, silken hair floating out behind her like she was a haircare model. She led us through the control room and down a long corridor of glass-walled rooms. There were all sorts of prisoners in there, most of which I couldn't identify.

One vampire was throwing himself repeatedly against a wall, bouncing off, then getting up and running at it again. It didn't even make a dent in the wall, but was banging him up pretty good.

Finally, we got to the right cell. Ariana flicked a switch beside the door, and a harsh spotlight shone down on the prisoner. It was so bright, I even winced involuntarily.

I didn't miss Ariana's subtle smirk at my expression. Bitch. They definitely used those lights for torture.

"Dahlia Laquesh. The distress of her fledgling vampire lover drew his nestmates. They got there just in time to prevent his death."

The girl in the cell was tiny, sitting in a wheelchair in the middle of the room, a rug thrown across her lap. She had lank, dark hair that hung over her face, and her shoulders were curled in.

"How could someone so small kill a vampire, fledgling or not?" I asked.

Ariana screwed her nose up in disgust, pressing a button on the intercom beside the door. "Get up, prisoner. There's someone here to see you."

Just like that, the girl moved from the wheelchair in a sinuous movement, her body stretching and elongating until she was coiled tall in the center of the room, the long length of her scaled snake body stretching.

Holy shit.

"She tried to swallow him whole."

I blinked. Then I blinked again.

X leaned over, pressing the intercom button. "Pro

tip, snake-girl—when a man says he wants to try deep-throating, that's not what he means."

I slapped his hand and swallowed down a groan, but couldn't help the smirk that curled my lips. I really couldn't take this bastard anywhere, but damn, he never failed to make me laugh.

CHAPTER
SIX

"**B**ut did he die?" I repeated for the tenth time. I'd been arguing with Ariana and the infamous Rebus for four hours. He'd turned up to argue for the death penalty, and the stink eye he was giving me was so venomous, it was a wonder my skin didn't melt from my bones.

It took everything in me not to flip him the bird. Honestly, I was exhausted. I wanted cheese fries. I wanted a bed, and to be bracketed on all sides by my naked lovers.

I wanted to be home.

"He says she just attacked out of nowhere. One moment they were kissing, the next she unhinges her jaw and is swallowing him headfirst."

I was about to protest that if she was eating him headfirst, then his ability to yell for help was impressive, but Rebus raised a hand to silence my protest. I wondered if I could get Judge to snap it off at the wrist.

"It is beside the point," Rebus continued. "It is the principle of the matter. She *wanted* him to die."

Dahlia the nagini was whipping her head from side to side like she could dispute his words with her vehemence alone. "No! He wanted to die. He asked me to do it. He wanted to be a part of me forever."

That was dumb. Even snake creatures pooped. He'd eventually just be vampire poop. But as I was meant to be defending her, I kept that to myself.

"See? It's not Miss Laquesh's fault that your boy can't commit. Now, as we've all established, no real harm was done here. I can take Miss Laquesh away with me, and she promises to never see your vampire ever again. Isn't that right, Dahlia?"

She hesitated, and I wondered if I should slap some sense into her. But her already large green eyes got bigger and filled with tears as she nodded softly, her voice tremulous. "I swear. I love Voltor. But he—" Her voice broke. "He's betrayed me. I'll go with Member Baxter. I won't see him again. I'll leave the city."

Poor kid.

"But—"

I raised a hand this time, cutting him off. "Rebus. I appreciate that you're protecting your people. It's admirable, really. But I have made up my mind. I am the authority in this room. I am happy to take this to Titus if you wish, but the girl is coming with me tonight. The discussion is *closed*." I allowed my voice to grow cold, losing all the cajoling nuances that I normally used when dealing with supernaturals. He'd jumped up and down on my last nerve.

Rebus snarled. "Listen here, you fucking little bitch —" He launched toward me, fangs out, clawed nails extended, but he didn't make it two feet before his heart was removed from his chest and held in the hand of Lucius.

"You all forget yourselves," Lucius said coldly. "You come for my consort, you come for me."

Judge winced, looking at the lifeless body of Rebus. "He attacked a Convocation Member. The penalty is death."

Ariana looked at the lifeless body of Rebus on the floor, then back at Lucius. "Witnessed and agreed." She toed the body with her boot. "This is going to cause drama. He was the leader of the largest nest in the city, and it's going to cause a power vacuum." She sighed. "Go. Take the nagini."

I wanted to say something about her giving us orders, but in the end, I couldn't be bothered. I pointed to the nagini, shooing her toward the door. Definitely wasn't going to look a gift snake in the mouth. I wanted out of this building and out of this city, before whatever bullshit the death of Rebus would produce, began to rain down.

We didn't wait for an escort out of the room. I followed Lucius, with Judge by my side and X at my back. As soon as we stepped out into the main control room, my bodyguards swamped me. Buddy gave Dahlia the side-eye, his gaze only briefly taking in her long, serpentine tail. I had a feeling that Buddy had seen some shit. He was huge and scarred, the pink slash on his face even worse than X's, leaving him almost disfigured.

So a girl with a snake tail? No big deal.

"I smell blood?" He didn't seem worried. After all, we were vampires, and the guys were... well, the guys.

"Not ours. Rebus got a little too handsy," Judge murmured softly.

Buddy didn't push it any further. Instead, he looked back at the girl. "Do you shift?"

She shook her head. "No."

I frowned. I saw where he was going with this. LA may be wild, but a girl with a snake tail was probably going to raise eyebrows.

"You normally use the chair as a disguise?"

Her big eyes were dark and haunted. Poor thing. "Yes. But they broke it when they brought me in."

I looked down at her tail, which was at least six feet long and as thick as her torso. Her skirt was a long boho one, and it would hit my ankles if I wore it.

Buddy was looking her over too. "If you coil tightly, I should be able to carry you out of here, and your skirt will cover the lower half of your body. Not all that unusual."

Dahlia looked between us, then nodded. She actually looked seconds from bursting into tears. "Okay. I'm heavy, though. Voltor always said I weigh a ton."

X snorted. "And I thought Lucius had no game. Kid, he's a vampire. If he can't lift a car, he isn't worth crying over. And you weigh considerably less than a fucking Chevy, that's for sure."

As if to underline the point, Buddy leaned down and scooped her into his arms, holding her easily. I reached over and straightened her skirt, so it flowed over her coiled tail, and then she looked like a perfectly human girl.

Kind of.

I sent a message to the pilots as we strode out of the laundromat that masked the Enforcer headquarters. "Let's run. Sooner we make it to Fox Falls, the better."

THE FLIGHT to Fox Falls was quick, thankfully, and our new charge slept most of the way. She looked exhausted, and I could imagine twenty-four hours in the tender care of the Enforcers might've felt like a lifetime.

The small plane landed outside the dimly lit town. It was nearly six a.m., but in winter, the amount of sunshine was lacking. It suited me well.

After I'd been shanghaied into being the Convocation Member for Endangered Preternaturals, the job role had promptly come with a group of people I needed to care for—all displaced, thanks to the Collector, a psycho who'd died trying to "collect" me. They'd been traumatized and scared. Some I'd been able to send back to their homes and families, but others... They had been in his care for the better part of a century, and they were the ones who needed the most help.

So I'd called up Eden Academy, a refuge for preternaturals that had turned into a school and safe haven for young supes. Not just shifters or half-breed supernaturals, but humans with special gifts as well. Demigods, Djinn, Fae. They were all welcome in the halls of Eden.

They'd built in the area between Brody's Packlands and Dark River, and garnered our promise of protection if anything went pear-shaped. But honestly, some of the people who were employed by the Academy—like the Lycanthropes who'd set it up—scared the ever-loving shit out of me. They didn't really need our help.

But after the Collector had dropped a whole bunch of people in my lap, I'd certainly needed theirs. A shiver ran over my skin as I remembered him, an old vampire who had seemed so lovely, but had tried to steal me and add me to his collection of unique supernaturals. I remembered Lucius literally cutting him to pieces, and X pissing on his burning remains.

Judge wrapped an arm around my shoulders. "Okay?"

I nodded, because I was an immortal, and I was going to have to come to terms with the fact that there were some things that would literally haunt me forever. Those first few years after my turning had been rough.

Fox Falls was an accomplishment though, something I could be proud of. Thirty miles east of Dark River, it was an abandoned village that had died out in the fifties, back when the mine it was supplying dried up. The mining company up and left, leaving it as a ghost town for ages, until I'd used my newly acquired Convocation funds to buy the whole town outright for a little under ten grand.

Not going to lie, it needed work. It had sat dilapidating through the harsh Canadian winters for over eighty years. Luckily, I had a motivated workforce who could operate at legitimately the speed of light and work through the night. Within two months, we had a functioning town for the displaced preternaturals, away from the prying eyes of humans and safe from people who wanted to hunt them down.

That last promise had resulted in my first interaction with Wilde, the Convocation Member for the witches, but eventually Miranda had talked him around. The town had a warding which sent up a warning signal for the leaders whenever anyone who hadn't been preapproved entered the city limits. It kept out anyone with ill intent. It physically repelled humans. Wilde himself had come up and undertaken the warding, which was why it was so fucking impressive.

Did I still owe him one for it? Yes. But I wasn't worried.

The plane bumped into landing, and I stood up. Thank god that was over. I'd get Dahlia settled in, talk to the Town Council here in Fox Falls, check on shit, and then go back to Dark River. To the rest of my guys.

I smiled at Dahlia, indicating the door to the plane. "Let's go."

She looked at Buddy, her arms raised to help him lift her, but he shook his head. "You won't need that here. You can be yourself."

Her eyes went wide once more, her lips parting in shock. She watched Buddy's back as he walked down the stairs, fear and hope warring in her eyes. She uncurled, moving toward the entrance and out into the dawn.

I patted her shoulder on the way past. "Welcome home, for however long you want to be here." She flowed like water down the aircraft's steps, and I watched her with awe.

X came up beside me, his arm wrapping around my waist. "Well done, Your Majesty. Another soul saved." He tilted his head to the side. "I can't be the only one wondering how they fucked, right?" Groaning, Judge slapped him on the back of the head as he stepped around us, and X gave him a petulant look. "What? You were wondering too. Don't fucking lie."

I mean, I'd wondered. I pulled him down for a kiss. "I love you, but you're a fucking teenage boy trapped in an immortal grown man's body."

He nipped my lip with his fangs. "Some things will never age. My humor, my perky balls and my love for you."

Romantic bastard.

CHAPTER
SEVEN

I quickly handed Dahlia over to the Fox Falls welcoming committee. But not before I put the fear into her. I had to put on my best grown-up voice, and I knew how ridiculous it looked coming from someone who still thought carrot cake was a salad.

"You are welcome here for as long as you want. However, you *cannot* return to LA. Ever. If you do, I won't be responsible for the actions of the vampire Enforcers. They will execute you, and there's nothing I can do about it. You know what, just avoid the West Coast altogether for a while. Do you have any family or friends you'd rather stay with?"

She shook her head, and Venelope, an elderly human with the ability to set shit on fire with her mind, rubbed her back soothingly. "It's okay, sweetness, you can stay here. We're family."

Dahlia burst into tears, and I froze like a deer in the headlights. I did not do tears.

"Uh, it'll be okay. Don't worry. Venny will get you set up in your own apartment, and they'll find something for you to do in the town so you can have some income. I, uh, have to return home."

Venny rolled her eyes at me, hugging the girl to her chest, muttering sweet things in what I assumed was German, though I was no linguist.

Venny was on the Town Council, along with five or six other townspeople. They elected them every three years, all official-like, which I thought was probably better than the system we had in Dark River. I'd never tell Catherine and Grim that though—Nico either. They'd argue that there was a difference between immortals and mortal preternaturals. Because almost all of my people were mortals. Immortals needed a stronger hand, with steady leadership. That was why almost all nests followed a single leader.

I was on the Town Council for Fox Falls too, but I didn't interfere too much, other than to drop off the odd stray here and there.

I gave Venny a grateful look, then said my goodbyes. The guys were waiting on the edge of town, just before the ward.

"Get her all squared away, Sugar?"

I nodded, but my smile felt too tight on my face. "I'm tired. Let's just go straight home." I'd messaged Brody and Tex to make sure they were in Dark River and not up in Nîso. Walker and Nico had started dinner, apparently. I just wanted to be immersed in their simplicity for a night.

"Same rules?" Lucius asked, his face serious. I rolled my eyes.

X rolled his shoulders. "You know it, old man. First one home gets dibs."

Judge slipped out of his jacket. "A gentleman's agreement. Rainy Day, you know what to do."

"Have I told you guys that this is dumb?" I asked as I walked toward Lucius and climbed into his arms. Lucius was old and, as Tex would say, overpowered. To give the others a chance, he had to do his sprint home with a distraction. Normally, that meant he was drinking from me, but sometimes it meant he was doing more interesting things to my body. The time he ran home with his fangs in my breast, literally sucking on my nipple, had been wild. Even with the distraction, he won three out of every four times, especially on a short sprint like thirty miles.

Lucius held me tightly, his eyes looking over my face with a wonder he still hadn't lost in all these years. He looked at me like he didn't know whether to eat me or fuck me, and most of the time, I didn't make him choose. I leaned in, capturing his soft lips with my own. He sucked my lip into his mouth, scraping the skin gently. Just to get a taste.

I pulled back. "You can have more than that," I purred, and a feral grin spread across his face.

"You're too sweet, Raine Baxter. It is an offer I'll accept. In three and a half minutes, after I secure myself victory." Then I held tight as he yelled, "Go!" and began running faster than a high-speed train.

There were shouts behind me, and someone shouted, "Fuck!" I laughed, snuggling my face further into Lucius's neck. These guys. They made me so fucking happy. I could only hope other people had the opportunity to feel this way one day.

I took my distraction job seriously though; I tickled his underarms, sucked on his neck, kissed his jaw, sucked on his earlobe. The outcome might be already decided, but I didn't often get to play with Lucius. He was a serious guy, and I guess his sense of humor had been the first thing that had burned out along with his humanity. If he'd ever had one. I imagine that the Iron Age might've been rough on the funny bone.

Despite my best efforts, Lucius still made it home first. He burst through the front door, laid me on the rug in front of the fire, and tore off my shirt so he could latch his fangs just above my left breast, hitting the major artery there and sucking down my blood. I wrapped my legs around his waist, trapping him between my thighs as I came. Honestly, the fact that drinking blood caused orgasms, and that he fed off those orgasms? Who said evolution was irresponsible?

"Lucius," I breathed, threading my hands into his soft blond hair as his teeth pulled out of my skin. He sat up on his haunches, looking down at me with a smug look on his face. In these moments, filled with my blood, coated in the scent of my release, he was almost like a different person. One who hadn't spent a thousand years bathing in blood and screams. He was almost boyish, which was weird. He was more like Nico, although both of them would disagree with the comparison.

I sucked in air I didn't need, and turned my head to the side to see Walker looking at me with a scotch glass in his hand and fire in his eyes. "Have a nice trip?"

"So good," I groaned, pulling myself up off the floor with the help of Lucius. I realized X was pouting in the corner, glaring at Lucius. The ire of X bounced right off him though, and he just smirked at the bad-tempered Brit.

"Don't sulk. I was going to suggest we share. Unroll your silk ropes."

And that right there was the power of succubi blood. Once upon a time, Lucius would have decapitated a man who suggested he wanted to taste what was his. Now? He wanted to help X tie me up.

"Just X?" Tex asked, returning from the back deck with a tray of barely cooked meat.

Lucius pulled me into his body a little tighter, but not out of possessiveness. He just liked holding me. "No. I think our consort may be in need of something a little more. She seems tense. I think that perhaps it might be time for—"

"A WHOLE PACK ORGY?" X shouted, pumping his fist. "Fuck yeah!"

Lucius chuckled deep in his chest, the purr of it sensual. "Would you like that, my consort?"

I nodded furiously. We didn't do it often—orgies, I mean—because it was a lot. There was a lot of dick and a lot of holes, and quite frankly, it was sexy, sweaty chaos. "If everyone else would like that too."

I could sense the heavy pound of Tex's heart. He was in. I looked between my more monogamous mates. Well, that was the wrong word. They just liked to worship me by themselves, which I was totally okay with.

Walker gave me a smirk which meant he was down to play, and my body immediately heated. When Walker got wild, it was something that I dreamed about for weeks. Touched myself in the shower to the memory. When he got his exhibitionist streak going, especially during our group lovemaking sessions... Little goosebumps rose over my skin as arousal flushed through my veins.

Oh yes.

Nico gave me a toothy grin. "Of course. It has been a considerable amount of time since we've had you between us all."

That just left Brody. He strolled over to me, lifting me into his arms until I could wrap my legs around his waist. He kissed me hard, his tongue pressing past my lips to stroke my own with his, dominating the kiss, teasing and tempting me with his warm body beneath my hands.

Pulling back, he looked into my eyes, his own deep brown ones molten. "I call shotgun." There were groans around the room, but my temperature was already at a hundred degrees. "Better put the steaks in the fridge, Pup, because it's going to be a long night." His grin was wicked, and I knew he was right.

In the words of the Prophet MC Hammer.

Stop.

Orgy time.

EIGHT

I kissed Brody like my life depended on it. He was so fucking hot, my fated mate, my Alpha. His skin burned beneath my fingers, and his tongue was like fire as he dragged it across my throat and the mate marks on my shoulder.

I moaned and wrapped myself around him tighter, grinding my core against his hardening dick. I felt Walker come up behind me, knew it was him by the way he felt, smelled, his whole vibe. If Brody and Walker shared, it was often with each other.

"Lay her down, Brodes. I want to strip her naked so everyone can watch as her body turns that pretty pink."

Brody grunted his agreement, dropping to his knees nimbly. He continued to hold me though, his hands large across the expanse of my back. He plucked at my clothes, undressing me with deft fingers. Having sex as a group was always amazing, because it forced us to slow down. When you could fuck at the speed of light, you tended to destroy rooms. But my shifters were still mortal, still breakable, so our lovemaking was slow and languorous.

Someone pulled my shirt over my head, and then Brody's lips were wrapped around my nipple. He laid me on the floor, his body covering mine, and he shifted his head to the side so my left breast was free for someone else.

Tex's dark, shaggy hair appeared in my vision, his lips curled in a smile and his eyes heavy with lust. Leaning over me, he brushed his lips across mine and then moved down my neck and over to my left tit. Unlike Brody, who seemed intent on making me orgasm with nipple play alone, Tex just scraped his teeth across the aching bud before continuing his path downwards.

"You smell too good to resist," he murmured against my skin, nudging a grumbling Brody from between my thighs.

Brody let go of my nipple with a pop, giving Tex a raised eyebrow. "I liked it there."

"You'll be fine. I'm just getting her warmed up— aren't I, baby?" Tex breathed the endearment over my wet center, cooling the heat.

Fuck.

"Tex, *please*..."

He slid his tongue against my still covered core. Somehow, he and Brody worked out some kind of synchronicity, because he was tonguing my clit in the same rhythm as Brody was drawing my nipple into his mouth.

A tearing sound preluded Tex's tongue inside me, and I moaned as I held his head closer. Someone caught my torn underwear as he flung them over his shoulder.

"Fuck..." It was a barely breathed sigh, but I could feel everyone's eyes on me as my own closed against the bliss.

"Move over, Snakelet. I'm going to give you a hand. Or a fang." My eyes popped open as my thighs were stretched wider, X tugging at one leg until it was up over his shoulder and he could run his hand up the inside of my thigh, his head pressed close to Tex's. "Share?"

Tex turned and kissed X quickly, nothing more than a small taste of my juices shared between them. X moaned, then turned his lips back toward my fleshy inner thigh.

"Hold on, Love. This is gonna be a bumpy ride." He struck, the venom in his bite coursing through me and electroshocking my system with an orgasm. My body bowed in the center like I was an extra in *The Exorcist*, and I screamed my pleasure into the room. That bite was really something else.

I ground against Tex's face, and Brody moved up to kiss me again. "Easy, Rainey. Tex is one of the few of us that actually has to breathe." He chuckled, even as I gasped against his lips. Brody placed his hands on my hips and rolled, so he was on his back on the faux fur rug and I was straddling his hips. It was an impressive feat of gymnastics. "I called it. These fuckers can wait," he growled, holding his cock so I could slide myself down on him.

Making love to each one of my men was different. Sure, some of the sensations were the same, but the feel was worlds apart. Making love to my fated mate? It was like the earth shifting around me every single time.

"Brody," I hummed, moving slowly. It was always a slow build, like creating a masterpiece that was going to rock your world, stroke by stroke. I leaned over into his chest, his hands moving down to grab my hips tightly.

"Take what you need, mate. You're going to need your energy," he purred, and he didn't have to ask twice. Brody's blood was... indescribable. Like sex in the sun, dipped in chocolate. It didn't make sense, but trust me, it was amazing for the both of us.

Luckily, Brody had worked on not coming every time I took a bite out of him, but it was always a race to the end. As he held my hips steady and thrust up into me, I dragged down mouthfuls of his blood and was soon screaming around his flesh as my orgasm ripped through me. I unlatched from his throat to pant his name, and he held me through it, his own body releasing into mine.

I'd barely regained my breath when someone else scooped me up into their arms. Judge. "Thanks, Juice Pouch."

Brody gave him the finger, though his lips were curved in a satisfied grin. He remained on the rug, one arm under his head, the other cupping his dick like it was a safety blanket. The look in his eyes was full of fire.

"I think you should reward all of Tex's hard work, Rainy Day. What do you say?"

I moaned my agreement as Judge's lips took mine, and he walked me toward where Tex was slumped against the foot of the bed. We often had to have sex on the floor when we did this, because there was just not enough space for all our bodies on the bed. With one last nip on my lips, Judge dropped me into Tex's lap.

"Mmm, you smell so fucking good, baby," Tex murmured, his arms banding around my back. He kissed me hard, his tongue stroking mine. I loved kissing Tex. "Spin on my lap, baby. Show me how you ride me, reverse cowgirl."

A low chuckle bubbled up in my chest. "Yee-haw?"

But I spun on his lap, and when his hand slid between us to grab his cock, sliding it inside me, all my mirth disappeared. This position was one of my favorites, because Tex's long cock hit places that made my eyes roll back in my head.

"Tex," I breathed, and he grunted as he rolled his hips sinuously.

Judge was now standing in front of me, his body stripped bare and gorgeous. His cock jutted toward me, and I reached out, grabbing it and using it to pull him closer.

"Easy, Sugar. That one's attached," he teased, but he shut up pretty quick as I slid him past my lips, swallowing him down until he grunted out a curse. I looked up at him smugly, and that lopsided smile was a reward of its own. I might be pinned between their cocks, but I felt so fucking powerful in that moment. The Goddess that Brody always called me.

"Mmm, you look so good taking my cock between those pretty lips, Rainy Day. Look how deep you take me," Judge groaned, and when Tex hit that sweet spot again, I moaned, making him shudder. "Is he fucking you so good, Sugar? Is he hitting all the right spots in that tight little pussy of yours?"

God, that mouth. I moaned my agreement, and then lifted a hand to cup his balls, rolling his sac gently in my hand. I gave them a gentle squeeze, making Judge curse and thrust into my mouth harder. I gagged, clenching around Tex, who doubled down on his thrusts. We were an undulating mass of pleasure until I was coming around both their cocks.

"Raine, I fucking love you," Judge breathed, his hands tangled in my bright red hair as he came down my throat. Tex wasn't far behind, pulling my hips down hard and grinding up into me as he unloaded inside me too.

I leaned backwards, glad I was flexible, and Tex turned my face and kissed me, his body softening inside me. He tasted the salty release of Judge on my lips and licked it off like a cat with cream. He didn't need to say he loved me with words; I knew it deep in my soul.

X was quickly there, plucking me from their arms. When Judge growled, Brody laughed. "Now you know how it feels, butthead."

The release of my guys was dripping down my thighs in a sticky mess, but X didn't care as it smeared all over his abs. "Oh baby, I've got a special thing planned. Just have to get the Sheriff on board."

Walker had a chair in the corner, where he usually watched our little exhibitions. He liked to watch. X strolled over and sat me down on Walker's lap. He was shirtless and his cock was out, and I felt the hard bar of it between my ass cheeks.

"Walker here won't let me tie him up because he's

a meanie, but I think if *you* were the ropes, he wouldn't mind quite so much. What do you say?" X teased, and I looked up into Walker's eyes, my lips tilted toward his.

He didn't resist, leaning down to kiss me despite the taste of Judge still in my mouth. He must have given his consent, because I felt the kiss of ropes on my wrists as X tugged my arms around Walker, until he was caged in the band of my arms. Then he tied my hands together at the back of the chair with a long line of rope.

I was bound tightly to Walker, the slow thump of his heart against my breasts. X pushed my legs up until my knees were either side of Walker's hips, then tied my ankles to the armrests.

We were both bound together, but there were no ropes on Walker. I was the rope keeping him in place. His cock was pressed tightly to my stomach, and I mewled that it wasn't inside me.

X stroked a hand down my spine. "Don't worry, Love. You won't be empty for long."

Nico's chuckle brushed across my overheated skin. "Aww, Sheriff. You look like you don't hate that nearly as much as you thought." He kissed a line up my back, then he gripped my hips and slammed inside me.

"Yes," I groaned. "More."

My ancient lover provided, moving his hands to the armrests, and Walker's hand's held my hips still as Nico moved in and out with a punishing pace. My clit rubbed against Walker's groin, and my vision began to blur with the pleasure. I was gasping between moans, Walker's fingertips pressing hard into my hips.

"Come for me, Raine," Nico purred from where he was curled over my spine. "Come for me so I can feel you milk my cock."

Damn these guys and their filthy mouths. I couldn't resist if I tried, my body arching against Walker, my nipples rubbing against his chest hair. "Yes! Oh god, yes... *Yes!*"

I exploded, blacking out a little, because when I came back to my senses, someone else was inside me. I didn't even need to look to know it was X.

"Oh baby, you like that, don't you? Being spread wide open for me." I could hear the heat in his voice. "Even your Sheriff is enjoying me fucking you into him, watching us come inside you as you're locked to him."

I gazed at Walker. His head was thrown back in pleasure, his hard cock leaking precum over my stomach, making it slide up and down the softness of my belly with every single one of X's punishing thrusts.

X was taking his time, each thrust slow and measured, like he was the maestro in a symphony, and I was the violin in his virtuoso. He leaned forward and kissed my throat, before sliding his fangs inside me, making me come again. All the cum inside me meant there was a sloshing noise with each thrust, a dirty, pornographic sound that just seemed to make me wetter.

X slapped my ass, making me moan again, and it was too much for Walker. He came in hot shoots between our bodies with a grunt. As X continued to thrust, it coated us both.

Finally, X found his own release, shouting my name before pulling out and stumbling back to the bed. "Jesus fucking Roosevelt," he muttered. I felt like he was mixing up his curse words, but my brain couldn't formulate a snarky comment since my whole body was now lax against Walker's chest.

Seconds—or maybe minutes—passed until someone cut the ropes keeping me tethered to Walker. The man in question slid me up and kissed me hard, maybe a little frenzied. Oh yeah, Walker had enjoyed that.

X was a genius.

But I didn't get to do much more, because Lucius was there, scooping me into his arms and lying me down on the bed. His hands were unexpectedly tender as they stroked over my body, tracing his fingers through Walker's release where it clung to my skin. He leaned forward, licking it from my skin as his hands moved down further. His fingers stroked through my overheated folds, and after a few slides, I realized he was scooping their cum back inside me.

A primal part of me made a feral sound, and when

his wild eyes met mine, I knew that the primitive part of the monster that was Lucius was mine too. Was *ours*.

He leaned forward, until his lips brushed over mine. "I'm going to fuck their release back inside you, and then I'm going to paint the walls of your cunt with my own seed. You're ours."

He did exactly as he promised, and my brain blanked out. We were just limbs and pleasure, until I was screaming his name so loudly, there was no way the whole town didn't hear me.

CHAPTER
NINE

I climbed out of bed the next morning, over the bodies spooned around my own and each other's. X took up the most amount of space, his limbs flung over any flesh he could touch. I loved it when we all slept in a cuddle pile like this. It made me feel adored. Happy. Lucky as hell.

The kitchen wasn't empty. Brody was there to hand me a cup of coffee, and I sucked it down like it was the only thing between me and narcolepsy.

"Thank you." I stepped into Brody's space, the bond between us almost like a warm hug of its own. "I know last night wasn't really your scene, but thank you for that too."

He kissed the top of my head. "Anything that brings you pleasure is my scene, Rainey, even if it does mean staring at a lot of assholes for a couple of hours."

I laughed, slapping his chest, but not moving from his arms. I could never get enough of this feeling. Of being bathed in his love through the bond. I wanted to stay here forever, but I knew I couldn't. Reality was a bitch like that.

"What's wrong?"

"I want to go to Amsterdam."

"For the baked goods?"

I snorted, because it was universally hilarious that vampires could get stoned. It had happened once here in Dark River. Bert liked to experiment, and well, there'd apparently been a lot of hungry vampires tripping balls on the grass in the town square that day.

I was sad I never got to see it. I wondered if I could convince Bert to give edibles another try, just for entertainment's sake.

"No, that's not it. Well, not just that anyway."

Brody wrapped his hands around my waist, lifting me easily onto the kitchen counter and stepping between my thighs. "Why don't you tell me what it is then?"

I rested my head on his shoulder, nuzzling my nose into his neck and breathing in his familiar, comforting scent. "I'm just tired, you know? Tired of the Convocation and the shit that comes with it."

"Heavy is the head that wears the crown," he quoted, his big hands trailing up and down my back comfortingly. "If anyone knows what that's like, Rainey, it's me. You're doing an amazing job."

I loved him so much it hurt. "Thank you, Alpha. That means a lot. But it wasn't a crown that I ever wanted. I don't want to be a leader. I just want to be happy."

He pulled back a little. "You aren't happy?" His face pulled down into a frown, and I quickly shook my head.

"With you guys, I'm deliriously happy. If it was just us, the pups, Dark River, and Nîso, I'd be the luckiest woman to ever die in a ditch. But the pressure of so many lives in my hands is wearing me down."

Brody nodded, his lips finding my temple as he dragged me closer. "So we fix it. My job as your mate is to make you so fucking happy that you wake up every morning with a smile on your face, and go to bed every night counting your blessings." He screwed up his nose, and it made my regal, imposing Alpha look almost boyish. I loved that expression, so naturally him. "But why Amsterdam?"

I told him about the throwaway comment Alexander the dragon had made after the Convocation meeting, about the Night Demon and how he'd be powerful enough to take my position.

The more I spoke, the more Brody frowned. "I'm not so sure about going across the world to meet a being referred to as a Night Demon. He doesn't sound particularly placid."

"I'm not exactly helpless. Besides, I've got Buddy and the team."

"Baby, if you think I'm letting you fly halfway around the globe to meet a mystery supe without coming with you, then you're crazy." He brushed his lips across mine. "We support you—you know that. Whatever you decide, we'll be behind you. But you're going to have to deal with the fact that we're all over-protective assholes and we'll be going to Europe with you."

"What about the Pack?"

Brody shrugged. "I haven't had a holiday in twenty years. Since you stumbled into town half-dead. Bobby is the same age as I was when I was made Alpha. He can babysit Nîso for a couple of weeks." He kissed me again, like he just couldn't help himself. "You aren't the only one who's tired of the crown, my love."

I pulled back to really look at him. Had I been so caught up in my own bullshit that I hadn't realized he was stressed? He looked older than when I'd first met him, the same as Tex. While the steady march of time had stopped for me, it hadn't for them. Slowed, sure. But they still aged. And one day, in a long time, I'd be in a world where Brody and Tex no longer existed.

The pain in my chest was like a knife, just at the thought of it.

Brody bundled me closer to his chest, and I wasn't surprised when I heard the soft sounds of Tex's feet padding across the hardwood. My pain always pulled at him like a leash. He didn't stop, didn't ask what was wrong. He just stepped into the hug that Brody was giving me, doubling down until I was surrounded by my mates.

"You're doing it again," Tex whispered in my ear. "Thinking about after. I told you to stop doing that."

"It's not that easy. It just hits me sometimes. Like I'll be halfway through a burrito and then I'll remember that in a hundred years, I'll still be eating burritos but you'll be dead and in the ground, and my heart will be buried with you."

Tex buried his nose in my hair, breathing me in. "I know, baby. That's the beautiful thing about love, though. You step into someone's arms for the first time, and from that moment, you'll never know if the next embrace will be the last time. Because there'll always be a last time. It might be tomorrow, or in twenty years, or a hundred. But the love you feel in those arms every single time makes the pain worth it, because then you'll know that you loved them with your whole heart. My arms might not be around you forever, but my love will be with you always, even when I'm gone."

He kissed my cheeks, and I realized tears were running down them. "You gave me your heart, put it in my hands, even though you knew one day I'd break it, and for that, I'm the luckiest man in the world."

They held me for a little longer, my mortal men, and I soaked in their love and warmth. Brody finally pulled back and kissed me softly. It was a touch filled with a love so tender, it threatened to break my heart right now.

"That day isn't today, Rainey. You're stuck with us for a long time yet." He pushed his strength down our bond, propping me up from the blues that had overtaken my body. "Now, go and wake up our Packmates. If we're going to Amsterdam, there's a lot of preparation to be done."

I squeezed them both tightly to me, like I could bond them all over again, then stepped away.

Tex was frowning. "Hang on, wait... Did you just say *Amsterdam?*"

CHAPTER
TEN

It had taken less convincing than I'd originally anticipated. Once Brody was on board, the rest had fallen into place. Nico had been with me after the Convocation meeting. He knew how desperate I was to be done with it.

Apparently, they all knew, because even Walker, who was the biggest homebody of all my men, got on board. Hanna was now the Sheriff in charge for awhile, I'd closed The Immortal Cupcake for a month, and that was all there was to it.

Well, that all took a week; it wasn't like it happened overnight. The hardest part had been getting permission from the Convocation to leave the country. Alexander had merely raised an eyebrow on the videoconference. Apparently, we didn't *actually* need to get together for every little thing—they'd arrived into the twenty-first century just enough to have someone set up their computers for them.

However, it had been almost unanimous, which should offend me but didn't. Half of them hated that I was even a Convocation Member and couldn't wait for me to be gone. The other half—Alexander and Titus—had a vested interest in me being happy. Wilde was just Wilde. It was hard to pick what the witch would do on any given day.

I messaged the kids, who were all spread out now, and told them what I was doing. Though they weren't kids anymore, not really. They had lives that ran independently of us, and of Dark River, but they'd always be Pack. They'd always be those tiny, scared little kids who softened some of the most bloodthirsty vampires on the planet.

Nico hung up the phone with a sigh. I winced at his frustrated expression. "No luck?" He'd been on the phone to every European nest he had good relations with, but so far, no one had any more information for us than Alexander.

We had been invited to six balls, two soirées and an orgy, though. We'd declined them all, regretfully of course, except for one by the head of the Amsterdam nest. We weren't exactly forthright with our reasons for coming to Europe, but no one would believe it was because we longed for the canals and pre-Christianity architecture.

"No. Francois still believes that you are a myth, so the very concept of a Night Demon is beyond the scope of his tiny mind."

Lucius snorted. "Francois is pretty, but has the intelligence of sludge from the bottom of the Thames."

Well, gross, but okay.

Diverting the conversation away from Francois before it devolved into a full rant, I rested my head on Lucius's shoulder. "So we head to Amsterdam and see what happens. If nothing comes of it, at least we tried."

X appeared behind me, wrapping an arm around my waist. I waited for his dirty comment about coming, but instead he licked a stripe up my throat. "We'll keep trying, Love. I'm not without my own sources in Europe. They're a little less official than that of the twins. And my methods are a little more..."—he scraped his fangs over my pulse—"brutal."

My whole body shivered with lust, but instead of taking a minute to have a quickie against a wall like normal, I just leaned my head back against his chest. "That's sweet."

His hand slid down my front, dipping just below the waistband of my jeans. "I'm nothing if not sweet. All the girlies tell me so."

I slapped at his hand and spun in his arms, grinning up at his handsome, scarred face. "Oh yeah, what girls?" Rising up on my tippy-toes, I nipped his chin. "I promise I won't hurt them. I just want to talk."

X growled low in his throat. "Mmm, you know it makes me hard when you act all psycho." Someone snorted, and he looked up over my head. "You too, Lucy. Watching you rend your enemies, *unff*—"

"If you're quite done?" Nico queried, his tone amused. "Titus has given us access to the family's private plane for the duration of our time away."

"You have a private plane?" I gasped. No way!

"*We* have a private plane," Nico corrected softly. "We are a clan. You are my consort. They are my family. Everything I own belongs to us. Now, let's go. There is no point wasting time."

"Fucking sweet bastard," X growled in my ear, and I couldn't agree more.

INTERNATIONAL FLYING WAS a lot different in a private plane. The food was amazing. With the eight of us— because none of my Pack were left behind—plus Buddy and Rio, my two lead bodyguards, we were basically a small crowd aboard the plane and more than enough to keep the flight attendants busy. Poor things—they'd almost had a conniption at the amount of powerful beings on one plane, but they hid it well.

What was it about luxury plane designers that

they loved the color beige? Actually, luxury anything. Always beige.

Brody and Tex were asleep on the armchairs that reclined into beds, while the rest of us sat around the dining table, forming a plan of action.

"So what do we know about this Night Demon?" Walker asked, falling immediately into his role of investigator. I think it physically pained him to leave the uniform at home, but he looked incredibly attractive in his tight jeans and t-shirt. The flight crew kept eyeing him like he was a buffet, and they were lucky I was so damn chill. Any other vampire would have plucked their eyeballs out of their head.

"Are you growling?" Judge suddenly scoffed, his midnight blue eyes twinkling in the soft overhead lighting.

"No." I cleared my throat. "Google wasn't very forthcoming. I got a lot of sleep paralysis demons, but they aren't real." I looked at the guys. "Right? Guys? They aren't real, right?"

Nico shrugged. "Once upon a time, there were all sorts of things roaming the earth that would now be considered demons. Gargoyles. Horned creatures. Dragons. I wouldn't rule anything out."

My skin crawled. Sleep paralysis demons. New fear unlocked. "Okay, I vote that if this guy is one of those, we leave him be. I'm not fucking around with anything with the word paralysis in its title. I'll suck it up and be the best Convocation Member ever," I swore, placing my hand over my heart.

Judge put his hand over my boob too. "Just checking."

Nico let out a laugh, his fangs pressing softly into his lip and making the flight attendant walking down the aisle toward us turn tail and walk back toward the nose of the plane. I pushed down my amusement.

"Let's assume it isn't a nightmare pulled directly from my childhood horror stories. Where do we look first?" I looked at Walker, because investigating really was his jam. We all had our talents—some more brutal than others—but Walker's had always been overthinking everything to death.

"Supernaturals are creatures of habit. When you live for eternity, drifting across the globe increases your ennui. We usually stay close to the place where we were created, or move to a new place and stay there forever. Those who roam tend to feel the effects of immortality faster."

We all looked at Lucius, who was staring at me with his unnerving gaze. Well, unnerving to everyone but me. "It is true. Also, I believe it would be best if you allowed me to feast on your delicious cunt before we land. It would be pertinent that I be more civilized while we are liaising with the European covens. We have a long history."

I frowned, because he almost sounded self-deprecating, which was very unlike Lucius. He knew exactly who he was, and was unapologetic for his actions. I stood up and went to sit on his lap, straddling his strong thighs. "I love you a little uncivilized. You know that, right?"

"I am thankful every day for what you've given me, Raine Baxter. I find I want you to be proud of me. I want people to look at you and know you're mine."

I scraped my nails through his hair, trailing them over his scalp and making his eyes close with bliss. "I am proud to be your consort, Lucius. I'm happy that my pleasure is what brings you back to yourself. I'd be delighted to ride your face."

Someone cleared their throat, and I looked over at Walker's amused face. "If we could hold off on this truly touching Hallmark moment, we might be able to get this squared away before you ride him into the European sunset."

I gave Lucius a grin, and merely spun on his lap so I was back facing the table. His hands roamed over my thighs, the gesture both comforting and arousing.

"So you're telling me that since Alexander thought he was in Amsterdam, if the Night Demon's alive, he's probably still in the city?"

"Hey, maybe it's a she. I've known my fair share of demons of the night. Most of them were Judge's ex-girlfriends, though," X added.

Walker chuckled. "True. We can't rule out

anything." He looked back at me. "If they're not still in Amsterdam, there will be someone there who'll know at least a name. We can track a name easier than we can track a myth."

Man, woman, or myth—they were coming home with me. I was going to unload this heavy mantle onto someone more capable, and finally get my happily ever after.

Amsterdam at night was like a beautiful woman with a knife. She was adorned with bright lights and baubles, but she hinted at a darkness that lingered just below the surface. I loved it immediately, and I could understand why a supernatural being would make this city their home.

It bustled with life, despite the fact the sun had set hours ago. We'd rented out an entire apartment with heavy drapes near the De Wallen district, which was the only solution when there were so many of us.

The guys all separated out immediately, going to chase down their own leads, and get a feel for the shadowy parts of the city's supernatural community. I stayed with Brody and Tex, both as added protection for Tex and because we had to go and pay our respects to the Alpha of the city. We were guests in their territory, and it would lead to drama if we didn't at least give our thanks that we were allowed on their land.

As if they could stop us.

I'd managed to convince the guys to just let me go without Buddy, because a huge show of force with some of the most feared names in the vampire world would probably make a bad impression. I had Brody, who wasn't exactly a slouch himself, and quite frankly, I could hold my own against the shifters now. I wasn't a fresh new fledgling anymore.

Tex wrapped his arms around my waist, kissing my neck. "Are you ready, mate?"

I was dressed in high-waisted black pants, with large gold buttons curving up over my hips, and a red silk blouse. I was practically dressed, but showing deference. Who knew pants could play an important role in politics?

"Ready." I spun in his arms, and my heart beat faster, like it always did when I took in how handsome he was. He still looked far younger than his true age, and I was fairly sure he would until the years started to truly catch up to him. But his jaw was sharper, his face more mature, then the man who'd first arrived in Dark River. He was so fucking handsome, it hurt.

He was wearing black jeans, and his signature leather jacket that made him look so deliciously bad. That couldn't be further from the truth though; Tex loved me like we were both still teenagers and I was his first love. He had "Mika" tattooed across his chest, a permanent memorial to the girl who'd died so that I could become Raine.

"You look delicious as hell. We don't really need to go out right now, do we?" I tugged at his jacket, and he laughed. His eyes slitted to his shifter form, allowing him to see me too. It took effort to partially shift, so he didn't keep his python eyes for more than a few minutes outside of his shifted form. But it was a sense that he relished after being deprived of it for the first two decades of his life.

"Not as beautiful as you," he said softly against my lips. "You steal my breath every fucking day." He kissed me again, his hands moving down to grab my ass with a groan. "But no, we don't have time. Being late would be an insult."

Tex had thrown himself into learning everything he could about the shifter world. Then he'd learned about vampire politics. He'd become so well versed on the intricacies of relations between the two that he advised me on things all the time, giving a more modern perspective that sometimes escaped Nico and Brody. The vampires were centuries behind when it came to individual liberties, and while Nîso was progressive, that didn't extend to the rest of the shifter world.

Not at all.

So when I became a Convocation Member, gathering all these weird and unusual supernaturals to me, it had been Tex I'd leaned on to help me create an expectation that was less about who had the most power, and more about a community that catered to the varying needs of each of its members. Our own little utopia.

I stepped into the living room, and into Brody's waiting arms. He rubbed his cheek across mine, scenting me as much as possible. "We should fuck you before we leave, so there's no doubt in anyone's mind that you belong to us. That you're our mate."

I looked at my watch. "We have time..." I trailed off, waggling my eyebrows.

Tex scoffed. "We really don't. Let's go." He sounded put out about it, like he wanted to stay home and "scent" the absolute hell out of each other, but I guess one of us had to be responsible.

We caught a cab across town, the three of us squeezing into the back. The driver had merely raised an eyebrow at the way their hands were resting on me, screaming intimacy. I just gave him my own brow raise back, my eyes saying *welcome to the future, old man*. Love wasn't finite.

The cab moved out of the center of the city, and the bikes became BMWs. The houses became less dilapidated, with luxury starting to ooze from the sidewalks. People strolled along the canals in fancy designer clothes, wearing the indulgent smiles of people who'd never had to worry about being robbed at knifepoint.

"Is this just a meeting? Should we have brought wine?" I whispered to Brody, and he squeezed my thigh.

"Just a check-in to pay our respects. It'll be fine, Rainey."

These things always made me nervous, especially when it was Pack-related. I still felt out of my depth in all things shifter, even after all this time. I was still an imposter, a barren vampire dooming a strong Alpha to a home without shapeshifter offspring.

It was something that still played on my mind, despite the pups, and despite Brody's words that it didn't matter to him. He had his Alpha Heir, and he was happy. I still felt like I was depriving the gene pool, and I knew that there were some in Nîso who believed that too. Like my mother-in-law.

The cab pulled up in front of a giant apartment building, though it wasn't like any apartment building I'd ever seen. It was a huge square box of red brick, and it must have had a hundred white-trimmed windows along the front. The roof was kind of boxy, like a barn, with dark gray slate tiles. It was at least four stories high, and it looked staid and imposing from the side-walk. A skinny garden filled with trees softened its austere appearance, at least a little.

"This must be hell to defend," Brody muttered.

I had to agree. It was close to its neighbors, had way too many windows, and there was a parking lot right in the front yard. Unless all these houses belonged to the Pack, this place was a death trap.

I tucked Tex's arm into mine, standing close to him so he didn't have to use his shifter vision during the meeting, or at least not too often. Brody gave me a half-smile as my mate melted away and was replaced by the Alpha of the North Western American Packs. He seemed bigger, harsher, more powerful at that moment as his Alpha power swept along my skin, and Tex shuddered beneath my hand.

Brody knocked on the door, and it was quickly opened by a short, square shifter with blond hair. He blinked as Brody's Alpha power hit him, and I saw him tilt his head slightly in submission, without really submitting. It was more out of politeness than anything else.

"Alpha. You are welcome in the home of the Amsterdam Pack."

Brody inclined his head respectfully. "Thank you."

The man swung the door wider, and we walked in, our footsteps echoing across marble floors. There was a grand staircase in the middle of the foyer, with doors off to either side of it. Our shapeshifter guide led us toward the first door on the left.

"The Alpha and Alpha Mate are waiting for you in the sitting room. Please, follow me."

Brody indicated he should lead the way, and we followed closely behind. The man's steps were even and unhurried, even with a vampire and an Alpha at his back. This one had some serious balls.

The sitting room had large windows, and I could tell they were tinted so those on the street wouldn't be able to see a thing. But the view over the waterfront was definitely glorious.

The man standing in front of the fireplace was not quite as tall as Brody, but equally as imposing. The Alpha of Amsterdam was no wilting bloodline.

"Alpha Brody, it is a pleasure to meet you. Your reputation as a kind and honorable Alpha precedes you."

I always found it kind of hilarious that the Alphas called each other by Alpha and then their first name. It was almost like daycare teachers or something. My daycare teacher had been Miss Annabelle and she'd liked to wear a dress that was covered in rubber duckies. I looked at the broad, scarred Alpha in front of me, and then superimposed a rubber ducky dress on top. I clenched my back teeth to hold back a laugh, but Tex still leaned into me a little harder, feeling my mirth down the bond.

Obviously, so did Brody, because he dragged me forward. "Alpha Dirk, may I introduce my Alpha Mate, Raine Baxter, and my Packmate, Tex Flanagan." A slight shift in the corner told me that Alpha Dirk was well protected in this room, and I heard at least eight varying heartbeats other than my guys.

No one seemed unduly stressed—at least, not to my senses—so I pretended that they were invisible for now. I gave the Alpha and his mate a bright smile. Lots of fang. "It's a pleasure to meet you both. Convocation Member Alexander has only positive things to say about you and your Pack."

Dirk gave a tight smile at my name drop. He bowed formally. "It is an honor to have a Convocation Member in my home. This is my Alpha Mate, Lieneke. Please, come and sit. Would you like a drink?"

Lieneke was far smaller than her mate, her frame almost waifish. Her power was barely a shadow of her Alpha's too. Definitely a love match between these two and not a position gained through might. Though maybe she was a monster in her other form. You could never tell with the quiet ones.

Lieneke's eyes went wide as she studied my fangs again. "We have a full bar selection," she said quietly, like I was about to shout, "Yes please," and launch myself at her throat.

Tex came to her rescue. "I would love some genever, if you have it. I have heard good things about Dutch gin."

Lieneke gave my mate a tentative smile. "Of course." She waved a hand, and the blocky doorman moved to the small wet bar beside the fireplace and began pouring drinks.

He returned with a glass that he handed to Tex. "I mixed it with lemonade. We tend to have it with a beer chaser, which you might like to try if you spend more time in the city."

Alpha Dirk waved a hand at the comfortable-looking couches set in front of the fireplace. "Please sit. Alpha Brody, we've been following the treatise of Inter-Pack cohesiveness that has been the topic of..."

I zoned out the talking Alphas as I let my eyes wander around the room. I counted four men in the corners of the room in their human form. They looked relaxed, reclining against the wall, one guy even perched on a stool. But I could feel their readiness in the air.

I wasn't a fool. I knew they were probably here because of me. I might be a young vampire, but I could easily overpower three shifters if they didn't get the jump on me. Any more than that would be pushing it, though.

I did have a reputation, being a Convocation Member and all, that was far grander than my actual abilities.

Okay, so four in the corner, plus the Alpha, Alpha Mate and Blocky, as I'd now dubbed the shifter from the front door. That meant there was one missing. I listened hard for the heartbeats, my face twisted in what I hoped was an interested expression, and then I heard it.

A wide grin spread across my face as I jumped to my feet, moving across the room and capturing a tiny furred creature in a second. I held it up by the tail. A mouse crossed its arms in front of me. Its little mouse face looked *pissed*.

"That's tricky. I like it." I laughed. "I didn't even sense you changing." The mouse just dead-eyed me. "All right, I'm putting you down. Don't want to do you any damage by holding you by the spine. Your tail is your spine, right?"

The mouse morphed right in front of me, unrolling into the hugest fucking shifter I'd ever seen.

"Well, it certainly isn't my dick," the behemoth growled. Naked.

I slapped a hand over my eyes. Sometimes, I still had human sensibilities. Sue me.

I spun back to Brody and Tex, hoping the *whoops* came across in my expression. "It still impresses me that a person your size can shrink into something so small. Not that it matters." I coughed awkwardly. "It's not the size of the shifter; it's the motion of the ocean."

Tex let out a strangled noise that could have been a cough, or could have been a contained laugh.

Alpha Dirk looked at me with an expression that I didn't even want to decipher, but I didn't think it was a good one. "This is my second-in-command, Jakob."

I turned, keeping my eyes above the equator. "Nice to meet you. Sorry for manhandling you."

Someone tossed Jakob some pants, and he caught them without looking. He lowered his head respectfully, even if his eyes said something entirely different. "It's an honor to meet you too, Alpha Mate."

I turned to Blocky, whose name I really should've asked. I couldn't keep referring to him by his shape, and clearly, I'd already made enough social blunders for one day. I gave him a bright smile, which seemed to just make him a little more terrified. "I think I might like that drink now."

CHAPTER
TWELVE

Three drinks and some stilted conversation later, we had relaxed into something less formal. None of us could really get drunk without trying, except maybe Tex, so I was just pleasantly buzzed by the atmosphere.

"What brings you to Europe?" Alpha Dirk said. "There are rumors you're looking for the Night Demon."

My whole body stiffened at the casual way he threw around the title, but Brody just gave him a polite smile. "Raine is here on Convocation business, and we are just along for the ride." Technically, not a lie. "We've heard about this Night Demon, though. Sounds like a myth to me."

"Like succubi?" Dirk asked, his grin smug.

I raised my drink at him. "Just like that."

Dirk leaned back in his chair, crossing his ankles. "Not a myth. Just a man."

"Just a fucking asshole," Jakob grunted.

Tex, who honestly was far wilier than the rest of us combined, gasped. "He's actually real? Is it true he's a sleep paralysis demon?"

Dirk gave him a bemused look that very clearly said *If you were my Pack, I would have put you down years ago.* "No. I don't know what his powers are. He keeps that shit close to his chest. He stays out of our way, and we stay out of his. He's no threat to us."

Jakob grunted his agreement. "Orthus is a cunt, though."

"Orthus? Is that the Night Demon's actual name?" I said eagerly, and then wished I could swallow down my words as both the Alpha and his second turned to look at me appraisingly. I straightened out my own face, trying to go for rich and bored, which these guys seemed to do so well.

Finally, the Alpha shrugged. "Orthus is the Night Demon's companion. He's a shifter, I guess, of a sort. But immortal. And as my right hand implied, a bit... abrasive. Extremely protective. No one has gotten close to the Night Demon in decades." He shook his head slowly. "If the Night Demon wants to spend his life in the shadows, then Orthus wants to spend it under a spotlight with his fists raised."

Well, that would make things easier. Brody

chuckled and changed the subject, because we couldn't seem too interested in the affairs of European supernaturals. We spent another thirty minutes with them, discussing mundane Pack problems and possible exchanges between the two Packs for dominant youngsters. I wasn't sure if anything would come from it, but it was polite conversation at least.

Finally, we stood to leave, and the Alphas shook hands. I thanked Lieneke for her hospitality and tucked my hand through Tex's arm, following Blocky out through the sitting room door and back into the huge foyer. Brody brought up the rear, protecting my back. I loved that man.

Finally at the doorway, I gave Blocky a megawatt smile. "Thank you so much for your attentiveness," I cooed. I frowned, like a random thought just popped into my empty head. "I should ask, where do they hold underground fights here?" I leaned forward, whispering conspiratorially, "I love some no-holds-barred cage fighting. I heard Amsterdam has quite the scene."

Blocky grimaced, but then gave me a small smile in return. I knew that smile. I'd enamored him. Yay for my succubutt.

"It's held in an abandoned underground rail station beneath the Red Light District. Underground rail was a terrible idea, no? But it helps the supernatural element of the city." He looked at me with large puppy dog eyes. "The fights are run by the vampires in the city. They're not like you; they aren't sweet."

I patted him on the shoulder. "Thank you for caring. But not to worry, I can take care of myself." We exited the building and stood out on the sidewalk, waiting for the hire car to come and pick us up. "They seemed nice," I said softly, and Brody smiled and nodded. But his eyes told me that we shouldn't talk more. Made sense, even though there was no one around. Jakob the mouse-man had proved that there really was nowhere private when your enemies —or your friends—could literally be a fly on the wall.

So instead, I described the surroundings to Tex. The tall brick buildings and gray paved walkways that were so unlike the concrete sidewalks of home. The deep canal that ran alongside us, its waters a murky greenish-brown with lily pads dotting the top. The baskets of colorful flowers that hung on the bridges.

It was a lovely city, but it wasn't home.

Finally, a car arrived, and we climbed in and headed back toward the city center. We'd go back to the apartment and meet up with the rest of the guys so we could pool our knowledge. Plus, I was starving, and by the sound of Tex's stomach, so was he. Food first, and then we'd figure out our next steps.

We didn't talk too much on our way back, and when we reached the apartment, Buddy was already there, pacing anxiously like a mother hen. It had taken a direct order to get him to stay behind.

I put out my arms and did a twirl. "See? Safe and sound."

He gave me a disapproving look. "I still don't like it."

Buddy liked me now. In the beginning, he'd been so damn formal that I'd wanted to kick his ass. Eventually though, I'd worn him down. Now he just looked at me like an annoying sibling that he'd really like to shake vigorously.

I patted him on the arm. "I know, Bud. I'll find what I'm looking for here, and then I'll be more careful." Actually, I wouldn't, but no one would give a damn about me by then. I hadn't really told him what we were doing here, mostly because he was an employee of the Convocation. I trusted him almost completely, but he wasn't family. Also, he could still be compelled.

Part of me was slightly worried that without Buddy and the protection of my Convocation Member status, the old vamps would come back out of the woodwork. But we'd made advances in treating the mental decay of vampires since it had been discovered I was a succubus. Treatments synthesized from my blood hadn't resulted in a cure, but enough to at least keep the madness at bay until we found something better. We couldn't hope for much more just yet, but it was the one thing the Convocation could all agree on: deranged, ancient vampires weren't good for anyone.

Besides, I wasn't a fledgling anymore. While I still wouldn't be able to hold my own against an ancient vampire, my senses were better, and I'd probably last just a touch longer than I would've once upon a time. At least, that's what I told myself.

Besides, I still had my guys, and they were all the protection I needed. I couldn't live the rest of my immortal life doing something I hated just because I was scared. Being scared to do something because of a hypothetical outcome was like buying a lottery ticket and then trying to buy a mansion with it.

I wandered further into the house to find Walker drinking a beer with X, looking out over the canal. I squished my body between theirs, and Walker kissed my head. "How'd it go?"

"You'd be proud. I only made one inappropriate dick joke."

Walker shook his head. "Look at you, all grown up," he teased. He dropped his voice. "The vampires here are assholes. I'm surprised Nico didn't start tearing out throats."

I winced. If it was that bad for Nico—who was quirky but definitely the most even-tempered of us, except for Walker—then it really was bad.

I looked at X. He smiled down at me, and it was a dark expression. "If it were me, I would have." His grin widened. "Instead, I spent the night talking to human prostitutes. You're welcome."

A normal, sane person might have a sliver of doubt hearing his words. A normal, human woman might even be jealous. But I had nothing but faith in X, despite the fact the man had once upon a time been an absolute manwhore. He just wasn't the type of person who'd lie to me about screwing other people—he'd very openly tell me about it. If it had been just me keeping his appetite sated, we might've had a problem. But if variety was the spice of life, then our little love nest had something of every flavor.

"They have any good news for me?"

He shrugged. "They were humans and totally after my cock. There's only so much information you can get out of a hot-blooded woman once they see all this." He gestured to his body. "They said that everything was good down there in the district, that they'd really cracked down on safety around twenty years ago, back when workers started going missing or turning up dead. They hired more bouncers, and the cops are now everywhere."

I frowned. "You think it was the Night Demon killing the girls?"

X shrugged. "I don't know. They're vulnerable, and there's a lot of supernaturals who would take advantage of that. Might not necessarily be our guy."

Did I want to hand over the reins to a guy who

killed women for fun? No. Fuck no. But I still needed to see him with my own two eyes before I ruled it out.

Nico came into the room. His smile was easy, but I could see the annoyance in his eyes. Whatever the vamps of Amsterdam said, it had pissed off my good-natured lover.

I spun and stepped into his arms. "Want to go watch people senselessly beat the shit out of each other?"

X whooped. "My favorite."

Nico's phone beeped, and his smile turned down at the edges. "I believe my twin has already beaten you to it."

Ah, shit.

THIRTEEN

The atmosphere in the underground fight club was feral. That was the only word for it. The sludge on the ground looked almost toxic green, people snarled and were generally unwashed, and violence was so thick in the air that I could taste it.

X looked like he'd stepped into a Christmas wonderland.

"Did that guy just headbutt that shifter?" He scoffed, and made like he was going to walk over there and join the brawl. Grabbing his hand, I pulled him back to my side. One psycho mate trying to climb into the ring was enough.

"Behave," I grumped, making him pout. I squeezed his hand. "I'll make you a deal. You watch over Tex so none of these vamps take a bite out of him. If they do, I give you permission to remove their fangs and their heart. What do you say?"

His eyes said he knew I was leashing him, but he still wrapped an arm around Tex and bent down to kiss him hard on the lips. "Come on, Snakelet, let's go see if we can't find some booze and maybe just a little mischief."

"X..."

He turned his head and kissed me too. "Don't worry, Love. I'll bring him back in one piece. See you at home before sunrise."

Then he was gone, Tex's hand in his. Shit, what had I done?

Judge walked up, watching the retreating backs of Tex and X. "Is that a good idea?"

I screwed up my nose. "Only time will tell."

His jaw tensed, but he let it go. I trusted X with my life and my heart. He'd said he would bring Tex back, and I believed him.

I stroked a hand up Judge's arm, bringing his gaze back to me. "Where's Lucius?"

His dark blue eyes sparkled as he lifted his chin toward the ring. "He asked for their fiercest warrior. I told him that there wasn't an honorable 'warrior' in this whole place, but you know what he's like, Sugar. They found him an opponent, and I don't know what kind of shifter the guy is, but he makes my skin prickle."

Of course, Lucius had gone for the bloodiest opponent. He was a chained monster, and this place allowed him to slip his leash for a while. Blocky's words about this fight being run by vampires echoed in the back of my mind, and I cast a look over at Nico.

"Is this going to cause a problem with the locals?"

He shrugged. "They know who he is. They accepted him into the fight. On their own heads be it."

I didn't think Lucius's reputation was quite as foreboding in Europe, although people knew who he was, of course. Nico and Lucius, as well as their brother Titus, were some of the oldest vampires in the world. They'd settled in North America, but that didn't mean they hadn't spent a number of years in Europe once upon a time.

If vampires had anything, it was long fucking memories.

My focus was drawn back to the cage. And it was a literal cage, made of mesh that couldn't possibly hold either of the men who stepped into the ring. One was the man who I'd seen literally tear a person to pieces, and the other guy, his warrior opponent... Well, I got what Judge meant when he said he made his skin prickle.

The guy was tall and broad, but moved with a grace that screamed predator. There was nothing lumbering about him, despite the fact that he was easily a full foot taller than Lucius. My ancient vamps, they weren't huge. They were just under six feet; in their time period, they probably would have been considered giants. But now, in the time of Wheaties and steroid-infused chicken, they were just average height.

All the better to sixty-nine with. Only short women would understand.

A vampire I didn't know—which was basically all of them in this city—leaped easily onto the side of the cage. He gave the feral crowd a broad grin. "A rare treat today, my friends." This vampire wore a long black coat with shiny brass buttons and no shirt beneath it. He kind of looked like a hot rockstar. "All the way from the New World, the one and only Mad King. The only vampire still living to have killed off an entire species."

I frowned. Well, that was new. "Which species?" I asked Nico.

He gave me a sympathetic look. "Yours."

Oh. Yeah. I'd forgotten about that. "Karma really bit him in the ass for that one." I leaned closer. "What's with the nickname?"

Nico sucked in a deep breath that made his nostrils flare. "We have a long history in Europe. Not all of it was pleasant." I got the feeling that not *much* of it was pleasant.

Well, clearly I was wrong about their reputation in Europe not being as bad as in the Americas.

But Rockstar Vamp was continuing. "We've paired

him with our very own unbeatable monster, whose hatred for my kind is well known. Orthus!"

Of course it was. Why *wouldn't* Lucius be fighting in an underground death match with the very man we were looking for? If I was a magnet for trouble, then Lucius was a bloodhound for it. He could sniff out trouble like it was as pungent as three-day-old fish in the sun. Fuck it, we'd deal with the problems later. By the looks of them both, there was no dragging them out of there now until they'd spilled some blood.

Rockstar Vamp cast the big dude a pompous smirk. "Undefeated until tonight. I know this fight is going to be the one we'll talk about for a century. So get your bets in now, because this one will be too close to tell."

There was a flurry of movement around the room as people raced toward the bookies, but I was too busy eyeing the man in the ring with Lucius. Orthus was heavily scarred, far more so than even X. The scars lashed across his body and up over his face. His hair was jet black, shaved close to his head. He had no tattoos, and he was wearing only a pair of tight shorts which hugged his butt in a way that should probably be illegal.

He was hot. I could acknowledge that. By the look in Lucius's eye, he was acknowledging it too.

No referee hopped into the ring with the two men. Walker shook his head. "This is going to be a bloodbath."

Lucius peeled off his button-down shirt with lazy hands, watching the pacing immortal. I could feel Brody at my back, his body stiff with tension. "Is he a shapeshifter?" I murmured.

"No. Not like me. Not like a two-natured shifter either. He feels... bigger. I don't know what he is, but he's powerful. Closest thing I can think of is Alexander."

My eyebrows drew together. Oh shit. Had Lucius bitten off more than he could chew right now?

I stepped forward, ready to drag him out of that ring if I had to, but Nico caught my arm as the vampire announcer shot a look in our direction, his shit-eating grin making my heart pound. He knew exactly what this guy was.

"Given the nature of our competitors tonight, there will be no holds barred. Any powers will be permitted. First blood or to the death—up to the opponents."

Lucius, now naked to the waist, grinned, stepping toward his larger opponent. Whatever he was saying was pitched so low, none of the others in the room could hear it. The man frowned at what my lover was saying, finally nodding without saying a word.

"What did he say?" I asked my men, because surely one of them heard. "He's not going to fight to the death, right? The guy is immortal; he can't die."

"How do you know?" Judge asked. Brody leaned

closer, quietly filling him in on our meeting with the Amsterdam Alpha, but I couldn't drag my eyes away from the two men in the cage.

Orthus, the big guy, inclined his head, then shifted. His body bowed and twisted in a way that still hurt me to look at. It was different for shapeshifters like Brody. Their shift felt more like nature's magic than the brutal, searing morph from man to beast that was happening in front of me.

Because what emerged from him was definitely a beast. I didn't realize I'd gasped out loud until Lucius turned toward me, looking like a kid in a candy store, as he pointed at the *fucking two-headed hellhound in front of him.*

"Holy fucking *hell*," Judge breathed. "Is that a Cerberus?"

Nico was shaking his head, and honestly, he looked as surprised as the rest of us. "Only two heads. Don't they have three?"

I felt Walker step closer to me, his body brushing right along mine. "Smell that?"

Now he mentioned it, the scent permeating the air was heavy with adrenaline, sweat, fear, but below all that, sulfur. "Is that... brimstone?"

Nico nodded. "Definitely a Hell creature."

I thought of Lucifer turning up in our Convocation meetings to stir shit, and fear swept through me. That guy was beyond powerful. Beyond anything a mortal

—or immortal—could reckon with. The fact that Lucius was fighting a creature that would have emerged from his domain? That scared the ever-loving shit out of me.

But my lover was more unhinged than ever, because he looked excited about the upcoming battle. I needed to feed him more of my blood, because that really wasn't a sane response to a six-foot-high, two-headed monster with fangs bigger than my hand.

Lucius's lips pulled back over his own fangs. Someone blew an airhorn, and the two of them clashed faster than even my eyes could follow. There was no dancing around each other, no pacing back and forth.

There was just blood and fangs and violence.

Blood splattered across my face, and I realized I'd moved forward through the crowd until I was almost close enough to touch the cage. I lifted my hand, wanting to cling to the protective mesh as I followed the fight with my eyes.

"I wouldn't do that. It's electrified during the fight," someone beside me said. I looked over at a man in a hooded sweatshirt, his hands tucked into the front pocket, blond hair peeking out from the neckline. I couldn't see much else about his face, and he didn't turn toward me as he spoke.

Someone smashed into the fence in front of me, and I sucked in a gasp. When I turned back to the stranger beside me, he was gone. Whatever. I dragged my eyes back to the fight, my heart in my throat.

I was glad I was immortal, because when Lucius slammed to the boards in front of me, the jaws of one of the heads around his throat, I died.

FOURTEEN

I should have known my lover better than that, because Lucius grabbed the beast's lower jaw and pried him from his neck, tossing him across the ring before bouncing back to his feet. He was bleeding in so many places, it was hard to count.

But Orthus was equally as battered. A hunk of flesh was torn away from his side, but it was already mending, thanks to his immortal healing.

They smashed around the cage again, blood beginning to make the floor slippery, and my fangs slipped out. The raw violence combined with the bloodlust and heavy scent of blood was stirring the predator. It was my first accidental fang boner in a decade, and I was pretty sure it had something to do with the blood of the hellhound. It smelled *delicious*.

Somehow, that made it worse. Judging by Lucius's

grin, he was enjoying the small snack as he fought. The blood did smell powerful, so it was probably giving him a little boost as well.

The heavy thuds of flesh meeting flesh became less pronounced as the crowd roared, stomping on the floorboards as they screamed at whoever they wanted to win. It was pretty evenly split.

Lucius's body tensed as he sprang, agile like a cat toward its prey, wrapping his arms around Orthus's neck and dragging him toward the ground. Unfortunately, he forgot to take into account the other head, or the general strength in those huge hindquarters. Orthus launched them both into the air, twisting and somehow getting Lucius under his big body, his second head crunching down right across Lucius's neck and shoulder as they slammed back to the ground in front of me again.

His huge front paws pressed down into Lucius's torso, claws digging in so deep that blood welled up around them. If Lucius tried to slide out from beneath him, he'd be disemboweled.

Lucius met my eyes with a grin, before patting the massive hellhound on the shoulder. "I concede," he said loudly, and the hellhound, its eyes flaming red, instantly released my mate. I could finally breathe again, even though Lucius looked like shit, battered and scraped to pieces, bleeding where he lay slumped on the mats.

Orthus shifted back, weaving dangerously on his feet but still standing. The announcer vamp climbed onto the mats beside the bars, proclaiming Orthus the winner. But the raw violence had spilled into the crowd, with fights breaking out over the outcome of the match.

I ignored it all, my eyes only for Lucius. He looked at me with raw lust, and I could see he was hard beneath his now shredded dress pants. "That was the most fun I've had in a century—not including when I have my cock inside you and my fangs in your throat, of course. Nothing beats that."

I looked at him incredulously. "Of course." I climbed onto the octagon, ignoring the look from the announcer, and walked toward the door of the cage. I ripped it open and strode in like I belonged there. People were shouting crude things, and they were lucky Lucius and X were preoccupied, because they'd probably have enjoyed dismembering people for even thinking those things. My other guys were more civilized. Barely.

I stopped in front of Orthus. "I'd like to speak to you after you've cleaned up, if I may?"

He narrowed his eyes. I suddenly realized the scars on his face and body weren't neat, straight lines, or even jagged ones from claws or knives. They were the soft silver of old burn scars.

"I won fair and square," the guy grunted. "I'm not

about to get jumped just because you fucking vamps can't take losing."

I raised an eyebrow. "Does he seem overly worried about losing?" I said, tilting my head at Lucius, who was licking the blood from his fingers. The man was the epitome of waste not, want not. "No, it's about something else."

Orthus's face shuttered, going perfectly blank except for those fiery, dark eyes. "Not interested."

I put a hand on his chest, pushing some of my succubus charm into his skin. "I'm going to have to insist."

The guy looked down at my hand between his pecs, then back at my face, his eyes ping-ponging around with way too much awareness. "Succubus?"

Lucius was there instantly. "That was a good fight, but I will remove your tongue if you don't watch it," he said in that creepy monotone voice he used when the psychopath came out to play.

The guy took in a shuddering breath, and I watched him shake off my compulsion. Of all the times for my fledgling abilities to fritz out. He glared down at me. "Still not interested."

I gripped his wrist. "I promise I don't want to harm anyone. I just want to talk. Civilly, if possible, but by force if I have to."

"The Mad King doesn't scare me, little bloodsucker. I just proved I can beat him."

I shrugged. "But can you beat the six others?"

Orthus's nostrils flared. His jaw tensed, his eyes burning with undisguised distaste. "Fine. You have five minutes. But I won't give you what you want. Especially not him," he said, tilting his head to Lucius.

"I thought we bonded in here?" Lucius huffed, his tone hurt, though I wasn't sure if he was really hurt or just being a jerk. Hard to tell, sometimes. Either way, I grabbed his hand before things escalated.

"That's all we need, I promise."

Orthus jumped out of the ring, and the announcer vamp came over, handing him a brick-sized envelope. "As agreed." He gave a smaller second one to Lucius. "Come visit anytime," he said, and I detected a faint accent. "I think people would pay just to see the Mad King bested."

Lucius gave the man a sharp-fanged expression. It might be construed as a smile, if you were an idiot. "I'll happily stand against you in the ring," he purred, and it sounded like the soft croon of death.

Orthus strode off, and we moved after him, dismissing the vampire. He pushed through a heavy wooden door marked *Staff Only*, and I suddenly realized they were changing rooms as he stripped off his shorts and stepped into a shower. "Speak."

Okay, don't judge me, but I looked at his dick. It was a nice dick. Did it inspire me to write sonnets?

Maybe. Was he hung? Like a unicorn. He had the hard body of a fighter, no matter how marred it was.

He was hot, but I was at capacity for dick. I loved my guys.

"I think you know what we're going to ask," I said, finally lifting my eyes to his face. He didn't seem perturbed by my perusal.

"You want me to fuck you?"

Lucius growled, but I held his arm tightly. "No. Thank you. I'm sure it would be wonderful, though," I replied awkwardly, not wanting to offend him.

I might have imagined his lips twitching as he tilted his head back into the water. "In that case, I don't know what the fuck you want at all."

I sighed. Guess we were going to do this the difficult way. "I'm looking for the Night Demon."

If I wasn't a vampire and couldn't hear the blood whooshing through his veins, or the steady pump of his heart quickening, I'd have almost believed him when he asked, "Who?"

I rubbed my hand over my face. "Don't fuck with us, Orthus. Alpha Dirk has already told us you're his keeper. I don't mean any harm; I just want to meet him." I chewed my lip with my fang, trying to work out how much to tell him in this place filled with ears. "I should have introduced myself. I'm Raine Baxter, Convocation Member for Endangered Preternatural

Species. It's literally my job to make sure he's safe." Whatever he was. "Please?"

Orthus's eyes ran over my face, hopefully reading how genuine I was. He turned off the shower, casually stepping into a pair of sweats without even drying himself, before pulling a t-shirt and hoodie over his head. He was definitely easier to talk to when he was fully clothed.

He narrowed his eyes on me. "No." He picked up his bag and left through the back doors, pushing them open into the darkness outside. We let him go.

"Want me to follow him?" Lucius murmured softly. I nodded, and he disappeared out the door, still shirtless and in shredded pants. I was left alone in the dressing room, but I knew it wouldn't be for long.

"You can come in now."

The door opened, and Nico, Judge, Brody and Walker all appeared. There was still no sign of X and Tex. I had no doubt the guys had been listening on the other side this whole time.

"What do we do now?" Judge asked.

I shrugged. "I don't know. Lucius is following him, but I don't think he's stupid enough to go straight to the Night Demon."

X appeared in the doorway. "Lucky you have such an amazing stable of lovers then, right?" He still had his hand in Tex's, and my mate looked... frazzled, but there was a grin on his face.

I moved toward them both, kissing X first. "Thank you for keeping our mate safe," I whispered in his ear as I scraped my teeth over his lobe. Then I moved to Tex. "Have fun?"

The flush on his face, the swollen puff of his lips, and the way his hair looked like it had been gripped in a fist all said *yes*. Still, he nodded. "It was interesting. But when I heard the name of the opponents in the ring, I recognized Orthus." He leaned in and kissed my temple. "I got X to bring me back here, and I put my cane tracker in his shoe."

My mouth fell open. Sometimes I seriously underestimated this man, or maybe forgot he wasn't the boy who'd played me rock vinyls in his garage. I looked at his cane, free from the little white tracker that we used to find it whenever he misplaced it. Being blind was tough, and he used little tracker dots to find his cane or his wallet, or whatever else, with his phone. It was a lifesaver if one of us wasn't around.

I pulled up the app on my phone, and there it was, a little dot on a map moving away from the abandoned subway station.

"You're a fucking genius," Judge grunted, watching the dot over my shoulder.

Tex gave us all a bright smile, the expression a shining reminder of why he was my literal heartbeat. "I know."

CHAPTER
FIFTEEN

We didn't track Orthus down straight away, no matter how much I wanted to. Instead, we watched. We watched him ping off other phones and towers, watched the places where the signal went blank, places he returned to several times, and we made a note of those.

We just watched for days. Apparently, the man lived in his Nikes. X had told us he'd lifted the inner-sole of the shoe, dug out a little of the rubber lining and nestled the tracker in there. Honestly, I was glad he used his powers for good and not evil.

Most of the time.

While we watched and waited, we had to attend a mountain of public engagements that I hated. Some-times with Nico, other times with Brody, and once I'd had to meet a member of the European version of the

Convocation, the Capi. That was awkward. Albert was the head honcho of the European witches, and honestly, he freaked me the hell out. I actually missed Wilde at that moment, for fuck's sake.

But tonight was the night I was dreading the most. It was a legitimate ball. A masquerade ball, which was great, until you realized that all the things that go bump in the night were probably attending too. Things that liked to hide in the shadows already, or behind pleasant facades, who either had a vendetta against the twins, or me, or just Americans in general.

It was like walking into a viper's nest, and it was giving me anxiety. But I was dressed in a beautiful gown in the shade of moonlight, and my guys? They looked like a wet dream.

We were a group, a team, a Pack, so no matter how much I wanted to hide Tex away safely, and even Brody, we would always attend these functions as a united front.

They were all dressed in tuxes, and my ovaries ached with the need to fuck them. Their shirts were varying shades of blue to compliment the silver of my dress, and they were scrubbed until they shone.

And *damn,* did they shine.

Brody groaned as I ogled them. "Rainey, I'm going to need you to stop thinking about whatever you're thinking about, before I peel you out of that pretty dress and fuck you all night."

Tex huffed. "And offend every powerful supernatural in a three-hundred-mile radius."

I sighed. He was the voice of reason. Again. Spoilsport.

X came over and ran his tongue up the side of my neck, right over my jugular. "I'm with Red. I say we stay home and fuck."

I wasn't sure how, but a tux made X look *more* dangerous. His tattoos peeked up over his collar, and his short hair was slicked back like he'd only run his fingers through it—which, knowing X, was probably true. He looked like a weapon, but the sexy kind. Like a sharp dagger dragged over soft flesh.

Everyone groaned, and I smirked. Whoops.

Walker wrapped an arm around my waist, tugging me out of the arms of my Executioner. "I think, for once, I might actually agree with the Brit." But he kissed me softly, so I didn't have to reapply my lipstick. He was thoughtful like that.

"I don't know when I became the voice of reason, but we must leave," Nico said with a sigh. He was looking at my thighs longingly, where my pale skin flashed through the thigh-high split in my dress.

"I haven't even shown Raine my surprise," X complained, and Nico rolled his eyes, waving a hand for him to hurry. "Snakelet!"

The look on Tex's face was amused, but also a little... slack with lust. Well, that was interesting. He moved toward me in that loose-limbed swagger that only he could master, his lips twisted in a smirk that I wanted to kiss right off his face. He shucked his jacket off, and I gasped softly.

X had run soft silk ropes up and around Tex's biceps, across his back, and down the other arm. The ties were intricate and well placed, and after a couple of decades of being the one inside the designs, I could appreciate how much time and effort would have gone into it. It slipped across his shoulders, over his shirt but under the vest of his three-piece tuxedo.

He was like a gift, but I didn't want to unwrap him yet. I wanted to grip the deep purple cords and ride him into next week. Instead, I slid my fingers under one of those intricate weaves and tugged him against my body. I kissed him hard, and I didn't need to give him promises—he could taste them on his tongue as it tangled with mine.

Someone groaned and wrapped their arms around my waist, tugging me away. "You're a fucking asshole, X." Judge's grunted words were beside my ear. "Sugar, you're gonna have to stop, or I'm going to fuck you both until you can't do anything short of whimper my name. Then that fuck Francois will come and track us down, and we'll all have to listen to a lecture from Titus about proper decorum in political settings." His hand skimmed down over my ass. "Might be worth it, though."

I sighed, because he was right. Killjoy.

With one last kiss, I picked up my clutch and strode out the door, my guys behind me. We were driving to the ball, because I didn't want to ruin this beautiful dress, and running in Louboutins was a nightmare.

The ball was at a large conservatory, and it looked like any other human gala, except there were no paparazzi here. None of us were famous in the human world. We all stayed in the shadows and ruled them with money and power.

Nico helped me out of the Hummer, placing my hand firmly in the crook of his elbow as everyone else fanned out behind me. We walked the short distance to the door, which was crowded by security of all different flavors.

"Good evening, gentlemen, ma'am. We're going to have to ask you to leave your weapons at the door."

I didn't even suppress the snort that passed my lips. It was like asking a rattlesnake to give up its rattle. The knives that X carried weren't what made him dangerous. Still, I shrugged, looking over at the guys.

X let out a long, put-upon sigh as he opened his jacket and started pulling out knives. And guns. And was that a crossbow?

I raised my brows at him. "Really?"

He just grinned and continued, moving from the

weapons stored around his torso to the ones holstered around his legs. Another six knives and a dagger long enough to be a short sword were placed in a tub that was labeled with his name. X was a moving armory. How did he not clank when he walked?

The security guard just gaped. "Uh, you can collect them after the gala?"

X grimaced, giving the vampire guard a glare. "They better all be there too. Or else I'll be collecting something a little more valuable from you personally."

They continued on, and I wasn't surprised that most of my guys were carrying some kind of weapon, though not to the crazy extent that X had been. Even Tex had a switchblade that he added to X's pile.

Only Nico and I were weaponless. He gave me a half-smile. "Raine Baxter," he whispered in my ear, his voice filled with thousands of years of experience. "I *am* the weapon."

Judging by the faces of the vampire guards—all of whom must be reasonably young in their years to be still working for other nests—they seemed to know it too.

We finally moved into the ballroom, and I was aware that I was under intense scrutiny, though everyone was pretty good about pretending they weren't staring at my group. Francois swanned up to us, his smile wide and his fangs fully on display. Sure, they were nice, but even I knew it was like the school jock pulling out his dick at a party and doing helicopters. At the time, you couldn't help but be impressed, but later you realized it was a pretty big social faux pas.

"Member Baxter, Nico." His eyes flicked behind me, their shine going flat. "Lucius." He just nodded at the rest of my men, like he either hadn't taken the time to memorize their names or had decided they weren't important. I kinda hated this fucker, just for that slight alone.

However, my mother had always told me to kill people with kindness, but never make yourself smaller to do so. So I pasted my own fangtastic smile on my face. "It's just a delight to be here. You host a beautiful affair."

He gave me a tight smile. "This is the shifter Alpha's doing, I'm afraid."

I'd known that, and given how they felt about each other, I knew the barb would hurt. "Oh? Where is Alpha Dirk? I should give him and his mate my compliments then. Excuse me." Then I swanned away, like this centuries-old vampire meant nothing.

Lucius's laughter was more a feeling than an actual sound as I moved across the room, my chin held steady. Walker grabbed a glass of champagne off the tray of a nearby waiter and handed it to me.

"Thanks, Sheriff," I whispered softly. Then we were in front of Alpha Dirk and his wife Lieneke. I gave them a genuinely warm smile. "Alpha. Good to see you again." I kept my eyes lowered with the proper respect. I could almost *feel* the burn of Francois' gaze on my back. I turned to Lieneke. "This party is glorious. Thank you for the invitation."

The Alpha Mate gave me a warm, if still wary, smile. "It is an honor." She bowed her own head in Brody's direction and gave Tex a smile.

I waved a hand at the great loves of my life. "May I introduce the rest of our Pack? Walker Walton, Nico and Lucius Flett, Judge and X." Neither Judge and X wanted their human surnames associated with who they were as vampires, so like Madonna and Prince, they went by single names. I could respect that.

The Alpha and his mate nodded politely, but they were clearly wary of Nico and Lucius. I was used to it now, and so were they.

Judge wrapped an arm around my waist. "Let's dance."

CHAPTER
SIXTEEN

A ball filled with unknown supernaturals was like the shark tank at an aquarium. It was fine, until someone threw chum in the water and then it became a feeding frenzy.

It started out fine, of course. We danced and ate fancy little canapés. We ass-kissed and networked. We grinned through weakly veiled insults and even more covert threats. All in all, it was going quite well.

But, like any party, it only took one asshole to ruin the delicate balance between civility and chaos. And this asshole decided to do it in the most spectacular way possible.

I was talking to an old witch—not the dick from the Capi, but definitely someone who could have taken him in a fight. She felt old and powerful, but she also grabbed the asses of the waiters who walked past, regardless of gender, and cackled at her own jokes, so she was somehow lower down the scale of scariness.

X was beside me, because if anyone could get down with inappropriate conversation topics, it was him. Judge was mingling with other vampires he knew, with Tex close by, and Brody was liaising with the other Alphas who'd been invited. I had no idea where Lucius and Walker were, but I hoped they were together; Walker would temper Lucius's more fiery responses. Nico was also nowhere to be seen, but he was a big boy and could take care of himself.

"How was I supposed to know that adding sweat to the incantation would turn it into some kind of hedonistic hex that made everyone take off their clothes and start copulating on the floor?" the old witch grumbled, but the sparkle in her eye told me that she wasn't the least bit repentant.

X laughed, but it dropped from his face like an ACME anvil as his eyes slid behind me. I spun, just in time to see a vampire we didn't know corner Tex at the bar. We usually let Tex handle his own shit—he was a big boy who'd stomped around in the affairs of powerful creatures for just as long as I had.

So we waited. We watched. And when the vampire grabbed Tex's face with rough fingers, we acted. X moved first, but we were both too slow to stop the vampire before his fangs were in Tex's throat. But only briefly, because then Nico was there, crushing the offending vampire's jaw in his fist.

The scream echoed through the room like a bomb siren, Nico pulverizing the other vampire's face as he carefully pulled his fangs from Tex's throat, preventing any further damage to my mate. He held the taller vamp in the air, his face that scary darkness that I didn't see too often but always knew was there.

People worried about Lucius, but he cloaked himself in the darkness, wore it on the outside for everyone to see and fear. But that dark beast lived inside his twin too. The predator lurking in the shadows just dressed in bright pink shirts and cheesy slogan tees, hidden behind that beatific smile.

Sometimes, he let the monster out to prove that it wasn't just one twin the world should be scared of, but *all* the Flett brothers.

No one stopped Nico as he reached up and snapped the vampire's fangs from his mouth, the screams now the only sound in the room. "You do not take what you want from those who belong to me." Nico's words boomed around the room. "You forget yourself." His snarl was more monster than man as he looked around the room. "You *all* forget yourselves."

This wasn't my Nico. This was the ancient vampire inside him who'd lived a thousand lives. He threw the sobbing vampire to the pretty granite floor. The guy slid across it as people jumped out of the way, his still bleeding mouth leaving a macabre trail of blood behind him.

He stopped in front of Francois, who looked down at the vampire with molten rage. It wasn't directed at the vampire who'd attacked my mate though—no, his rage was all for Nico. For me. For us.

"This is not your wild west playground, Nicolai. You have no authority here. No power."

Lucius appeared beside his brother, his lip curled back into a disdainful snarl. "You have power here only because we *allow* it. Let us not forget who ruled before you, and who will rule after you if you push us. I conquered these lands by myself before most of you were even born, against vampires older and more powerful than any of you. If you do not think I will band together with my twin and wipe every trace of you from this continent, you have a short memory."

The moment was tense, and I placed a soft hand on both their spines. I loved them so fucking much. I wouldn't undermine them, but I also didn't want to create an international incident over some fucking moron who couldn't keep his fangs to himself.

Just the idea of him trying to bite Tex without his permission made my sluggish, undead heart pound with fury.

Nico sucked in a deep breath. "They belong to me," he repeated, his voice more reasonable. "Any creature who thinks of touching what is mine will not fare as well as that one." He tilted his head toward the now unconscious vampire. "Consider yourselves fairly warned."

With that, he bundled us all up and swept from the room. I held Tex tightly to my side as the others circled around us, making people move out of their path or be walked over.

I took a moment to look at the people in the room, and noticed that the crowd had split into definite sections, each member segregating back to their own race when things got tense. There was some fear, and more than a little disdain permeating the room.

I didn't care. I didn't need the drama of these people and their fucking politics. I didn't want to be here at all. I wanted to be home where Tex was safe, and where we were all together in one community instead of warring factions, like this was still the sixth century.

I swept out past the security, and X grabbed the entire tub of weapons from the shaky-looking security guards. I didn't know who exactly Nico had defanged, but apparently it made an impression.

Buddy was standing at the end of the short pathway, his eyes scanning the surrounding buildings and the back door of our Hummer already open. The guys bundled me inside, then climbed in after me. No one spoke, and I wrapped myself around Tex like I was the snake shifter. Someone had closed up the wounds on his neck, but there was still a small trace of blood on his pale skin that felt like a dagger in my heart.

Tex rubbed a soothing hand over my back. "It's okay, baby. I'm okay."

He was trying to console me? I choked out a sound that might have been a sob or a laugh. He pulled me into his lap, holding me tightly as I buried my face over the spot where the ragged bite marks had been.

I shuddered. "I hate that I can't protect you."

Lucius, that sweet fucking psycho, snorted. "You don't *need* to protect him, Raine Baxter. We are your consorts, your mates. We will protect you both." He said it like it was obvious. Like it didn't even bear mentioning that if anyone tried to hurt me, he would tear them to pieces. Again.

Tex sighed beneath me. "Raine, baby. I've come to terms with the fact I will always be your weakest link. I hate it, I do, but I wouldn't be anywhere else but with you. I'd hate it even more if you were here without me."

Nico ran a hand over my head, and then over the styled locks of Tex. "You're not the weakest link, Tex. You're the lynchpin. You give our girl something that none of the rest of us can. A connection to her past, a link to her humanity. Not one of us has seen our humanity in the last hundred years. Even the Alpha." Brody didn't seem offended by that, nodding his slow agreement. "We can give her protection and love—

137

hell, we would give her our lives if that's what was needed. But only you can give her that special thing she needs to feed her soul. You should be proud of that."

I felt the tears start to fall. Fucking Nico. I buried my face in Tex's chest, let the bond between us soothe me as much as his hands. "Let's go home. I don't want to be here anymore. I don't care if I have to sit on the Convocation forever."

Brody grabbed my hand, filling his own matebond with strength and reassurance, lifting my fingers so he could kiss every single one. "We've come this far, Rainey. We can finish this, then go home." He gave me a soft smile that was probably meant to reassure me, but somehow, just made me cry harder. "You're many things, Raine Baxter, but you aren't a coward. You're the toughest, most resilient, most beautiful woman I've ever met, and there's not a single supernatural on this godforsaken continent who isn't going to know it."

I sucked back a hiccuping little breath. "You guys are really good for my ego—have I ever told you that?" I joked, because that's what I did when I was scared or the vibe of a conversation got a little too serious.

Judge cleared his throat. "Maybe we can get home quicker than we thought." He held up his phone. On it was the mapping system from Tex's GPS tag. "This is where he stays. He goes there, stays for hours, and doesn't leave. I've looked it up, and the only things there are a few warehouses and what used to be a flophouse in the twenties." It was hard to know if Judge meant the 1920s or the 1820s. Hell, with them being this old, it could be the 1720s.

X, who'd been uncommonly quiet, nodded once. "Let's fucking go then."

Despite the fact that it was nearly three in the morning, and the docks should have been empty, I wasn't surprised that they were full of activity. If you were a human driving past, it would probably appear empty. But I wasn't a human. I could hear the heartbeats as they echoed off shipping containers. Smell the stench of forgotten humanity. I saw the movement of men covertly weaving in and out of containers, probably doing something illegal. But that wasn't my business—not here, at least.

Behind all the warehouses and shipping containers, squashed somewhere in a back alley but somehow covered on all four sides, was a tiny little shack. It looked like the kind of place you'd store machinery or something, and calling it a flophouse was probably giving it a sense of grandeur it didn't really deserve.

The guys moved through the darkness like shadows, Lucius remaining at my back along with Tex and

Brody. The house was surrounded, and there were at least seven heartbeats inside. Maybe more.

"You think this is a crack house too?" Tex whispered so softly it almost sounded like the whistling of the wind through the buildings. I didn't put anything past Orthus and his senses. I shrugged, because I honestly couldn't tell. There was definitely the chemical scent of drugs around here somewhere, but it could be from one of those containers being offloaded on the dock, or the guy a hundred feet away shooting up.

All I knew was that nothing in the house had changed yet. I stepped forward, going to knock on the door, Brody and Lucius on high alert. Lifting my fist, I'd almost knocked when a shadow appeared from nowhere and knocked Lucius to the ground. Pushing Tex behind me so quickly that he would have gotten whiplash if he was human, I recognized Orthus immediately, at least in his human form.

Lucius seemed to be half-heartedly fighting him, his blood still up from the fight at the gala, and it was a testament to how far he'd come that he didn't just reach inside the unshifted man's chest and rip out his heart.

"Orthus, stop!" I yelled, breaking the silence of the docks. I felt like I was breaking a rule, but I didn't care.

Lucius just grinned up at me. "Go. I've got this under control."

And if that didn't just make the enraged hell dog madder... Orthus launched at Lucius's throat, but without being in his hellhound form, he didn't stand much of a chance.

I pulled Tex through the door and walked into... an orgy?

My feet stopped dead, and I just blinked. "What the actual fuck..." Tex breathed, and I had to agree.

Everywhere around us were women and men writhing on the floor in pure bliss. One guy had a woman bent into a position I didn't think was even humanly possible, but they were definitely human.

In the middle of the room, on a dirty floor that I wouldn't want to look at with a blacklight, was a man in a hoodie. He sat cross-legged, his elbow resting on his knee, propping up his chin. He looked bored. Super bored.

His eyes flicked to us, and he frowned. "Who are you?" He sighed. "Doesn't matter." He flicked his fingers in our direction, and suddenly, there was a hand tangled in my hair and Brody was bending my head back so he could kiss me.

Like, *really* kiss me. Tex was behind me, sucking on my neck, his dick hard in his tuxedo pants as he ground himself against my ass.

Whoa.

"What the fuck?" I hissed, and tugged on my bonds with my guys. Brody pulled back with a frown, but there was still lust clouding his eyes. I jumped out from between their bodies and marched over to the seated fuckboy on the ground. "Turn it the fuck off," I growled, and the first real expression crossed his face. He looked shocked, like I'd slapped him.

"Excuse me?"

I gripped his hoodie and pushed it off his head. He had shoulder-length blond hair and eyes so clear, it was hard to name their actual color. Green, maybe?

He looked surprised as hell, as he flicked his hands toward me. I flashed my fangs, my eyes sliding to Brody and Tex, who were currently kissing each other. Eesh, that one was going to be hard to explain later.

"I said TURN. IT. OFF."

The guy was on his feet so quickly, I jumped back a step. "Orthus!" he yelled, but I reached out and grabbed his shirt. He tried to yank himself away, but I was stronger. He might be huge, tall and broad, but he wasn't a vampire. "Who the fuck *are* you?" he hissed. "Orthus!"

I shook my head, pushing my succubi powers at him. "Orthus is busy," I told him, as the rest of my guys broke in through the door, Orthus unconscious between X and Lucius. "I'm Raine Baxter, and I just want to talk... Night Demon."

CHAPTER
SEVENTEEN

I wasn't sure what I thought was going to happen at my words. Maybe we'd sit down and have a conversation. Maybe he'd run. Maybe he'd fight.

I hadn't expected him to kiss me. It wasn't a romantic gesture—it was a mashing of his lips on mine, but damn, it stunned the shit out of me.

Ten points to the Night Demon.

He pulled back and stood there, staring at me expectantly. I screwed up my nose. This was awkward.

The Night Demon rocked back on his heels, his face folded into a frown. "That usually works."

Orthus was still growling, and then he shifted into the two-headed hellhound while the guys tried to work out how they kept their hands on something that was doubling in size and bulk. Which meant I had exactly three seconds to make my case before I became dog food.

"I want you to come to America and be the leader for rare supernaturals!" It all ran out in one long sentence, and the guy looked like I'd slapped him upside the head, but in the next second, Orthus was free of Lucius and X, and had his teeth wrapped around the Night Demon's arm. They disappeared into the shadows within the space of a heartbeat.

"*Fuck!*" I shouted.

With the man gone, the people doing the devil's tango on the floor seemed to wake up from their stupor. Not to say that they stopped—one guy was mid-stroke, and he looked down at the girl who seemed really pissed to stop that close to coming. She said something to him in annoyed Dutch, so he kept pumping away like a champ, and I knew we'd over-stayed our welcome.

"Let's go. Dammit."

Tex wrapped his arm around me, pointedly not looking at Brody. I mean, we'd been together twenty years. Swords had crossed, saliva had probably been exchanged. But Brody was absolutely hetero, and he didn't lean to guys the way some of them did. So the fact they'd made out was definitely going to be weird for both of them.

"It's okay, Rainey. You got out what you needed to say, and the rest is up to him."

I pouted. "If I had more than three seconds, I might have been able to convince him." Orthus was going straight to my shit list. We shut the door on the orgy behind us. "The guy just disappeared into the shadows. What the hell *is* he?"

Nico shook his head. "I don't know for sure."

I huffed in frustration, resisting the urge to stomp my foot. We were so close. I hadn't assumed it was going to be easy to find the Night Demon, but damn. This was ridiculous. To make matters worse, when Orthus had shifted, he'd lost his shoes, the ones we were using to track him. Now we were fucked. They'd go to ground, and it would be impossible to find them.

I toed Orthus's shoes with my own stilettos, then picked them up. They were coming with me. Was it petty to steal his shoes? Yes. Did I care? Not even a little. If he wanted them back, he could come and get them himself.

I didn't fool myself, though. They were gone.

We melted back into the night, and I caught an Uber back to the apartment with Brody and Tex while everyone else ran. I still wasn't running in Louboutins, and honestly, I had no urge to run through the street barefoot if I didn't have to. I mightn't be able to get tetanus anymore, but it was also seriously gross.

When we made it back to my pissed off body-guards, I gave them a tight smile as proof that I hadn't been bodysnatched, then stomped into my bedroom. I threw my shoe hostages across the room and got out of my own stilettos. Your feet still ached walking around in heels, undead or not.

Judge appeared behind me, wrapping an arm around my waist. "It'll be okay, Rainy Day."

I huffed, lifting my shoulder so he'd get the hint and unzip my dress, and he sighed against my nape, but still did as I wordlessly asked. The dress slid from my shoulders, the heavy beading sending it straight to my feet until it pooled around my ankles.

Judge hummed softly in his throat at the sight. "Still the most beautiful woman I've ever held in my hands."

I snorted, in a seriously unsexy way. "I've met the Witch Miranda, Judge. Don't screw with me."

Miranda was... gorgeous. Like, you didn't know if you wanted to hate her, or switch teams so she'd give you just a little bit of her attention. I'd hated her at first, but now we were friends, of a sort.

His lips brushed over the curve of my shoulder. "The fact you still think I just mean the outside packaging, Sugar, breaks my heart." He nipped my throat, the gentle scrape of his fangs an erotic promise. His hands roamed down the sides of my body. "You're beautiful, Raine. Just looking at you sometimes makes me hard as fuck. But it isn't your outer beauty that makes it hard to breathe, Rainy Day. It's that sassy fucking mouth, and your wildly big heart, and the fact you make me laugh every day... That's why you're beautiful. I love you, and I'd love you even if you were a scarred old hag with body fungus."

Someone chuckled by the door. "You were going so well," Tex said. "Maybe we should have gone with X's suggestion that she ride his face until she felt better."

While a pep talk was nice, doing my best to smother a man—who didn't need to breathe—with my vagina was usually a world of fun.

But I wasn't really feeling that either. "I just want to puppy pile tonight. I just want you all around where I can touch you, like the old days."

Judge wrapped his arms back around my waist, holding my near naked body tightly to his. "Anything you want."

And that was how I ended up in the middle of a mattress on the floor, surrounded by the great loves of my life, and still unable to sleep. The sun was bright outside the windows, and the soft snores around me were soothing in their own way. Not all of them were asleep; vampires didn't really need to sleep often. They basically only did it to conserve energy, especially as they got older. Some slept to keep away the ennui. But we tended to not break the silence when it was like this. Everyone deserved time with their thoughts.

Unfortunately, my thoughts just continued to go

around and around and around. I was going home. I knew what Walker would say—that I was quitting at the first hurdle. I knew Brody wouldn't care, because he would be missing home already too. X was probably enjoying raising hell, but honestly, he just wanted me to be happy, along with Tex. Nico and Lucius... Well, who knew what either of those two wanted. Judge was used to roaming. He'd go where me and Tex went.

"You're thinking hard," X grumbled. "It's keeping me awake." He reached out an arm and pulled me closer, despite the fact he was dragging me across Lucius. Lucius's hands reached out and stroked my body as it moved across his, but didn't try and hold onto me. He was better with the sharing thing than I ever could have imagined. I was thankful for that.

X snuggled me into his chest, his lips pressing against all the exposed skin he could find. "Sleep, Red. There's time to worry about this shit later. We're all here now, and there's no point worrying about what hasn't happened yet." He said all this with his eyes closed.

"Love you, you crazy asshole," I murmured against his chest. "You make me so goddamn happy."

"You're lying basically naked in the middle of a bunch of predators, and I'm the crazy one?" he scoffed. "You make me happy too. You know I love you more than I love blood splatter. Now go to sleep."

I couldn't help the stupid grin on my face. "I'm just going to make a warm drink. Might help. I'll be right back."

A hand stroked up my thigh. Nico was awake too. "Try the A-Pos. It's nice warmed up."

There was a time when discussing the different blood types and their vintage would have been weird. But not now. It was better than going out to find a random Joe on the street and sucking his blood, then killing him.

I climbed carefully over the limbs that seemed to be tangled, avoiding a sleeping Tex who was curled around Judge, one foot on Brody because they were Pack and Pack slept better when they were touching. They'd overcome their weirdness, obviously.

I finally made it to the door, and looked over the real Sea of Love. Sure, it was actually a Sea of Dick and Orgasms, but that didn't fit so nicely into a song. I grinned, humming the Honeydrippers song under my breath as I walked through the kitchen toward the fridge.

Buddy was asleep, and Rio was guarding the door. I gave him a little wave, no longer shy about being partially nude since they'd all seen me getting railed over the back of the couch three months after starting as my security detail.

So awkward.

I looked in the fridge and pulled out the A-Pos. I

felt the cool displacement of air behind me, and smiled. Part of me knew Lucius wouldn't stay spooning without me there.

But when I turned, it wasn't Lucius. It was Orthus.

The guard shouted and threw a knife, but it was too late. I was wrapped in shadows and then disappeared into nothingness.

CHAPTER
EIGHTEEN

Fuck! Fuck, fuck, fuck, fucking Fucker McFuckin', Mayor of Fuckington!

"Are you done?"

As quickly as I'd disappeared into darkness, I reappeared in... not shadows. My cursing was apparently not as internal as I'd thought. Where the hell was I?

"No, I'm not fucking *done*. Where the hell am I, Orthus, you fucking asshole?"

Honestly, it looked like nowhere I'd ever seen. Almost like a desert, but the sand on the ground was so black that it absorbed the light. The mountains in the distance were jagged, and one was coated in lava. I spun in a circle. There wasn't a single speck of green in the otherwise barren landscape. Hot wind whistled across the near empty plain, creating an eerie sound.

Some part of me knew I wasn't in the human realm

anymore. I went for Orthus's throat, but he just wrapped a big hand around my own and slammed me to the ground. "Apologies, vamp. You can't overpower me here. This is my domain."

His domain.

Orthus was a hellhound.

Surely this wasn't... "YOU BROUGHT ME TO HELL?!"

Oh god. I mean, oh Lucifer.

"Calm your tits, vamp girl. You're fine. It's not like you need to breathe oxygen, so the sulfur isn't gonna hurt you," he scoffed.

Just like that, I clamped my lips shut and stopped breathing. "Don't tell my tits what to do, Fido. Take me back."

There was a sound behind me, and I spun, teeth bared, my hands curled into claws like I could actually fight off any kind of demon. I was so screwed. But behind me wasn't a heinous creature.

No, it was a really damn hot Night Demon.

He gave me a tight smile. "You're fine, succubus. Part of you belongs here too."

"I just wanted to talk, for g—" I caught myself. "For *gouda's* sake."

Orthus snorted. "Pretty sure Luc would be just as pissed if you took cheese's name in vain."

"Look, I'm sorry I stole your shoes—"

"You stole my shoes?"

"And interrupted your weird little orgy ritual—"

The Night Demon looked offended. "I was feeding."

I held my hands up to stop them both. "Whatever. I just wanted to talk to you, not torture you with my presence. This is extreme. You have to take me back; I swear I'll go home and leave you to your weird little flea hovel on the docks."

Bravado don't fail me now.

"You're a succubus."

Fat lot of good that was doing me with these two. "Barely. Doesn't matter. Take me back." I was annoyed at how my voice trembled.

"You don't understand—"

I held up a hand again. "No, *you* don't understand..." Then I burst into tears.

You know what? Don't judge me. I'd been dragged into the shadows and ended up in Hell. Say what you want about my lack of lady balls, but until your feet felt just a little too hot with the brimstone burning your goddamn soles, you can't tell me you wouldn't cry too.

It was almost worth it to see the absolute panic on their faces, but I couldn't appreciate it. "I just want to go home," I hiccuped, and the two of them looked at each other, then back at me, then back at each other. "I don't want to be the stupid Convocation Member anymore. I just want to bake, and kiss my boyfriends, and eat deep-fried shit at the diner. I just want to *live*."

Orthus rolled his eyes. "You're already dead."

I narrowed my eyes at him. I was about to tell him where he could stick it, but then I remembered where I was. "HOLY SHIT! Did you *stake* me?!" It didn't matter that I no longer needed to breathe, I was hyperventilating. Go figure. "Oh my god, I can't believe I'm dead-dead."

My first thought was this was going to kill Brody and Tex, the severing of our mate bond, but hopefully their bond with each other would keep them from following me into death. Judge would protect Tex; I knew that with my entire soul. Because his heart was split into two, and I knew he would keep Tex going for as long as he could.

A sob built up in my chest as I thought about the kids, my pups. How they would've thought they'd have me forever, and now I was gone. I pushed the emotion back down, because I didn't want to cry in front of these assholes. The others would take care of them, love them enough that the wound of my death would heal eventually.

Maybe not Lucius, because if any one was following me to Hell, it was him.

X would protect the pups, because he adored them too. And Walker. My precious Walker would carry on, because that was who he was.

Nico? I didn't think he'd stay either. So much loss, it sat on his shoulders like a mantle of grief.

I couldn't breathe. I slumped to the ground, grappling for my matebonds, but there was nothing. Emptiness.

I was dead.

My tears dripped onto my hands as I cried even harder.

"Hey, hey, it's okay. Hey," the Night Demon murmured, squatting down in front of me. "You're not dead. You hear me? You're fine—I swear it. I just needed to talk to you somewhere safe."

Safe? Hell was safe?

"You're fucking insane. We are in *HELL!*" I screeched. "Listen, Night Demon—"

"Vali. My name is Vali."

At one point, that would have mattered to me. Now, nothing mattered. "Safe was just talking to me in your shitty little crackhouse. Safe would have been Orthus setting up a date in a damn coffee shop. We could be having this conversation over pot brownies and coffee, not standing in my goddamn underwear in Hell," I hissed.

As if they hadn't noticed until that point, they both looked down at my bare legs, my undies with *Don't get me wet* and a picture of a Gremlin on my ass and a Mogwai on my hoohaa, and my plain white tank.

"None of those options are safe when you're with

the man who eradicated your entire damn species, succubus," Orthus spat. "You might like to play with death, but not all of us are disloyal to our own species."

I looked at him, staring him dead in those dark abyss eyes. "I don't play with Death—I ride his face until Death is begging *me* for release," I snarled. "Don't talk to me of traitors. You have no fucking idea who Lucius is, or anything about us." If I trusted any man to chase me to Hell and save me, it was that lunatic. "Neither of you are succubi, so I don't know why your panties are in a knot. Pretty sure hellspawn and demons have nothing to fear from Lucius, regardless of his past."

"Incubus," Vali stated calmly.

"*Vali!*" Orthus hissed.

I just blinked at them both. "Excuse me?"

Ignoring the hellhound who looked seconds away from tackling him to the ground to shut him up, Vali replied, "I'm an incubus. The last of my kind, just like you. We're only kind of demon-ish."

"Excuse me?" I repeated, because there were lots of things in that sentence that didn't make sense.

One: I had no idea incubuses... Incubi? Incubussy? Whatever. I didn't even know they'd existed at any point.

Two: Why were there no other incubi, and why

was he looking at me like I was a Christmas turkey and he'd been on a diet of lettuce for a lifetime?

Three: What did he mean, not *really* a demon? And why did he keep saying *we?*

Orthus tilted his head to the left, looking like a Doberman even in his human form. "The gargoyles approach."

"Ah, fuck."

And just like that, two miniature dragon-looking things appeared on the ground in front of us. Orthus stood, positioning himself slightly in front of Vali, but not shifting into his hellhound form. He was alert, but not tense. Were these miniature dragon things friends?

I said miniature because I'd seen Alexander in his full dragon form, and he was the size of a football field. These guys were the size of a Mom van.

Before my eyes, they shifted from stone lizard things to men. Hot men. Naked hot men.

Was I supposed to cover my eyes?

"Orthus. Vali. What are you doing here?" one of the men growled.

The other one gave a lopsided smile. "What Romanus means to say is, hey, it's good to see you, but is that a fucking mortal in Hell? If Luc catches you using Hell like a Starbucks, he's going to chew you out."

The other guy, Romanus, snorted. "Literally."

My eyeballs felt like they had a mind of their own. They bounced from the gargoyles, to Orthus and Vali, to the gargoyles' dicks just hanging there in the sulfur breeze, and then back to their faces. I was stuck in a loop I couldn't escape.

Vali gave them a soft smile, and their eyes went big. Like kawaii-big. "I'm sorry, Rouen. We'll get out of here right now."

Romanus reached out and slapped Rouen's hand as it reached for the incubus. He gave Vali an unimpressed look. "I'd quit that shit, otherwise it isn't Lucifer you'll have to worry about. Rella doesn't share her mates," he growled, a friendly warning with bite. His eyes fell on me. "Vampire." He sucked in a deep breath, scenting me. "Succubus?" He looked back at Vali. "I see. Good luck, friend. But get the hell out of here now."

Vali nodded. "Sure thing. Give my love to your queen."

I wanted to flex, just a little, so they couldn't just throw me in the River Styx and be done with it. If that actually existed. "Tell Lucifer that Raine Baxter sends her regards," I said lightly, and everyone turned to look at me. "Yeah, bitches. I mightn't be hellspawn, but I'm not without connections."

Orthus cursed, and then I was wrapped up in shadows again and sucked back into darkness.

Fucking hellhound.

CHAPTER
NINETEEN

I knew we were back on my normal plane of existence because the bonds came rushing back into my chest like a freight train, dropping me to my knees as I gasped under their pain, fear and confusion.

"You guys have exactly five minutes before my mates arrive and whatever I said about you being safe from Lucius goes right out the damn window," I said, coughing as I replaced the tainted oxygen in my lungs with the sweet aroma of garbage and stale piss from the back alley we were standing in.

I almost preferred brimstone.

I sent reassurance down the bonds in huge waves. I was okay. I'd been to Hell and returned reasonably unscathed.

"It's going to take more than five minutes to

explain, but I think, perhaps, we can help each other." Vali was standing close, so close that the scent of him almost washed away the stench of human filth. So close that I could see the sharp line of his jaw and his stupidly high cheekbones.

So close that I could tell his lips were soft and kind of pillowy, and that his eyes were seafoam green. In their depths, I could see something that tugged at my heartstrings more than his words could—I saw despair.

Shit. Damn bleeding heart. Not even a real bleeding heart; I was hungry and could actually consume one of those.

"I'd appreciate it if you stopped the Flett twins from tearing out our throats before we talked," he said softly. He was lucky I was feeling charitable and that I had an insane amount of curiosity. Honestly, curiosity might be my eventual downfall.

I didn't make any promises though, as I counted under my breath. Five. Four. Three. Two...

The displacement of air let me know my men had arrived. That, and the "Oof!" of Vali hitting the pavement.

"Wait!" I yelled at Nico, and launched myself at Lucius, who had Orthus's throat between his fangs. I poked him in the butthole, hard.

Lucius reared back and looked at me like I was the insane one.

I gave him a sheepish smile. "Just wait. You can kill him later."

There was nothing human in Lucius's expression at that moment, as he tossed the hellhound to the side, and I winced as Orthus hit the wall on the other side of the alleyway. But I knew what was coming and braced myself.

Lucius grabbed me, dragging me into his arms. His rough hands gripped my face, tilting my head to the side. "You were *gone*," was all he said before he sank his fangs into my throat. The madness had a hold of him.

Or maybe the madness was just an excuse we used to justify the fact that when he pushed my panties to the side and sank his cock into me, I liked it.

I liked Lucius's desperate hands more than I cared to admit out loud. I loved that he needed me more than he needed oxygen. Was that weird? Probably. But as he thrust harder, one hand still wrapped around my throat as he pinned me up against the wall, his other hand slipping between our bodies to rub my clit, I didn't care. I loved his tenuous hold on the predator. I loved the fact that he needed to center himself in my body because he loved me. I loved him too.

I clutched at his shoulders, moaning into the night. "Lucius, please," I breathed. He pinched my clit, and that was all I needed. I came around his cock as he kissed me, consuming my pleasure like it was heroin. I should be worried that he was addicted to me like this, but I wasn't.

Not even a little.

Especially not when he lifted the hand that had been rubbing my clit to his lips and sucked down my release. My pussy pulsed around him, and he made this growling noise deep in his throat which I knew, after a couple of decades, meant that I was going to bring him to his knees.

Unfortunately, we had an audience, and absolutely no time.

Lucius lowered me to my feet, but kept me close to his body. I looked past his shoulder at the rest of my guys. Brody was heaving deeply, like he'd run a marathon—which maybe he had, considering I had no idea where we were.

"You okay, Lucy?" X asked softly. He eyed him warily.

What the hell had happened while I was away?

Lucius didn't speak, just gave a tight nod. With that, the others all rushed me. I was passed from one set of arms to another, and I hugged them each to me tightly, emotion clogging my throat. I apologized repeatedly, even though it hadn't been my fault. Sometimes you just needed to say sorry to someone because they were hurting, even if it wasn't your fault. Showing your empathy didn't have to be an entire flash mob of feelings; sometimes it could just be a single word.

Saying sorry wasn't a weakness.

Walker pulled his shirt off, then settled it over my head. It fell mid-thigh, like a t-shirt dress, covering me from stray eyes. "You scared the shit out of me, Raine Baxter. Again."

Nico was still shaking with rage when I made my way to him. He wrapped me tightly in his arms and didn't let go. "I'm okay," I whispered softly against his chest.

"I want them dead. They stole you in the middle of the day. Directly from our arms. They are a *threat,* and they need to die."

I stroked a hand down his spine. I could see the tension in the two men who were still backed against the wall. "There are a lot of people in this world who are more of a threat to me than these two. We can't kill every single one of them."

"Why not?"

I snorted, tilting Nico's chin down so I could kiss him. We never mentioned it out loud, but every single person in my Pack knew—the madness was creeping at the edges of Nico's mind too. He'd held it off for so long, but it was there now. Just flashes when his emotions ran high.

"Because we aren't monsters, Nico. We're the good guys, remember?"

He took another shuddering breath, and I could see him push the crazy back down. I couldn't handle both twins being crazy. No, that was a lie; I would absolutely love Nico despite the madness, but I'd fight hard to keep Nico as the man I knew and loved.

When I looked over at the two men who'd stolen me from the kitchen, Orthus looked perturbed, but it was Vali's expression that caught my attention. He looked like he was having a heart attack. His eyes were big and shining so brightly that they were almost surreal. His gaze was bouncing around, and he was sucking in air through his nose so hard that his shoulders were heaving.

"Are you okay?" I went to move toward him, but Nico's fingers latched around my wrist. I looked at Orthus. "Is he okay? Vali, are you choking?"

Nico was frowning now too. "I didn't do any damage." His voice was steady and sure.

Orthus was watching the incubus, his eyebrows low over his eyes. They seemed to have a silent conversation, and he turned back to us. His body was between Vali and the rest of us, protecting him, even though he wouldn't stand a chance against all of us in a fight. "He's fine. He's feeding."

I blinked. "Pardon me?"

Honestly, it looked like he was having a panic attack.

Vali took a ragged breath in. "You don't feed?"

"On blood? All the time." I waved a hand in his general direction. "I don't do whatever it is you're doing right now."

"What the hell is going on?" Walker grumbled, and I reached a hand over to him. I needed his steady reassurance.

"The Night Demon is an incubus. A sex demon."

"Like you?" Tex asked softly.

I shrugged. He didn't seem overly like me, but I wasn't a typical succubi. "No? Maybe?"

It was Walker who stepped forward. "We should discuss this somewhere more private." He shot a quick look at Lucius. "Not at our lodgings."

I raised an eyebrow, because who gave up home ground?

Orthus huffed a sigh. "I know a place. Let's go." He eyed Lucius warily. "I need your word that he won't attack."

I screwed up my nose, looking over at Lucius, who raised a single brow. I shrugged. "I'm his lover, not his leash. You fucked up; you're gonna have to live with the consequences." I rolled my eyes as Orthus stepped close to Vali. I'd worked out somewhere on our exit from Hell, that it was Orthus who had control over the shadows. "That being said, he knows what this means to me, and I'm sure he won't attack either of you unless you provoke him. No more stealing me into the shadows, and don't touch anyone without permission."

"Fine. The gargoyles will be watching the shadows now so I doubt I could sneak you back into Hell anyway."

Brody spun on his heel and stared, while Tex gasped. "Hell? He means figuratively, right?"

"Is that why our bond snapped?" Brody added.

"Yes. And he meant literally." I shuddered.

Now that I wasn't down there, I could acknowledge the whistling wind hadn't really been wind at all. It had been screams.

Orthus led us to what looked like an abandoned building in the Red Light District. The windows were boarded up, and the heavy door was weathered. He watched the streets, watched the cops up on the corner, and the tourists with their money belts out still getting ripped off by pickpockets—though I had to give it to them, they were fast. It was almost mesmerizing, and they never took the whole lot. Just little bits here and there. Clever.

A kid walked past us, and I watched him size X up and go for it. There was a slight smile on X's mouth as the kid—who was probably about seventeen—bumped into him. X let him get his hand all the way into his pocket before he spun supernaturally fast, gripping the boy's wrist.

It would have been comical if the kid's face wasn't totally petrified.

"Choose your marks better, boy. There are scarier things in the dark than the cops," X growled, and maybe he flashed a little fang. He held the kid's wrist easily as he pulled his wallet from his pocket, taking out two hundred euros and handing it to him. "Take the night off. Get something to eat and take a bath— you smell like asscrack." He released the kid, who ran so fast, I wondered if maybe he had a little supernatural in him too.

X moved up behind me, pushing me through the door of the abandoned building. I leaned back against his chest. "You're getting soft in your old age, you know that?"

"Shh, don't make me spank you, Red. I'll do it. Your Night Demon looks like he might enjoy it too." I followed X's line of sight, and without a word of a lie, Vali looked like he was about to come in his pants. Again.

I pointed a finger at him. "You need to stop that *right now*. I can't believe I'm having this discussion again, but you can't feed off people without their permission."

"Apologies." His face didn't look very apologetic. "Please, come in."

The room we walked into was like a time capsule for a brothel. The heavy velvet curtains screamed luxury, and even though the white-washed paint was flaking away, it still managed to look cozy. Orthus stood beside an unlit fireplace, looking vaguely annoyed.

"Please, have a seat," Vali said softly, indicating the seats behind us. I nodded, sitting on a light blue fainting couch. A small cloud of dust puffed up around me.

X sat beside me. "Think of all the ancient bodily fluids this couch has seen."

Ew.

Vali cleared his throat. "I think it's best if we start over. Hi, I'm Vali, an incubus. The last incubus. This is my companion and best friend, Orthus."

"More like his attack dog," X whispered from the side of his mouth. I hushed him, but he made a good point.

"Alpha Dirk suggested he was your protector."

He nodded. "We protect each other. We aren't affiliated with anyone in Amsterdam, so we have each other's backs out of necessity and loyalty. Unfortunately, Orthus bears the brunt of that load. A lot of people are less than impressed with the Night Demon."

We'd come back to that. But first... "Raine Baxter. I'm from North America."

Orthus snorted, muttering something that may have been the word, "Obviously."

"I'm the Convocation Member for Endangered Preternatural Species. I'm a vampire, and surprisingly enough, a succubus, as you guessed."

"Pleasure to meet you," Vali responded, and then we fell into silence. Awkward, sweaty silence.

I cleared my throat. "These are my consorts. X, a former assassin, and his partner Judge." I pointed to Judge, who was between Brody and Tex. "My mates, Brody and Tex. They're shifters. Walker, Sheriff of Canada's only community of vampires who don't feed off humans." I gave him a soft smile. I looked to my left, where my twin statues sat, glaring death. "You know Nico and Lucius."

Orthus snorted. "How did the last succubi end up with the fucking decimator of her species? Fate is a fickle bitch."

I mean, he wasn't wrong about Fate. She was a mercurial ho. "It's a long story, but it involves severed heads and a man who wanted to collect me like I was a Pokémon card. And not just any card. A really good one."

"1999 Charizard holo," Tex whispered beneath his breath, the same way Captain Ahab might have talked about Moby Dick. Deep down, that guy was a dork, and I was all about it.

Unfortunately, neither Vali or Orthus had any clue what he was talking about. Nico was smiling though, because we were slowly indoctrinating him into pop culture.

"It's a rare... You know what, it doesn't matter. All that matters is Lucius is mine now, and he's not exactly the same man he was all those centuries ago. What happened in the past can't be undone. The only thing that matters is the future." I sucked in a deep breath. It was now or never. This was my moment to make my pitch, woo this guy over to America, and live happily ever after. He just had to be stronger. "Do you think you could beat me in a fight?"

They both stared at me. Guess that might have been a bit of a random question.

"Perhaps? It would be close." Vali answered cautiously, like I was insane.

X tilted his head to the side. "You can do that lust bomb thing, but what else do you have? She's a vampire."

He snorted. "Well, I've got these." In a blink of an eye, wings appeared behind him and, oh my god, was that a tail?

"I get the demon reference now," X muttered. "What do you think he can do with that tail?"

I nudged him with my knee, hoping Vali hadn't heard. I didn't want to think of this attractive man, his wings spread wide, his tail holding my arms above my head.

I was happy. I had my guys. This was just the

incubus lust bomb thing.

Vali's jaw tensed as he let out a shuddering breath. I noticed the top arch of his wings had an extruding sharp claw, almost like a tusk. The fleshy wings were a deep red color, like when you closed your eyes and faced the summer sun. The very bottom point of his wing bone also had a sharp claw thing as well. They'd make fairly decent weapons.

I looked at Lucius. "Why didn't I get wings?"

He shrugged. "Want me to take his for you?" No inflection, like he hadn't just threatened to dismember a person who was standing less than ten feet away.

Everyone in the room tensed, and I shook my head. Fucking Lucius. "I'm good. Thanks, though."

Orthus was looking at us with wide eyes. "You think this is *better?*" He pointed at Lucius, which was probably dangerous in itself.

I lifted a single shoulder. "I mean, at least he asked first. Once upon a time, he would've just taken them and given them to me in a bloodied box as a gift, regardless of what either of us wanted." I looked at Vali's wings, which were pretty spectacular. The tail that whipped behind him slowly would also make a decent weapon if the point was as sharp as I thought it might be. "I think you're right. It would be close. That's good enough for me." And good enough for the Convocation, hopefully.

Someone moaned loudly from the building next

door, and I looked in that direction. Then the sound came again. Geez, the girl was either being murdered or was having the orgasm of her life. It could go either way.

Orthus looked at Vali, who shook his head, and the hellhound relaxed.

"Noisy neighbors?"

Vali smiled, and fuck, it was a good smile. It lit up his whole face, and until that point, I hadn't realized how much sadness weighed down his features. "The noisiest, but it is easy to feed from them here, and in return, we keep them safe. Even if they don't know it."

X leaned back in his chair, his feet stretched out in front of him. My eyes were drawn to the long lines of his muscular thighs. "Let me guess. You guys moved in twenty or so years ago?"

Orthus growled. "Who have you been talking to?"

X gave him that cocky smirk that always made me want to get naked. "Humans. They are more observant than any of us give them credit for."

Had they stopped the prostitutes being murdered, or had they been the cause? Gah, now I had more questions. I wanted them to be the saviors. Vali seemed nice, and I'd learn more about him when I took him back to the States. Wasn't like I had to hand him over the Convocation until I was content; there were no deadlines.

Vali nodded softly. "We are symbiotic, the women

of the night and me. I think that because humans have always needed to be willing participants in my sustenance, I view them less like livestock than other supernaturals." His eyes flicked to Lucius. "They aren't disposable, as most people think. We need them far more than they need us. In fact, they don't need us at all. We are leeches attached to the undercarriage of their short, fruitless lives."

I leaned forward, propping my elbows on my knees, my fingers steepled under my chin. "I have a proposition for you." I sucked my bottom lip between my teeth. I didn't want to fuck this up. "I want you to take my place on the Convocation. I want you to become the representative for rare supes like us, the endangered species, the last of their kinds."

The look this near perfect stranger gave me almost broke my heart. It was one of defeat. Of need and desire, of wanting something so bad but knowing it was impossible. His shoulders curled in on themselves, his wings wrapping around his body like they were trying to comfort him. Those soft eyes almost wept with pain.

"I would give anything to take that burden from you. But I can't. I can't leave Amsterdam." He sucked in a shaky breath, and Orthus's shoulders tensed as he rested a hand on his friend's back. "The only place I can go is straight to Hell. As per my curse."

Excuse me? Did he just say *curse*?

I'd read fairy tales, and one principle seemed to pervade them all: men ain't shit.

Joking. Mostly. It was actually that true love's kiss could break any curse. I was skeptical, because as Vali told his story in that quiet, melodic voice that seemed to be almost like a physical caress, I was beginning to think my first thought might have been correct.

"It was several centuries ago now. Maybe six or seven hundred years?"

Orthus shook his head. "Nearly eight hundred years, Vali."

The man in front of me looked sadder, if that were possible. His eyes were too wide, filled with too much pain. Too many years. I could almost taste the bitterness of his despair on my tongue.

He shrugged. "Decades run together like minutes sometimes. It was how I met Orthus, really. There was a woman."

X raised an eyebrow. "Isn't there always?"

Vali nodded. "Well, there were actually lots of women. It was an easy time to get laid if you were a man like me. I traveled with the Vikings for a while, right before they went home and stopped raiding, but long enough to pick up a few of their habits, like actually bathing. It was easy to woo a woman into your bed if you didn't smell like a dirty ballsack and changed your clothes at least once a year."

Romance at its finest, ladies and gentlemen.

Vali continued. "We'd just been drifting around when we came to the Netherlands, my brethren and I, though it wasn't called that yet. It must have been the thirteenth century? The incubi were more plentiful, but we were obliviously on our way to extinction. We didn't realize he"—he pointed to Lucius— "had started killing off the succubi. We avoided them if we could." He shook his head. "I'll get into that later."

He shifted in his seat, as if the next part made him uncomfortable. "Anyway, it was a smorgasbord in the Middle Ages, as I said. Feeding was easy when I could just walk into a brothel and women would fall at my feet. I could stroll into grand balls on the arm of society matrons and debauch whoever I pleased. I was drunk on power and sex. It was at one such ball that I... might have messed up."

Orthus snorted. "You think?"

Vali gave him a soft smile. "I have no regrets." The look that passed between them was almost loving. Holy shit. Did they—were they—you know, partners? Not that I cared, but I wouldn't have guessed.

"Your consorts will tell you that all supernaturals were more plentiful in those days. There were shifter packs all over Europe, and vampires roamed in large nests, decimating villages and blaming the plague. Witches pushed back at Christianity, or sometimes set themselves up in the church and used it as a cover for their covens later. But I'm getting off track.

"I was at a ball held by a powerful witch in Nijmegen, and I found myself in the kitchens, making love to two scullery maids. Let's just say, one was very adept at milking—"

I was no prude, but... "Spare the details."

Vali gave me that smile again. "I promise you, they both left happier than when I met them. I doubt they'd ever felt sexually powerful in their lives, but I gave them that. A brief moment of pleasure in a world that just wanted to use them and toss them aside, as if they had no more worth than a barn cat." He raised an eyebrow as if daring me to contradict him. I kept my lips firmly closed.

"Anyway, I smelled Orthus before I saw him. That

brimstone scent that only Hell creatures can pick up from each other. I wondered what this witch was doing in his basement that smelled like the fiery pits of Hell, so I looked. I found Orthus in chains. He was naked, runes burned all over his body. They'd dragged him up from Hell and shackled him right there in the basement, siphoning his magic for... who fucking knows what. He looked rough, Raine. Very rough. For an immortal being to look that bad? Well, I knew whatever they were doing was not good. That kind of magic practice was banned, even back then. I promised to get him out, because he looked quite pitiful."

Orthus growled, but the angry sound didn't actually reach his eyes. He looked pained at the memories. I wanted to tell Vali to stop, but I couldn't. I needed to know. It was important for us all.

Plus, what kind of cliffhanger would that be?

"I went back to the party, laughed and smiled, and then left. The following day, I met with the lady of the house and I seduced her. Probably gave her the only orgasms of her life, knowing her husband. The guy was... not good. Can't imagine he'd been too worried about his wife's pleasure. But I'm getting off track." His eyes flicked to Orthus. "I used my abilities to beguile her into undoing the hex holding Orthus captive. She wasn't very powerful, but I fed Orthus some of my strength, and with him pushing from the inside of the circle, and Mara undoing the complicated weave outside, we managed it."

Mara. He still remembered her name. I don't know why that mattered to me, but it did. I nodded, reaching out with my own abilities, pushing something good toward him. Not pleasure, but something similar. Security? Contentment? That was the thing about being a succubi; it wasn't just all lust and sex. Those weren't emotions really, not by themselves. They were a cocktail of sensations like comfort, trust, obviously a primal desire. Nico had said that the original succubi had been able to wield all of those feelings individually, as well as together. I wasn't that good yet, but I'd try for him.

Vali gave me a tight smile. "Thank you. I got Orthus, and we ran. I wasn't dumb enough to stay in Nijmegen. We got to Amsterdam—though it was little more than a village then—before they found us. Mara, the witch's wife, was dead. Murdered by her husband, though he accused us of killing her. The witch wasn't exactly doing anything coven-sanctioned though, and when they investigated, they found evidence of his dark practices and ordered him to be executed. He was hunting us, and the Council of Witches was hunting him. They found him, but not before he made it here to Amsterdam."

He let out a shuddering breath. "As they dragged him away, he cursed me. He had nothing left to lose. I was never to leave Amsterdam for all eternity, unless I went straight to Hell. Then his dark magic pushed into me, cursing me with immortality—which again, is illegal magic. It pulled the life force from everyone in that village at the time, killing them all to grant me immortality. A hundred and fifty people. Men, women, children. He knew what he was doing. He was giving me a lifetime of torture. There was no one here to feed on, and I couldn't leave to find sustenance. When they dragged him away to execution, the Council of Witches left me here. To suffer.

"I buried every single one of those one hundred and fifty people, with Orthus's help. It took us weeks, until they were more sludge than body. Over the next year, I made a headstone for every person. I didn't always know who they were, so sometimes I made it up. But I memorialized them all. Even the infants. Their headstones lie under the dirt to this day if you know where to look."

His voice was scratchy now. I could feel his remembered hurt, and it made me want to cry. X pulled me tightly into his side, his hands brushing across my cheeks. Oh. I *was* crying.

"Save your tears. It was a long time ago," Orthus growled, looking uncomfortable.

"We've been here ever since. Orthus pledged himself as my protector in return for saving his life, and in those early years, when I was starving in a village filled with the dead, he saved me just as much, if not more. He fed me, even when we were both so weak we could barely stand. We were even a long time ago," he whispered, looking at his friend. Boyfriend? Lover?

Orthus shrugged. "I stay because I like you now."

I resisted the urge to go "awwww" because it probably wasn't appropriate for the gravitas of the moment, but it was hard. I mightn't know the status of their actual relationship, but the love was there, whether it was platonic or more. You'd have to be blind to miss it.

"What happened afterward?"

"People returned. It was a prosperous fishing village at one time, and as people forgot about the mass death that had occurred here, as it faded from human memory, more people returned. It was easier for me to feed, even gradually. I didn't want the people to leave again. A couple of decades passed before a new problem occurred. I was immortal. I didn't age, but I couldn't leave so people didn't notice. It took us a couple of centuries to work out how to hide in Hell, and in that time, I was burned at the stake at least three times as a demon. Once, I was buried alive in a disused well. It was not a good time." He sucked in several deep breaths. "But the village turned into a town, and the town into a city, and now it isn't so bad."

Better than being burned alive? Seemed like the bar was on the floor with that one.

"That's it? In almost eight hundred years, you haven't managed to break the curse?"

He shook his head sadly, and I knew this wouldn't fucking do. I had to help him, even if he didn't want to help me in return.

Nico was frowning. "I'm no expert, but curses always have to have a breaker. It's in the balance of nature."

Orthus turned his cold eyes to me, but didn't say anything. No, it was Vali's deep sigh that echoed around the room. "There was. I had to bond myself to a succubus." Oh shit, I had a feeling I knew where this was going. "Two problems with that. One was the obvious problem, which I didn't know at the time, but would later become the shackles that held me to this place—your boy Lucius was having a temper tantrum and had slaughtered hundreds of them."

"Seven hundred and sixty-three," Lucius corrected. I shot him a look. We'd talk later about how huge that number was, and how he still remembered it.

"And the second problem?" Nico prompted, though his face said he already knew the answer.

"The succubi hated the incubi. We were the balance that kept the other in check. We could enhance or neutralize each other's powers as necessary. We could also feed each other until we were fully sated, without the need to feed off humans. But we could also draw too much and kill our partners. We were symbiotic, but we were also each other's weakness. The succubi at the time were trying to grasp for status by beguiling powerful people—like Lucius Flett, arguably the most bloodthirsty vampire created, though back then his reputation wasn't as bad as it is now. Speciecide will do that to you." He looked at Lucius and shrugged. "Not everyone appreciates being blinded by sex and controlled like a puppet, so I understand."

I looked back over at Lucius, and his eyes were hard and distant, lost in memories.

Vali continued. "Kings and queens fell at the feet of the succubi, waged wars at their whim. The succubi didn't want a balance. They abhorred any weaknesses. So they had the incubi assassinated quickly. In one week, before warning could be sent, all my brethren perished."

"Except you," I said softly.

He made a choking sound as he swallowed down his emotions. "Except me. They tried. An assassin appeared and stabbed me in the back in my sleep. But I'm immortal. She died that day, Orthus tearing her to pieces, but with her went my last hope of release." Finally, his eyes met mine, and the hope in them stole my breath and made goosebumps race along my skin. "Until now."

The silence in the room was visceral. Once again, someone *needed* me, the very thing I was trying to escape.

Lucius cleared his throat. "Well, now I don't have to pretend to feel guilty anymore, right?"

CHAPTER
TWENTY-TWO

I needed some air. "Excuse me for a moment." I stood and strode to the small balcony that was beyond a pair of ornate French doors, pushing out into the brisk, pre-dawn air. We'd have to head back to our apartment soon. Otherwise, we'd be stuck here all day.

I felt Brody at my back, and when his warmth wrapped around me, I couldn't help but melt back into him. "Are you okay?" he murmured.

I wished everyone would stop asking me that. It had been a hell of a night—no pun intended.

"I will be. Just needed time to digest all that." That my kind had killed his kind, and my lover had killed the last of my kind, and that bullshit curse which was *so* awful, I almost wanted to summon the ghost of that asshole witch and kill him all over again.

We liked to think of time as linear, but really, she was an incestuous bitch. The amount of huge events that happened simultaneously in history, but which your brain processed as centuries apart, was actually astounding.

"Take all the time you need, Rainey. No one is going to tell you that you need to do anything. His past is not your problem. He made his choices, whether you agree with them or not. You aren't his savior."

"Aren't I, though? Would you leave him here to rot for eternity? Be honest."

I felt Brody's breath on my cheek. "No, I wouldn't. But I've been raised and molded to bond my people to me from the day I was born. I've prepared for all the different connections inside me. You didn't have that benefit, so no one will begrudge you your decision. And if they do, fuck them."

I sighed, gripping his hand where it was wrapped around my torso and holding it tightly. There was no point panicking about this until I'd heard what bonding with an incubus entailed. Maybe it was just a handshake, or like a vow. Maybe we bared our throats and pledged allegiance to each other, like shifters did.

But we were sex demons, so the chances that we could bond fully clothed seemed miniscule. Not that he wasn't an attractive guy; when he turned that heated expression my way, it made my lady bits go wild. However, there was a difference between appreciating how attractive he was and tying myself to him for life.

"I think the problem," I whispered, and I felt Brody's body stiffen slightly behind me, "is that we would have to fuck. And I don't know what this will mean for our group. We're a team. A Pack. It's been twenty years, Brody. We're *happy*. Can I willingly risk all that for a stranger?"

Brody spun me in his arms, his hands coming up to cup my cheeks. "Raine Baxter, one of the things that I love most about you is that you've always been willing to risk it all for a stranger. Except normally, it's your life you're gambling with," he said sternly, though his eyes were alight with mirth.

I gave him a lopsided grin, but let it fade. "If it was just my life and my happiness, we wouldn't even have this conversation. I'd be the brand new owner of a slightly used incubus. But it's not just me."

He brushed his lips across mine. "Mate. You have us all wrapped around your little finger. You just have to say the word, and we'll learn to live with it," he whispered against them softly. "Now, you better come inside before the sunrise. Lucius destroyed the apartment we were staying in when you were taken, so we have to find somewhere else to stay."

He did? Holy shit. "How bad?"

Brody grimaced. "I'm not sure the place has maintained much structural integrity. Needless to say, we probably won't get our deposit back. Buddy was out looking for you as well, but once we messaged him that you were fine, he went to fake an explosion to explain the destruction."

I swiped a hand down my face. I mean, I didn't blame Lucius. In his position, I probably would have gone crazy too. I just didn't need this right now.

"You can stay here," a voice said from the shadows, and Orthus appeared. "We have plenty of rooms for you and your consorts."

I frowned at the huge hellhound. "Were you eaves-dropping?"

"Yes." He didn't even sound remotely guilty.

I narrowed my eyes in his direction. "I don't think I like you much."

He gave me a full, blinding smile. "The feeling is mutual, vampire. But he needs you, and I vowed to do anything I can to keep him safe." His tone sounded a little disgusted that it was me saving him, but he could suck my lady balls.

"It's rude, and I don't appreciate it, but thank you for your offer of a room. We happily accept your hospi-tality tonight." I looked at Brody. "Call security and tell them to take the night off."

"Raine…"

"It's fine, Brody. What's the worst that could happen? I go straight to Hell? Been there, done that today." Orthus snorted, walking back in from the balcony first. I could tell by the guys' faces they hadn't even realized he'd left. "That's a hell of a party trick, walking in the shadows."

Orthus just shrugged, looking at Vali. "The Mad King trashed their accommodation. They are staying here tonight." He gave him a pointed look, the kind of non-verbal communication that came from being around someone for a long, long time. Whatever silent argument they were having was getting a little heated, until Vali ripped his eyes away.

"You're welcome to stay as long as you like. Let me show you to the top floor rooms." He uncurled his body, and I realized he was a lot taller than I'd originally thought. It was like his wings made him seem more imposing. When he hid them away, that tail disappeared like it had been a hallucination. I was a little mad, in all honesty.

"Did old-school succubi have tails and wings?" I asked Lucius, because if anyone knew, it would've been him.

He nodded. "Smaller than those of an incubus, more decorative than battle-ready. Obviously." He didn't say it smugly. Lucius honestly didn't care that he'd eradicated an entire species. No, that wasn't true; he did care. He just didn't do regrets. He'd once told me he couldn't go back and change it, couldn't wipe away the madness and the pain, so what was the point of feeling guilty about it?

Remorse was something he was slowly learning. Say what you wanted about my killer, he did have empathy. Deep inside, where the madness still hadn't touched, was a man who loved his twin. He cared deeply about the family we'd created. And I knew that he loved me more than he loved death. It didn't matter that his body count was probably in the thousands—his death one, not the sex one—because that wasn't the same vampire who'd woken up beside me nearly every day of the week for nearly two decades.

I didn't even want to think about his other body count. I avoided the conversation of how many women he'd been with like my sanity depended on it. I'd avoided that talk with all of them. Even Tex.

I laughed at the direction of my thoughts, considering we were walking up the winding staircase of an honest-to-god brothel. I ran my fingertips over the wallpaper, only to realize it was furry. "Is this carpet?" That was weird.

"Someone decided to do a makeover of the building in the seventies. It didn't go well."

"You weren't here in the seventies?"

Vali shook his head. "No. I was in Hell, and then down on the docks. It's easy to disappear into the shadows down there. We didn't return here until twenty years ago. We thought we may be able to do some good in our endless eternity, and it's in Orthus's nature to protect. To guard. If not me, then the whores of the Red Light District."

I begrudgingly raised Orthus in my opinion a single notch.

Vali pushed open the first door on the landing, and I gaped. The room was... intense. There was red and gold everywhere, and the bed? It was round. Vali clicked a button by the door, and the bed began to spin.

"Oh my god, it *spins!*" I gasped, taking a running leap toward it but pulling up at the last second. How many people had fucked on this bed?

"The sheets are clean, I promise. This place hasn't been used in sixty years, so I'm fairly sure any remaining bodily fluids on the mattress are well and truly dried up now."

That was oddly not that reassuring. Then I thought about how many people must fuck in hotel room beds. Hundreds? Thousands? At least any STDs in this bed would be geriatric by now. It should be fine.

So I launched myself onto the bed as it spun and... "Oh my god, it vibrates too?" I said with wide-eyed wonder, making Vali throw back his head with a laugh. The cadence of the sound, the way it felt like it hummed through every atom of my body, made me still.

Holy hell.

I knew I must have been staring at him with my

mouth open, because when he looked at me again, the smile fell quickly from his lips. "It does. There are settings on the switch attached to the nightstand. If you'll excuse me, I'll open up the other rooms, and you guys can get settled. I know today has been a lot for you."

With that, he was gone, not walking into the shadows like Orthus, but moving equally as quickly and quietly.

Judge and Walker winked at me as they walked past my room, but Tex came inside. "Straight in, Tex. The bed is about seven feet in front of you." I murmured the directions automatically, even if he didn't need them all the time. When he reached down to the bed, I realized it was still spinning and vibrating. "You're going to have to jump aboard the Pleasure Express, big guy. Just make the leap of faith."

"Promise to catch me if it flings me off the side?" he joked, and my lips twisted into a smile he couldn't see.

"I'll always catch you, Tex. Always."

"I know, baby." He climbed on the bed and slumped down beside me, wrapping me up in his arms. "You think it would be weird if I took my pants off and let this thing vibrate my balls?"

TWENTY-THREE

I would like to say that I used that spinning, vibrating platform to its full advantage, but in all honesty, I curled up in the arms of Tex and went straight to sleep. It had been a big night. It wasn't every day you went to Hell and then had a life-altering crisis. Granted, these things tended to happen to me a little more than the average person, but still, it was exhausting.

I woke up smooshed between Lucius and Tex, and I couldn't help the smile that curled my lips as I realized that while Lucius was so wrapped around my body I was basically anchored to his side, he also had one hand gripping Tex's forearm, holding him tightly in his sleep. Apparently, me getting stolen had affected Lucius a little. I didn't blame him, but it made my heart hurt. After all this time, I was still the only anchor he could use to withstand the insanity in his mind.

But the fact that he protected Tex as well, even when he was asleep? It got me right in the feels.

I was mesmerized by Lucius's face where it rested on the pillow inches from mine. I kissed his sharp cheekbones, tracing the light blue tattoos that swirled across his skin, evidence that he was from a different time. That he'd lived a thousand lives before me. Lives that he'd forgotten, or chosen not to remember. Lives where he'd been as happy then as he was now with me. Lives where he'd bathed in blood and madness.

His eyes snapped open, and I watched the panic and madness recede as his mind caught up with his sight. He pressed his cheek against my hand, chasing the feeling of my touch.

"I love you," I whispered softly against his lips.

His hand slid up my side until he was cupping my face with his big, rough palm. "I don't love you, Raine Baxter. That word is too small. Too overused. You are my *world*. My sanity. My happiness, even if it took me a long time to recognize what that sensation in my chest was. When you disappeared—" He made a choking sound. "When you were stolen from me, the despair I felt..." He trailed off, his head shaking. "I don't want to live like that. If anything happened to you..."

I placed my finger over his lips. "The only thing that's going to happen to either of us is that we are going to go back to Dark River. We're going to bake cakes, and fuck in the moonlight, and be ridiculously happy for the rest of our long-ass lives. We'll see the world—or not, I don't care. As long as I can spend it with you"—I looked over my shoulder at the still sleeping Tex—"and him. And the other five people who love and care about us."

He kissed me then, desperate and rough. He always kissed me like he might not get to do it ever again. The only exception was after he'd gone down on me. Then his kisses were soft and sweet, like the sun coming out from behind heavy rain clouds.

I kissed him back, my nails scraping against his scalp in a way that I knew made him purr happily. "We have to get out of bed," I laughed as I moved away, but he chased me with his mouth.

It took me ten minutes of kissing, and one fast and furious orgasm, before Lucius, Tex and I finally made it out of bed.

Today, I had to make some decisions, but if life had taught me anything, it was that I shouldn't jump into shit without being fully informed. Which probably meant I was going to need to make some calls.

As I made my way downstairs, I realized everyone but us was already awake. Walker and Nico were sitting by the window, having a quiet but intense conversation. Vali was on a seat in front of the fire, a large coffee mug in his hands and a faraway look in his eyes. I noticed the slight tremble to his limbs. I couldn't see Orthus anywhere, but I was beginning to suspect that it didn't mean he wasn't actually here.

Brody looked a little bleary-eyed, so I walked over to him, kissing him softly. "Sleep okay?" I asked, as he handed me the extra coffee he had waiting. It was perfectly hot. "How did you know when to make this?"

He grinned, his eyelids hooded. "I know the sound of your orgasms now, Rainey. I knew how long it would be between the first moan and Lucius getting you off. Just had to time it right."

My cheeks flushed, and my eyes darted back to Vali. This was awkward, even though he was an immortal sex demon who lived in a brothel and had probably heard more orgasms than the creator of the Rabbit.

So I mumbled out a "Thank you," and took the mug from Brodie, leaning into his body.

X bounced over to me, a grin on his face. "Guess what, Red?"

That smile never meant anything good.

"What?" I said hesitantly. With the amount of glee on his face, this conversation was about to go one of two ways. Either he'd killed someone he shouldn't, or I was about to have a lot more orgasms.

Or he'd found an expensive teacup in a thrift store. Yeah, that always made him obscenely happy too.

"This brothel has a sex dungeon. An actual *sex*

dungeon." I could swear he was bouncing up and down on the balls of his feet. "It has swings and furniture and *paddles*! So many paddles. And the eyelets, Love. You should see the amount of eyelets. I could tie you and Snakelet and even the psycho up all at once and play with you at my pleasure." His excitement was tempered with a whole cloud of lust. "Can we play?"

A whole new sex dungeon was like kinky Disney for X—if Mickey put away his red pants, strapped on a black studded harness, and got out his riding crop.

"Sounds like a date," I said, trying to hide my mirth at his enthusiasm and failing miserably.

He stepped into my space, his hand bracketing my jaw. "Laugh it up now, Love, because today I'm going to have your mouth stuffed so full of my cock, the only thing you'll be able to do is moan around it."

Oof. Maybe I didn't have anything better to do today.

"No wonder she isn't starving. She gets more cock than the highest paid worker in the district." Orthus had appeared out of nowhere—again—and I rolled my eyes. He didn't seem disdainful, though. More amused than anything.

Vali slapped him on the stomach with the back of his hand. "We should all be so lucky, O."

I frowned. "You're starving? But you live in the middle of De Wallen." I could literally hear people having sex next door, and it wasn't even nine at night yet.

Vali shrugged, getting up to put his mug in the sink. "It's not the same. How do I put this..." His eyes dropped to Brody. "You're a vampire, so think of it like this. Feeding from a human is nice. It's filling. It takes the edge off, most of the time. But feeding from other supernaturals? It's a whole class of its own, am I right?" I nodded, and he continued. "It's the same for me, but slightly more complicated. Feeding from humans having sex with each other is like a snack. Feeding from a human while having sex with them myself is a little bit more, but still not enough. I'd need to have sex with ten to fifteen humans in a day to be fully sated, even briefly."

Eesh, that sounded like hard work. I looked at Vali with his piercing eyes and soft blond hair. His skin was a light gold that begged to be touched, and his body was strong enough that you could picture him throwing you against the wall and fucking your brains out.

Okay, so maybe not such hard work for a man like Vali.

"When two supernaturals have sex near me, it's better than with humans, but similar to them, the sation that comes afterwards lasts a day, maybe a few hours more." His eyes danced beneath the chandelier, and my cheeks flushed.

Lucius snorted. "You're welcome for breakfast then, incubus."

"When I fuck another supernatural, it's like a gourmet meal. And so filling, I don't have to eat for a week." His eyes flicked to Orthus, whose face was impassive.

Yep, they definitely had sex. Well, that might make things more complicated.

"And when you have sex with a succubus?"

Vali sucked in a deep breath, his jaw taut. "I don't really remember much. It was a long time ago, but the sensation of our essence twining, the feeling of completeness, of power, of just *humming* with life..." He ran a hand over the back of his neck, his eyes distant. "That isn't a sensation I'll ever forget, even if it's torture to remember it now."

Well, now I felt even more like shit.

X, bless his perverted little heart, slapped Vali on the back hard, sending him stumbling forward a couple of steps. "That's tragic, fuckboy. Don't worry, you can come to X's Pleasure Fest tonight, because the more the merrier. You can stand in the corner and pull your dick, because I can promise you, it's going to be a buffet." He grinned, his fangs denting his bottom lip. "You can look, but you can't touch, because I'll snap off your fucking fingers." He patted Vali on the back a couple more times, then walked back into the kitchen to make some tea.

"Uh, thank you?"

Only X could threaten to maim someone and they weren't sure whether to thank him or run away.

"You're welcome. Besides, you're hot, and Walker is a voyeur. Makes shit interesting."

"X!" Walker chastised roughly, making X laugh harder.

"Enough, you two." My cheeks still felt hotter than they had any right to be, considering I was dead. "I have to make some calls to a witch I trust, to see about this curse and the bond." I let all signs of mirth slip from my face. "I'm taking your predicament seriously, Vali. If I can help, I will. But..."

He held up a hand. "I get it. Thank you for trying."

I excused myself and headed out to the balcony again, sucking in the atmosphere of the area. The streets were overrun with people again, including the police. Pulling up Miranda's number, I pressed Call. I was shit with time differences, but was pretty sure she wouldn't be in bed. Hopefully.

"Raine? Is everything okay?"

"Miranda, have you heard of an incubus?"

"Like the nineties rock band?"

I snorted. I was pretty sure she was fucking with me, which was something that always tripped me out. She'd mellowed over the years, and now she had an actual sense of humor. "Like the species."

"Not much, only what they teach us about extinct

species... No fucking way! Your Night Demon is an incubus?"

"Yeah, an incubus with a huge-ass problem, and I'm going to need yours and Wilde's help."

Then I laid it all out there for one of the few people I trusted who hadn't been inside my vagina at some point.

Apparently, once a species had basically been extinct for eight hundred years, information on them became pretty scarce.

But curses? My girl Miranda knew curses inside and out. "Not that I'd ever use a curse," she said indignantly. "That kind of magic is for fools. It takes as much as it gives. Because the magic wants balance, even if it's sucking it directly from your soul." I could hear her flicking pages, with the soft voice of Wilde in the background. "But they are an individual thing, so if anyone has any copies of his grimoire or even familiarity with his practices, that'll help. The incubus says you have to bond to break the curse?"

I looked through the window at Vali, who was talking in a low voice to Judge and Walker. Tex was napping beside Judge, probably because jetlag had finally caught up with him.

"Yeah, but I'm not sure exactly what that entails."

Miranda snorted. "Yes, you do."

I huffed an annoyed breath. "Fine, I know it involves sex, because *duh*, but that can't be all, right? Otherwise, every time a succubus and an incubus did the forbidden hokey-pokey, they'd bond. That doesn't sound ideal to me."

"The forbidden... You know, there might actually be something wrong with you," she said seriously, and I couldn't help but laugh. I could hear chuckles in the background, but Miranda just continued. "Look, I'll keep looking into it, but this isn't our area of expertise. The incubi and the succubi were already gone by the time North America was discovered. It might be worth asking the local Council leader." There was muffled cussing from Wilde. "On second thoughts, Wilde said he's a fucking asshole who wouldn't know a hex from a hat trick. Will the vampire Council over there help? Or the Capi?"

I snorted. Un-fucking-likely. But then I remembered the horny old witch I'd been talking to before shit went down at the ball.

"I might know someone."

CHAPTER
TWENTY-FOUR

"Just a minute!"

Marta's house reminded me of the house from *Hansel and Gretel*, minus the candy. Marta, the old witch, might as well have put a *Free Candy* sign on the door, because the place looked like a gingerbread cottage. There were leadlight windows and white-trimmed gables, an arch-shaped door, colorful touches here and there. It was quaint. It was inviting.

Common sense said to never trust any place which looked that inviting.

We'd left Judge, Lucius and Tex back at the brothel, because temptation went both ways and Lucius was still a little volatile. Walker and Nico were hitting up some library that Wilde had suggested might have some information.

I stood on the sidewalk with Vali and Orthus, as well as X and Brody. Buddy, my guard, stood on the street, his eyes haunted. I'd tried to tell him it wasn't his fault I'd been stolen—that shit just tended to happen to me—but he'd just grunted and gone back to super soldier mode.

Oh well. We'd fix that later if we had to.

I knocked on the door again, and a voice came from within. "I said, just a flipping *minute!* Unless you want your insides to liquify, I can't just stop what I'm doing," the voice snapped.

Ew.

"Maybe we should have this meeting out here," I murmured to Vali.

He nodded but before he could agree, the door was pulled open. Marta stood in the doorway, her hair sticking up in every direction and something smoking behind her from the kitchen. "What in Hecate's name are you doing here?"

Well, at least she remembered me. "Hi. Sorry to interrupt you, but I was hoping to have a word with you, if we could."

Her eyes bounced around my motley group. "No." Then she shut the door in our faces. Asshole.

Orthus snorted behind me. "Looks like you're zero for two with that tactic, succubus."

I glared at him as I knocked on the door again. "Please, ma'am. Just a second of your time." I continued knocking and didn't stop until she wrenched open the door again.

"What is it? I'm busy."

"I just have a question about a historical member of your coven..." I trailed off, looking over at Vali.

"Pieter Stormson."

The old witch stopped, her eyes moving around us quickly. "Where did you hear that name?"

I shrugged nonchalantly. Just because Miranda and Wilde had looked into the old witch and given her a hesitant tick of approval, didn't mean I'd trust her.

"From an acquaintance."

Her lips pressed into a tight line. "Come in. It is best not to talk about the Dark Betrayer where other ears can hear."

The Dark Betrayer. Seemed apt, considering what the bastard had done. We all filed into her little gingerbread house, which became seriously cramped. X was a massive guy, as was Orthus, and Brody wasn't that much smaller. Vali's shoulders were deceptively wide, not that I noticed until I was pressed tightly against his spine as we all tried to maneuver into her sitting room.

"Oh, sod it," she huffed, muttering something under her breath and making magic tingle across my skin. A popping sensation pressed against my eardrums, before the room suddenly quadrupled in size.

"Holy crap. It's like the TARDIS in here," X breathed, and I was kind of impressed with his *Doctor Who* knowledge. Tex and I had kept them all young, I liked to think.

"Would you like tea? Coffee? Something a little stronger?" she asked with a wink. I wanted to believe she meant booze, but I wouldn't risk eating or drinking anything in her home. Usually, it was only Fae you had to worry about accepting hospitality from, but honestly, it was better to have the policy across the board.

"No, thank you."

"So be it." She waved her hands in the air, and a teacup appeared in her hands.

X gasped. "Is that genuine eighteenth-century Delftware? Look at the traditional blue and white glaze, and see how it's becoming more Oriental in pattern? That happened when the Dutch East India Company really took off and brought influences from Chinese porcelain back to the Netherlands."

I stared at the man who had once tied me to the ceiling and paddled my ass with a studded flogger until I begged. Sometimes, it was hard to reconcile the teacup nerd with the bloody killer.

It wooed Marta the witch, though. "A man who knows his earthenware. I am impressed, Mr...?"

"Just call me X. Teacups are a little hobby of mine."

I hoped to god she didn't ask what his other hobbies were.

"Indeed. Ask your questions then."

I cleared my throat nervously. "We just want to know if there were any techniques that Stormson was known to use, or particular curse balances he used repeatedly."

Marta shook her head. "No, after he was found guilty of Dark Practice by the Council of Witches, his notebooks were burned and his house razed to the ground to deter any of the younger practitioners from following in his footsteps." She shook her head in disgust. "He murdered his wife, the daughter of a well-respected member of the Council, so his fate was already sealed with that one action. When they found out he'd been harvesting the life force of a demon beneath his house, opening himself and his coven to demonic possession, well, that was unforgivable."

"Pah!" She made an odd spitting gesture, without any spit, as her disgust turned into something darker and more potent. "When he was finally captured, he killed an entire village in order to curse an—" She jerked to a stop, and her eyes ping-ponged around our group. "Oh my. Oh. *You.* The two-headed Cerberus who protects the Night Demon. Not a Cerberus at all, but an *Orthus*—that's the name of the two-headed hound demon," she seemed to add for my benefit.

She flicked through a book to her left, which appeared to be some kind of encyclopedia, then looked back up from the page at Orthus. "It's right there in your name. I feel like such a fool. And *you*." She pointed a gnarled finger at Vali. "Not a demon at all, but an incubus."

Orthus's body trembled with readiness to defend his friend, and I reached out to rest my hand on his arm, steadying him. Or distracting him, at least.

But it was Vali who answered. "Yes. The Night Demon persona came about after one too many wives sought me out. While their husbands were out with their mistresses, they were 'ill' having 'taken to their beds.' When in fact, I was taking them to their beds." He snorted. "Sexual liberation was a long time coming for women. I feel like I just gave them a small taste of what was to come."

"A regular philanthrope," I teased, but turned my attention back to Marta. "We'd appreciate your discretion, but I understand that a coven is a many-layered thing and you don't always have a choice." I knew Wilde's coven had a geas against malicious secrets.

Marta nodded. "Indeed, but I have a few hours before I will need to inform them. Now, tell me about your curse."

AFTER A FEW HOURS, we found out that other than impromptu orgies and making her own elixirs, Marta's one true passion was history. She showed us her library—another room that was far too large to fit in her gingerbread house without the aid of magic—and to be honest, it gave me some serious envy. It was the kind of library every little bookworm dreams of. When she hopped up on that little wooden ladder, and wheeled down past the shelves, honestly, I thought about trying to beguile her into letting me have a go.

"Aha! Here we go. Catch, vampire," she shouted, tossing a book over her shoulder, and X obligingly caught the ancient tome she'd so haphazardly lobbed. "And this one as well." Three books later, she finally came down off the ladder. "Now, let's see. I assume you want to bond the incubus? Permanently?"

I winced. "Probably not permanently, if possible." I gave Vali a tight smile, darting my eyes back to Marta quickly. "I want to help, but I don't want to help him leave Amsterdam only to be trapped in a prison of a different kind."

"A fair point, young one. Ah yes, here. I knew I'd seen something about the ancient rituals of coition demons."

"Coition?" I whispered to Vali, who was standing beside me.

"Sex demons," he murmured back.

I blinked slowly at him. I liked being a demon in bed, but not literally. I didn't know how I felt about being a demon full-stop. I'd met Lucifer, and although his presence was terrifying, he was a lot more laidback than Tex's Bible-thumping parents had made him seem. But what did I know? Maybe in Hell, he got a thrill out of poking pitchforks in places pitchforks should not go.

"Let me see. Here we are—descendents of the original sin. Freed from Hell during the biblical reckoning, blah blah blah. Ah, here." She slid the book across to me and Vali, and I looked down at the crumbling text. There were illuminated drawings along the margins of forked-tongued demons fucking in ways I wasn't sure were even in the Karma Sutra. Good to know the tail was, uh, prehensile.

I read the beautifully written text:

"Coition demons, better known as INCUBI for the males and SUCCUBI for the females, are physiological very similar but not the same subspecies of demon. Incubi have the ability to breed with humans, whereas succubi are barren unless they bond and then mate with the incubi or another subspecies of coition demon, such as VARICUBI."

What the fuck was a varicubi? A question for another day.

"Coition demons are obviously not monogamous by nature, and have been known to form large family groups with other coition demons. What is interesting from this researcher's point of view is that not all members of the family group appear to have sex. In fact, some of the coition

demons do not copulate at all; rather, they feed from the collective bond of the family group."

I looked at Vali, who was frowning down at the page so hard, his face looked like granite. I wanted to ask what he was thinking, but not in front of the witch.

"The bonding process is a relatively easy process, similar to a Fae handfasting (See FAE and FAIRIES) where their hands are bound with ribbon or leather strapping, which has been anointed with their blood and bodily release. They wear the strapping from dusk until dawn under the light of the full moon, then exchange a kiss to seal the bond. This researcher has noted that some of the more close pairs will undertake bites similar to that of shifters (see SHIFTERS AND TWO-NATURED) while mid-coitus, which bonds them even further, creating a bonded pair within the larger family group."

I looked up at Marta. "Can we take some pictures of these pages for future reference?" I'd ask to take the book, but honestly, I didn't trust it wouldn't turn to dust in my hands or get eaten by termites or something.

Marta gave us a sad smile. "Of course. I doubt I will ever meet another incubus and succubus, and it is only right that you have as much information about your kind as possible. I don't believe that withholding information creates power." She looked at Vali. "I apologize for the historical sins of my coven. You should know though, that there is a chance that breaking the curse will also remove the immortality curse. You may perish."

"He's going to die if we bond?"

Marta shrugged. "It's possible, but without knowing the very nature of his curse, and the exact wording, it's hard to predict. It's possible that he'll just continue to live out the normal life cycle of an incubus. It's possible that his bond to your life force will mean that when you meet the final death, so will he. It is also possible that his immortality was a separate curse to that of his prison curse, and he will be truly immortal forever. The amount of life force used to power the curse would suggest this is the case; curses with that much dark magic don't normally have a balancing break. The death of the townspeople was the balance. But again, I can't be sure."

So there was a one in three chance he'd die. I looked at Vali, and then beyond him to Orthus's hard face.

Well, fuck.

TWENTY-FIVE

We were a subdued bunch when we returned to Vali and Orthus's brothel home. Marta had offered us cookies, but I wasn't wholeheartedly convinced she wasn't going to stuff me in the oven at some point. She was sweet, but old preternaturals were hardly ever selfless.

Luckily, Judge had cooked chili while we'd been away, though given the amount of bread flour covering both Tex and Lucius's body, they'd skipped to dessert early. I pouted at them, though it didn't bother me even a little when they had sex without me. I was only one person with one vagina. I wasn't so greedy that I'd prevent them from finding pleasure with each other, people they'd loved and cherished for years now.

Their feelings for each other didn't diminish their love for me. If anything, they enhanced it. We were content, fulfilled, and emotionally connected on so many levels. Polyamory for the win!

Lucius heard us first, of course, and he had me in his arms before I'd even finished stepping over the threshold.

"This guy has serious attachment issues," Orthus grumbled, dodging around us.

I flipped the bird at him over Lucius's shoulder. The vamp in question just gave him what I affectionately liked to call his "murder eyes."

I slapped his shoulder. "Stop it."

Lucius huffed. "How did it go with the witch?"

I sighed heavily and just let him carry me around like I was a princess. He enjoyed it. I enjoyed it. Sue me.

"Okay, I guess. Have Nico and Walker returned?" Lucius shook his head, walking me to the kitchen where the other guys were. As he put me down on the countertop, I laughed at the incriminating handprints on Tex's black skinny jeans. "Been busy?"

Tex grinned, the pink flush along those sharp cheekbones endearingly mortal. "Making chili is hard work."

I heard the front door open and close again, heralding the return of Walker and Nico.

Judge leaned in and kissed me. "Come on, Rainy

Day. Let's go feed the family." His voice dropped, his Southern accent getting stronger as he said, "Then later, I'll eat ya out like my favorite peach pie."

Well, I was never going to say no to an offer like that. I wrapped my legs around his waist as he lifted me down, and he kissed me with those full, soft lips. I pulled back and looked up into his midnight eyes. "You doing okay?"

He gave me that cocky half-smirk that always made me fall in lust with him. "You're not gonna believe this, Sugar, but I miss home."

He was right. I couldn't believe it. My Drifter missed home? Mr. "I'm not made to stay in one place" wanted to go back to Dark River? I couldn't keep the shit-eating grin from my face, and he huffed out a sigh.

"Don't gloat, Rainy Day. I've grown attached to the place. It's kind of like a plantar wart you draw a face on and somehow become attached to."

I wasn't going to unpack that one, so I gave him another quick kiss. "I miss home too. We're almost there." I wiggled out of his arms and picked up a bowl of freshly baked bread. Guess that explained all the flour. Throwing Judge a saucy look over my shoulder, I sashayed out of the room. Granted, it probably looked like I was limping, but half of the battle was being confident, right? I just confidently looked like I was lame.

The guys had set the big table with mismatched china and cutlery, and someone had picked up bright red tulips. Those romantic bastards. I kissed Nico and Walker, and smiled at Buddy and Rio.

I felt bad that their trip had been so tumultuous, but they hadn't complained, even when Lucius had apparently nearly killed Rio after Orthus stole me from the kitchen. They hadn't told me that little fact until I'd spied Rio all banged up with my very own eyes.

"Sit down, you two. I know you love Judge's chili."

Buddy huffed at me. "I couldn't feel my butthole for a week after the last time. Just because you guys have some insane masochist streak, doesn't mean we all want to burn our lips off when we eat. I swear, there's still a stomach ulcer in there."

I laughed, nudging him with my shoulder. "Don't be such a baby."

Vali and Orthus were looking at the table with strange expressions on their faces. Had we gone too far? Made ourselves too at home? My guys were used to people bending to their whims, but this wasn't our home.

"Is this okay?" I asked Vali softly, my eyes darting between him and Orthus.

The hellhound gave me an intense look that I couldn't quite decipher; it could be anything from angry to appreciative. Vali's was easier to read. He was buried in his feelings, somewhere between longing and sadness.

Neither one of them answered me.

"Sit down. Judge can't cook much else, but his chili is legendary." Until they said no, we would go on. I didn't want to hurt Judge's feelings either.

When Vali sat down, Orthus beside him, I smothered a sigh of relief. I put the bread in front of them, and Judge placed the cast iron pot of chili in the center of the table.

"The cookware in this place is like a vintage dream. You should check it out, Nico. You'll come in your pants," Judge teased, ladling chili into my bowl first. He handed the ladle to Vali. "Try it. I made it a bit milder than I normally would. I know some of you aren't used to any heat." He shot Buddy a grin.

Orthus took the ladle, pouring some into Vali's bowl first and then his own. I tilted my head at him. They had a weird dynamic, one I still couldn't work out. They'd definitely had sex in the past—that was obvious from Vali's story. Were they still having sex?

Why did I even care?

I put the fixings on top of my chili and passed the bowls to Orthus. The guys got their own chili, and soon enough, we were all sitting around eating. Like a family. Vali and Orthus were still subdued, but they ate their food.

"You didn't answer me," I murmured to Orthus. "Is this okay?"

He tilted his head at me. "Too late now if it wasn't, succubus."

"Stop being such an asshole," I grumbled, and he raised an eyebrow at me. I ignored him and looked at Vali. "Do you like it?" He nodded, taking another mouthful.

"Then why do you smell so damn sad?" Brody asked the question I was dying to know. Orthus sighed, picking up a piece of bread and tearing it in two, stuffing an entire half in his mouth.

Vali cleared his throat. "It's just been a long time since we've done something like this."

"Had someone else cook for you?"

"Eaten in the company of others. Like friends. It has been just me and Orthus for a long time."

"How long?" Walker asked softly.

Vali shrugged. "Three hundred years or so. Since Tineke died."

"Tineke?"

Orthus slammed down his spoon. "My wife. Excuse me." His chair scraped as he pushed it back, stomping out of the room. I could hear his heavy footfalls as he climbed the stairs, before the sound of a door slamming upstairs made me wince.

Shit. I was kind of fucking this up. "Sorry. I'm not normally that insensitive."

Vali shrugged. "It was a long time ago, but certain things bring back up old pain."

"She made chili?"

Vali laughed, but it was a soft, bittersweet thing. "No, Raine. It's not the chili."

Now it was my turn to frown. "Then what?"

He just shook his head. "You'll have to figure that one out, I'm afraid."

Dinner went on, more subdued, but eventually, conversations picked back up. Vali talked softly to Buddy, who was sitting beside him, their heads close together as they chatted. The expression on Buddy's face was slightly awestruck, and I wondered if maybe Vali was using his powers on my bodyguard. I'd have to talk to him. My security wasn't his snack pack.

I filled Nico in on what Marta said, showing him and Walker the photos I'd taken on my phone of the pages about bonding coition demons.

X pointed to one illustration where the incubus was dicking an upside-down succubus like he was trying to dig a posthole. "We should try that one."

I snorted. "Would you drop me on my head?"

X looked truly affronted. "I would never!"

"You dropped Tex on his head a month ago when you were trying to do that standing sixty-nine," Judge grumped from the other end of the table.

"Snakelet was fine, and he shouldn't suck so good if he didn't want me to lose control of my muscles."

Tex grinned, totally fine despite the rather large egg he'd been sporting for a week after. For all his bravado, X had babied him like he had actually been in mortal peril.

Nico had a small smile on his face. "So what are you going to do?"

I shot a quick look at Vali. His attention was solely on me, like his life might depend on it. And in a way, his immortal life kind of did.

"No offense, Vali, but I don't think either one of us wants to commit to like, uh, a relationship forever, right? You're nice, but you're basically a stranger. But I like you, and I want to help you, so if you're open to the idea, I think we might have a family bond?"

His whole body deflated with a sigh. "I think that would be excellent, Raine Baxter. I would have taken whatever option you'd given me at this point, as long as I'm free."

Brody leaned back in his chair. "And if you die? If the immortality curse lifts immediately?"

Vali shrugged. "So be it. I'm ready to be free, one way or another."

"And in exchange, you'll take over Raine's role on the Convocation? You'll protect those you govern with respect and care?" Nico queried, and I could sense his question was lined with his truth-telling power. He didn't use it often anymore, but when he did, it was impossible to deny.

"Yes. I would do anything required to leave Amsterdam. To be free. I'll care for them as if they are my kin. Whether my lifespan is decades or centuries. Or longer."

I nodded, swallowing hard. We had a plan. I just had to hope it didn't backfire in all our faces.

Everyone went their own way after dinner, while I helped Nico and X wash up. Well, I sat on the countertop and talked, while they were sexy and domestic. Foreplay starts in the kitchen, boys.

They'd gone on a run to the local blood bank today to get us some supplies, since relying on Tex and Brody was unfair. They didn't need to be iron deficient just because we were lazy.

As I walked down the maze of hallways, I heard voices. Slowing my steps, I recognized the pull of Tex's bond in my chest, and the low murmur of someone else. When I got closer, I realized it was Orthus. I needed to apologize to him, for barging into his life and turning it on its head.

Anyone with eyes could see he cared about Vali.

And I knew that while I was freeing the incubus from his curse, I was also turning Orthus's entire life upside down. What if he didn't want to leave Amsterdam? Nico had said that supernaturals were creatures of habit, and they didn't like to move once they'd created a territory. Would he stay here? Was I stealing his best friend from him?

"You play?" Tex's soft voice was a soothing balm. It always eased something restless in my soul.

"Yes. I taught myself many centuries ago."

"What about that?" Tex asked, and I desperately wanted to poke my head around the door jamb to see what they were doing. Instead, I stayed in the hall like a creeper. "Can I see?"

"Yes," Orthus's gruff voice answered.

I heard the soft sounds of an acoustic guitar as Tex's skillful fingers played something that was vaguely familiar. "You know this one?" I didn't catch the hellhound's response. "Here, listen on my headphones." They were silent for a moment as they listened to the song.

I thought about leaving, but I was curious about Orthus. He was handsome, that was for sure, and something about his abrasive manner felt exhilarating. Yeah, I knew that made no sense, but my therapist was like, two thousand years old and enjoyed fucking me on his office furniture.

The sound of the piano drifting through the door

was a surprise. Orthus didn't seem like a piano player. He hit a few chords, did a couple of runs, and then silence.

"Got it?" Tex murmured.

I didn't hear Orthus's response, but it must have been yes because the opening chords of Taylor Swift and Bon Iver's "Exile" began to echo around the music room. Tex's surprisingly deep voice kicked off the lyrics, and while he never believed me, he had a beautiful voice. He softly strummed the guitar, the words haunting as they floated through the hallway.

Orthus could really play. The piano crooned the sad melody, and I leaned my head back against the wall as I let their music wash over me. When Orthus joined in on the chorus, I nearly startled and gave away the fact I was listening.

Tex harmonized with his low tenor voice, and honestly, I wanted to cry. It was beautiful. I sank to the floor, and just listened.

When I glanced down the hall, I saw Vali standing at the end, his head cocked to the side as he listened too. I smiled softly, but didn't beckon him closer. We could appreciate this moment together, separately.

Finally, the song trailed off, and I crept away, back toward Vali with my finger pressed to my lips. He nodded, following me toward the living room. He looked over his shoulder at the empty hall. "It's been a long time since he played. I'd forgotten how good he is. He prefers to use his hands for more violent pursuits these days."

Like cage fighting for the vampires.

"The full moon is in three days, and I'd like to be home by the end of the week." I sucked in a deep breath. "Is that okay?"

He nodded. "A week is long enough to wrap up my affairs."

"And Orthus? Is he coming with you?"

A small smile curled his lips. "Why do you want to know?"

I shrugged. I didn't really care, did I?

I was saved from answering by X bursting into the room. "Red, it's time for dessert. You too, Dickubi." I screwed up my face at the name. "No good?"

I patted him on the arm. "Keep trying, big guy. You'll get there."

X made a low growling noise and grabbed me, slinging me over his shoulder. "One of us is going to get there, and it's going to be you. At least four times before I even give you my dick." He started striding toward a set of stairs that went down, then stilled at the top. "I was serious, incubus. Let's go. I intend to make you so full, you won't need to eat for a week."

There was indecision on Vali's face, and I gave him the most reassuring smile I could muster while bent over someone's shoulder like a sack of potatoes. "It's totally up to you. We don't mind, but we aren't going to care if you'd rather not. I know we're basically strangers."

Vali threw his head back and laughed. "I've had sex with more people whose name I didn't know than I have with friends, Raine Baxter."

"Then what's the problem?" I asked, as X huffed out an impatient sigh.

Vali chewed his full bottom lip between his teeth. The light was hitting him just right so that he seemed almost angelic. "This seems more important."

X sighed. He put me down and strode over to the incubus. "Look, Vali. Red here has already committed to you in her mind. She's probably picked out where you'll live, what room you'll have, and how to introduce you to the kids. She's figured out your astrological sign and designed you a 'Welcome To The Family' cupcake flavor." He reached out and gripped Vali's shoulder. "She cares about you already, because that's the kind of person she is. She sees past your history, your failures, the blood that has wet your hands in years gone by. She forgives you for the heinous shit you've done, even if you don't deserve it. All she cares about is that the person you are now is kind, that you treat everyone with respect—whether they deserve it or not—and that you don't stand in the way of her orgasms."

Pretty sure that last bit was for X's benefit, rather than mine.

I cleared my throat. "Regardless of all that, there's no obligation. I'm sure you'll feed just as well up here as down there." I tried not to blush, but it felt like every drop of blood I'd fed on was now in my cheeks.

Vali was silent for a few more seconds, his eyes running over me appraisingly, but I could see the war behind his eyes. Desire and fear were oscillating through his eyes like a movie reel.

Finally, he let out a shuddering breath. "Please."

X whooped and picked up Vali, stuffing him over his shoulder like he had me just a moment ago. "Come on, Love. I've been waiting for this for hours. SNAKELET!" he shouted back into the house, and I couldn't help but laugh.

I loved this man, but he was a serious handful sometimes.

We'd made it to the bottom of the stairs before Tex appeared. "What?"

"It's kinky time, so get that sexy fucking ass down the stairs. Grab the growly one if he wants to come. He makes Red wet, even though she won't admit it out loud. Plus, he might want tips on how to please a woman."

Vali was now chuckling, and I was so furiously red in the face that my head was going to explode. "What the *fuck*, X?" I hissed.

"Pfft, every single one of us has enhanced senses. I can smell how slick you get when he makes that weird growly noise under his breath." He looked at Vali. "Well, maybe *you* didn't know. I didn't read anywhere about incubi having increased senses. More stamina, yes. Way better in my opinion. No one likes a two-pump chump. Talking about you, Lucy!"

Lucius yelled obscenities back at him from somewhere behind the dark wooden door at the bottom of the stairs.

X put Vali back on his feet at the top of the stairs so it was still his choice if he descended them. Sweet, if somewhat impatient man that he was.

Orthus's head appeared through the doorway, his lips curled into something that might have been an amused smile. "I was pleasing women before your grandparents were born, vampire." Then he disappeared back inside the house.

"So has Lucius, and he still sucks," X shouted after him.

Lucius himself appeared. "I swear, I will cut out your appendix and fuck your stomach cavity if you keep besmirching my skills like that."

Um. Ew.

"Stop talking dirty, Lucy. It's not time yet. Still gotta show our girl the surprise." With that, X bundled us all down the stairs, his hand hooked around my wrist as he dragged me forwards. "Close your eyes and open wide."

"I swear to god, X, if you put your dick in my mouth, I'm going to bite it off."

"Normally that would turn me on, Love, but we don't have time for foreplay." He walked me forward, and I could almost feel his giddy excitement. "Ready?"

I laughed out a "Yes" at his excited tone.

"Three, two, one... Open them."

I opened my eyes to a room filled with tall pillar candles and every type of sex furniture you could imagine. A couch that was sloped to raise my ass in the air, a St. Andrews cross on the wall. Pommel horses and enough rings on the ceiling that we could probably hold an Olympic gymnastics event in here. On the wall was a whole range of... accompaniments. Paddles, floggers, cuffs, even a vibrator that had to be plugged into a damn wall and would probably electrocute me from the inside, it was so old.

X wrapped me up in his arms. "Are you ready to enter the happiest place on earth?"

TWENTY-SEVEN

All my guys were standing around the sex den. Lucius looked hungry, as did Nico. Walker sat atop something that looked like a throne, all gilded accents and heavy red velvet. His jeans were unbuttoned and his shirt was untucked, showing me a delicious sliver of his abs. So different to my normally buttoned-up Sheriff. I loved Exhibitionist Walker just as much, though.

He was positioned right in front of the sex chair, where he'd get a bird's-eye view of me being fucked. There was a smirk on his lips, and I wanted to climb onto that throne and fuck him like the king he was.

X, of course, had other plans. He looked at Vali, and pointed to two slightly less ornate chairs over the other side of the room. "Remember—you can look, but you can't touch. If you touch without permission, I'll cut off your fucking hands, and you can pray to whoever it is you believe in that they grow back."

There was no Orthus, and I don't know why that bothered me. Not everyone wanted to watch group sex like it was live action porn. Let him hide away on the first floor; I hoped he had headphones, because I predicted the night was going to get loud.

Vali tipped his chin. "Noted, vampire. Ask first if I want to be able to jack off again."

X grinned, and it was all fang. "Excellent comprehension for a man who was born when they still wrote with charcoal sticks." He grabbed me up into his arms and spun in a circle. "I've waited all day for this, and I don't know where to begin." He spied Judge, leaning against the wall nonchalantly with one shoulder, an amused expression on his face. "Judge! Make her come while I decide which toy to use first." He kissed me hard, full of frenetic energy, and then passed me off to Judge, who was chuckling silently.

"He's like a kid in a candy store. We should buy him a red room for Christmas," I whispered against his ear.

"Mmm, Sugar. I think we'd all like that." We watched X for a moment as he perused the wall of toys, then Judge's grip on my chin turned my face back to his. He kissed me softly in a way that only Judge could really do. Like a caress that somehow traveled past my lips and right down to my core.

I was fairly sure it was his gift. If X's kiss was venomous, producing an orgasm that was like a two-by-four to the ovaries, then Judge's was like a slow-release poison which snuck up on you, until you were coming all over his thigh like a nun who hadn't had sex in three decades.

I buried my fingers in his hair, holding it tightly in my fist. His hands slid down to my ass, and he moved me until I was grinding on his cock, the friction of our clothes amazing but also aggravating. As if he read my thoughts, he peeled off my shirt, baring my breasts to the room. I should have been embarrassed that Vali was right there and I was almost naked... but I really wasn't.

Almost everyone in Dark River had seen my boobs by this point. Walker's exhibitionism, combined with the fact my guys were horny bastards, meant I had a lot of outdoor sex. It was an unwritten town rule that we all pretended it never happened.

Judge undid my pants, and I got to my feet to wiggle them off. Leaving my panties on for modesty, I straddled his thighs once more, launching back into the kiss. He leaned back on the S-shaped sex chair, and my knees had the perfect placement to grind.

"We definitely need one of these," I groaned. He flipped me over until my back hit the cushioned chair, my legs over his shoulders. He ground down deep, hitting my clit with achingly amazing pressure. "Yes!"

"Nope!" X announced from above us. "Brody, your girl is looking awfully tempting with that mouth open. Come over here and fill it. I know it's not doggy style, but you'll have to deal with it."

When Brody sauntered over, a grin on his face, I knew I was going to need my super healing to be able to walk properly tomorrow.

I WAS PANTING, my body suspended from the ceiling, horizontal and facedown like the perfect tribute, with my limbs tied together behind my back. Tex was strung up behind me, his feet still on the ground but his hands attached to a ceiling hook. His cock was positioned at my core, and he was using what momentum he could to move inside me.

X was an artist. A sadistic, amazing artist. He walked around us, an impressed look on his face. "Beautiful. A fucking masterpiece." He looked down at Lucius, who was kneeling beneath my suspended body, naked, his fangs in my breast as he sucked my nipple. "Are you sure you don't want to be up there too?"

"Not today, Executioner."

X pouted, but then he rocked me back into Tex's body, making us both groan. I looked around the room, at Walker's cum spread over his abs, though he was already hard again. I wanted to lick it off him. He must have seen the desire in my eyes, because he stood and walked over, his jeans still low, held up only by his juicy ass.

"Do you want a taste, Sweetheart?" I nodded furiously, and when he stepped in closer, I lifted my head to run my tongue over his salty abs.

Being such a damn giver, he gripped my waist, moving me back and forth against Tex, whose wide-leg stance was holding him steady against the force of my body, allowing him to hit places that I didn't know were possible.

I moaned as I licked, Walker's encouraging voice washing over me. "That's it, good girl. Lick up every drop."

X groaned. "Hold still, Snakelet. We are going to desecrate Isaac Newton's legacy by making what I'm calling the Fucking Cradle."

I couldn't turn my head to see what X was doing, but I heard Tex's groan, and I could use my imagination, especially as he suddenly thrust into me with more force. I came hard, but they weren't done.

Lucius collapsed beneath me, sated, my blood staining his lips as he watched whatever the hell was going on down there with heat in his eyes and his hand on his dick.

Tex was breathing heavily, chanting "Fuck, fuck, fuck," under his breath.

Back and forth they swung us, Walker stroking his

once again hard cock. Someone else appeared in my periphery, and I didn't even care that Vali had left his chair and gotten close.

"Can I..." he breathed, his whole body trembling. "May I stand here?"

X grunted, plowing back into Tex again. To the left of us, my other guys had their hands on their dicks, watching the live action porn take place. "Just remember the rules. No touching. Cutting off your hands would only add to the experience for me at this point," X joked gruffly. At least, I assumed he was joking.

X continued his punishing pace, and I dropped my head, the pleasure so intense that I'd fly apart if I wasn't strung so tightly. A cool liquid sensation on my breast had me opening my eyes, and I realized Lucius hadn't closed off the wound. Instead, he was letting my blood drip into his mouth where he lay below me.

There was probably something wrong with me that I thought it was hot. If vampires drank blood as food, but also drank and used it during sex, was it blood play or sploshing?

That was a question for another day as Tex suddenly twisted his hips, creating a different angle inside me and making stars appear behind my eyelids. "I'm going to come," he moaned, his tone begging, though I wasn't sure if he was begging me or X or the whole room in general.

X upped his thrusts, his hands holding my hips now as he took control. I took Walker's cock in my mouth and let him fuck my face as an orgasm ripped through me, followed closely by Tex's own shout of release. Walker was close behind, his abs contracting tightly as he came in hot ribbons down my throat.

Hats off to Sir Isaac, because holy fucking shit. He had really been onto something. My whole body was limp, and when X finally untied me from these ropes, I was fairly sure my body would never operate the same way again. I was going to need a wheelie walker thing from being bow-legged from sex.

When I opened my eyes, Vali was on his knees beside me, his face so close I could feel his breath cooling the sweat on my cheeks. "Please," he breathed.

Call it all the endorphins running through my well-pleasured body, because I whispered, "What do you need?"

He didn't look over his shoulder at X, or down at the killer lying beneath me, his eyes solely on mine. "A kiss," he whispered, his eyes painfully hopeful, and I couldn't have said no at that moment, even if I had a heart made of stone.

"Then take it."

"It would be worth my hands," he murmured, and then his mouth latched onto mine.

Oh. Oh hell. The kiss was somehow soft but firm, but that wasn't what had my body twitching like there were a hundred volts coursing through my veins. It was the *connection*, the filling of a well inside me that I hadn't even known existed. Power poured between us as the kiss deepened, filling, filling, filling until I felt so full that the world would bow before me if I requested it.

Vali dragged himself a way with a gasp, falling backward onto the wooden floors with a thud, his chest heaving like he couldn't get enough air.

Orthus burst through the door, his feet halting as he took in the room. Me and Tex suspended from some of the many rings attached to the reinforced ceiling. X still buried deep in Tex. My guys lining the walls of the room, or lying back naked on the chairs that littered the place. Lucius beneath me, his face smeared with blood, and Vali lying unmoving on the floor beside him.

That shook him out of the stunned disbelief at the scene in front of him. He dropped to his knees beside Vali, his eyes on us all as if we were about to jump up and attack him. Uh, hello? I couldn't even scratch my nose right now.

"Vali, what's wrong? I felt something through the bond..."

Wait, they were *bonded?*

Vali started laughing. It was an almost hysterical laugh, and when I turned, he was crying through the gut-wrenching laughter. "O, it's..." He gasped, struggling to form words. "It's everything I could have expected. It's... more." His eyes met mine. "It's amazing. I haven't felt this satisfied in an eternity." His body was still shaking, and I realized he was orgasming.

Orthus looked between us, then leaned down, lifting Vali into his arms and striding from the room.

X pulled back, staring at the door. "I thought Judge was quick on the trigger, but not even he's blown his load with just one kiss."

Lucius climbed out from below me, leaning up and kissing me hard, as if he was trying to lick the taste of Vali from my flesh. He sucked and plunged his tongue inside my mouth until I was gasping.

When he finally pulled away, his eyes were wide, so fucking wide that his lids almost disappeared. "Well, this is a problem, Raine Baxter. Or maybe a miracle." He turned, looking over his shoulder at Nico. "It's good to return, *Scáth*."

Nico's whole body went rigid. "Lucius?"

The man I'd lived with, the man I'd loved for two decades, smiled an expression I'd never seen. It was free of pain. Free of madness. It was like the sun. "Brother." He turned to me. "My lover." Then he kissed me again, gently, without desperation.

Who was this man?

S ometimes, sex was a revelation. But this? This really took the cake.

We were all dressed once more, scattered around the brothel's sitting room. I'd even called Vali and Orthus down, because they were important to the topic. Integral, even.

Good communication made the dream work, or something like that.

I looked at the smiling, happy Lucius like he was possessed. Nico stared at him like he was a ghost. The rest of the guys stared at him like he was about to bust out a machete and go on a killing spree, even though he hadn't ever been more placid. It had been fifteen minutes since he kissed me, and he'd been grinning the whole time.

"Is he high?" Brody asked, and I shrugged. I didn't know.

It was Nico who answered, after taking a long, shuddering breath. "No. I don't think he's ever been more grounded, at least not in my memory." He swallowed hard. "He used to call me *Scáth* when we were little. It means shadow."

Lucius gave an amused shake of his head. "You all need to stop looking at me like that. I can feel the effects of the incubus's kiss wearing off already. I'll be the same psychotic madman you know and love soon enough." He sighed, leaning back in his chair. "It's nice to have a break from the voices in my head, that's all."

Orthus growled low. "Does someone want to tell me what's going on? Vali is still giggling like he's been into the brownies in the cafe down the road, and the Mad King is smiling at me like we're going to Mass for Christmas. It's freaking me the fuck out."

I turned to Lucius, then slid my eyes to Vali. "One of you guys want to take this one? Because I'm confused as fuck."

Vali shrugged. "I can answer my part, I guess. I feel sated in a way that defies belief. I'd been starving for so long, but that gnawing pain in my chest that refused to leave, is finally soothed. I guess it's a coition demon thing?" His blue eyes stared intently into mine. "Don't you feel it too?"

The worrying thing was that I did. Even now,

power was thrumming through my body. It was like a painful hole in my chest—one that I didn't even know I'd had—was now filled.

Like walking around for years with a splinter in your foot that you couldn't get out—disconcerting at first, but you'd work out how to deal with the niggling pain, how to work around it, until suddenly it's just a part of you. Your body adjusts to tolerate the pain. Then one day, someone with a steady hand and a badass pair of tweezers comes along and pulls it out—suddenly, that pain you were so used to disappears, and you realize how much it actually did hurt.

"I feel it. I feel powerful, like the succubus has had a power boost. I could take on the world." I looked over at Orthus, giving him a saucy smile. "Kneel, hellhound," I purred. Orthus got to his feet jerkily and bent his knees. Then he jerked back, his eyes narrowed and a sharp smile across his face.

"Not today, succubus."

A part of me was happy that he could still resist the succubus. "Lucky."

Judge was leaning forward. "So do we think it's Raine's power boost that has turned Lucius into a Stepford Wife, or a combination of their fluids?"

I screwed up my nose. "Don't say fluids like that. It gives me the ick."

"Sugar, I just watched you lick fluids off of the

Sheriff's abs like it was cream and you were a sweet little pussycat," he crooned back.

I shot him the finger, but my body still clenched with desire at his words. That guy could master my body without even touching it, like one of those instruments you played by waving your hand over it and making alien noises come out. What was it? A theremin?

Lucius laughed, and it shocked us again. "It's so nice to watch you all flirt, without having to push down the urge to attack you for touching what is mine." He looked blissed out. "Possessiveness is a side effect of the madness. The man—me—loves you guys almost as much as I love Raine. But the monster wants her all to himself, and I'm not sure she'd survive his kind of love."

I look into his clear, beautiful blue eyes. "That's disconcerting to know."

"You've always had the reins to my control. They were safer than most."

"Is there anyone you didn't want to murder in their sleep?" Walker asked, his face impassive, though I knew he was probably apprehensive of this new side to Lucius.

Lucius tilted his head to the side. "Raine. The pups. Even the monster loves those three, as much as a monster can love anyone. Nico, though I enjoyed tormenting him. Titus." I nodded, not sure of what I

should do with this information, but Lucius continued. "I think it was a combination of the two coition
demons' saliva, tinged with lust, that made all this
happen." He looked at Nico. "It could be a solution to
the madness. If we could just harvest—"

Orthus let out a growl. "Hold the fuck up. That
isn't what we agreed to. Vali isn't your toy to play with
until you satisfy the vampires. You made your bed—
you can lie in it."

Lucius's mouth slammed shut, his jaw tightening.
"You're getting something out of it too."

"An escape? To what? Become a lab rat? This agreement seems to involve you taking and taking, adding
things on, and Vali is the one who's giving."

I chewed my lip. "I'd like to amend our agreement,
if you want. This?" I pointed to Lucius, whose frown
wasn't concealing murderous rage like usual. "This
benefits *all* of supernatural kind. I'll maintain my
status as a Convocation Member if you will help me
find a cure for the ennui madness in vampires." I swallowed hard. "So many desperate supernaturals, just
looking for a way to beat back the demons."

"Not everyone is meant to live forever, Raine
Baxter," Orthus said gruffly.

I nodded. Was he talking about vampires or
himself? "I understand, but everyone should be able to
make that choice with a sound mind."

Vali's soft eyes watched me intently. "You'd give up

your chance at happiness for this? Give up freedom from the heavy mantle of power?"

I nodded firmly. "In a heartbeat," I said quickly. Because I would. No one deserved to suffer.

"What would it entail?"

I shrugged. "I don't know. All I can tell you is what happened from my experience. Regular samples of saliva and blood, and uh, other fluids. That's about it."

Vali shook his head. "Your Executioner was right about you. You are good." He gave me a tight smile. "I know the madness. I'm willing to help, as well as take over the leadership in the Convocation."

"Vali—" Orthus interrupted.

"*No*, O. We both know this is the right thing to do. When have we ever just done what was easy and safe? Besides, she's right. This is for the good of us all. No one needs crazed vampires roaming the streets."

Silence fell over the room, and Brody leaned forward in his seat. "When were you going to tell us that you and Orthus are bonded? You know if Raine bonds Vali, then you're automatically included in that bond. That's probably something you should have been upfront about."

Brody was using his disappointed Alpha voice, and that shit worked on me, even though I wasn't any kind of shifter.

Orthus just frowned, then looked at me. "I didn't

see how it was relevant. Would it have changed your mind?"

No. "Maybe."

Brody growled this time, his Alpha power spreading through the room. "That isn't something for you to decide. I know you've been on your own for a long time, but we are a Pack. We invited the incubus to be a part of that Pack, and lying your way into our bond isn't the way to start a life together."

"I never lied," Orthus muttered, his knee jiggling, but he didn't look at me.

It was Tex who answered him. "A lie by omission is still a lie, Orthus."

Silence fell around the room, and I got to my feet, smoothing down my nightgown. "There are two more nights until the full moon. Think it over, both of you. A bond is forever, and it isn't a short-term fix. If you're going to start out with lies and omissions, I'll do what's best for my Pack now. For my family." I sucked in a deep breath. "I need to be able to trust you."

I walked out of the room and up toward my bedroom. I was tired, my thighs felt like jelly, and I was still reeling from the discussion. My brain needed the blissful nothingness of sleep, just for a little while.

CHAPTER
TWENTY-NINE

I hardly saw Vali or Orthus the following two days. Vali had given me a big smile as he finished his coffee this morning, but then he'd disappeared out the front door again. I hadn't even seen the shadow of Orthus since I'd confronted him about already being bonded to Vali.

I worried that we were doing this against his will. Brody had just shrugged and told me it was up to me if we went ahead, but I could see the hesitancy in his eyes.

Ugh. This. It was this type of bullshit I'd been trying to avoid by coming to Amsterdam in search of the damn Night Demon. I didn't want to make life-or-death decisions about people anymore. I didn't *want* the weight of an entire species' mental wellbeing on my conscience.

Instead of easing my burden, I'd gathered more. The souvenir edition, as it was.

Tonight was the night of the full moon, and if we were going to bond, it had to be now. Luckily, the guys were taking care of most of the details. This morning, Nico had gotten me off by teasing me with one of X's silk ropes until I was a moaning mess, and then made me come on his tongue.

The man had a talented tongue. I remembered the time that he and Tex had a contest to see who could learn to tie a cherry stem in their mouth first. Nico won, but only by a couple of hours.

I was a lucky girl.

I wasn't sure if they'd handed off that debauched rope to Vali, but I assumed I'd find out tonight, if they ever returned to the brothel. I spent the remaining daylight hours checking on the kids, on Fox Falls, on Dark River. Everything was fine without us.

Sometimes I wondered if they needed us at all. Maybe I could just run away, and everyone would be fine. Probably not, though. It had only been nine days since we left.

The front door opened, and I tried not to look like I'd been pacing in front of it all day. It wasn't Vali and Orthus; instead, it was Walker.

Lifting his sunglasses onto his head, he gave me a lopsided smile, placing a paper bag down beside him.

"Evening, Sweetheart." He stepped toward me, bundling me up into his arms. "How are you feeling?"

"Nervous," I said honestly, because no one understood me quite like Walker did. Not to say he understood me better or worse, but he just seemed to know when I was feeling out of sorts.

He nodded, his lips touching my temple. "That's an understandable emotion. But it'll all be okay. Or it won't. Doesn't matter either way, because I'll have your back always." He tilted my face up so I was looking into his burning eyes. "We all do."

"I love you too," I murmured softly, and when he kissed me, I didn't hesitate to kiss him back. "What's in the bag?" I knew it was food; I could smell it, and it was making my mouth water.

"Poffertjes." Seeing my confusion, he grinned. "Mini Dutch pancakes."

I squealed, diving for the bag. I'd seen them on the street the other day, but we'd had no time to stop. He smacked away my hands until he could pull out a square cardboard container and a fork. "Pancakes always make you feel better."

I gripped the box to my chest, wrapping my free arm around him. "*You* always make me feel better. The pastries are just a bonus."

"I just want you to be happy, Raine. It's all I've ever wanted."

That was why I loved Walker. He wasn't showy. He

wasn't clingy or prone to huge displays of love or lust. He didn't insert himself into every part of my life unless I asked. But he was always, *always* there when I needed him. My rock. My life preserver. My calm in the storm of my life.

"I know, Sheriff," I said softly. "I don't deserve you sometimes."

Walker snorted. "Raine Baxter, you deserve the damn world." He lifted the paper bag. "I got souvenirs for the kids too. Enit will never forgive us if we come all the way to Amsterdam and don't get anything for them. I wanted to show you, and then I'm going to post them back home this afternoon."

He pulled out a long, gold box, and when he opened it, a dainty glass tulip was well padded inside. It was glorious and intricate, and I gasped, noticing the end tapered into a sharp point. "Walker, did you get our daughter a glass flower dagger?"

He grinned. "Carmen's going to love it. This is why I decided to send it home by mail. Wouldn't want to get it confiscated at customs."

I shook my head and opened the next box. A small mechanical windmill was inside, and when I turned the base, the blades spun and it played a lullaby that I didn't recognize. Enit would adore it.

The last thing in the bag was a single yellow clog, with the name of a famous Dutch beer along the side, next to a little man holding a beer.

Walker grinned. "Apparently, you drink beer out of it, but I'm sure he won't until he's twenty-one."

Yeah, sure. And I was Mother Teresa. Sure, shifters had a higher alcohol tolerance so he'd have to shotgun like four in a row to even feel tipsy, but I wouldn't put it past Christopher to do that.

That was who he was. Enit was the empathetic one, Carmen was the wild child, and Christopher had a self-destructive streak from the trauma of his past. I'd sent him to therapists; he knew the jargon. He had the tools, and now he had to work through things himself.

"I worry about them."

He wrapped an arm around my shoulders. "I know you do. It's what makes you a good mother."

"Do you think they'll react okay to having two new figures in our family group?" You could never tell with those three. We'd been a constant in their lives, but they still reacted badly to outsiders, even now.

He shrugged. "I think so. If not, they'll get used to it. They aren't babies anymore. They're going to leave the nest and live their own lives. They have their own Packs. Christopher is... Christopher. He'll sort himself out sooner or later."

I sighed. Sometimes, I wondered if me being the Convocation Member had been good for them or not. I'd been away so much while they were growing up, but they'd had the guys, and the Pack in Nîso. They'd had all the people in Dark River, who spoiled them like mad. They hadn't lacked love.

But I'd been their mother. I really hoped I hadn't compounded Christopher's abandonment issues.

"Come on, Raine. I'll feed you your poffertjes, then I have to head to the post office before tonight's festivities. Just a family bond?"

I nodded, despite the heat that had been between us in X's dungeon. I wasn't ready to completely jump aboard the crazy train just yet.

"I'm doing the right thing, right?" I asked one last time.

"Yes." I loved it when he didn't try and emotionally bring me around to the right decision and just told me what I needed to hear.

He bent down to pick up some fallen tissue paper, and I swung my hand back, slapping his juicy butt. Honestly, I don't think I'd appreciated butts until I had such a wonderfully squeezable collection of them at my disposal.

"I swear to god, Raine, if you try to slap the other cheek..."

"You'll what?" I teased, flexing my fingers like my hand was a weapon. It was a small quirk of mine that I had to slap both cheeks. It was like both or none. What if the left cheek felt more loved than the right? What if Walker felt lopsided for the rest of the day?

I was all about fairness.

"I'll eat all your pancakes. No! I'll chew them up and then spit them back in the box so neither of us gets to appreciate them."

I gasped at the sheer brutality of it. "Sheriff Walton, who *are* you? I've been married to a monster all this time."

He just laughed, kissing the top of my head. "The lengths I have to go to in order to protect the sanctity of my ass cheeks." He dropped a small kiss on my nose too. "I'll be back before dusk."

He ducked back out the door, and I continued my pacing. At least, until Orthus popped out of the shadows. I caught him looming out of the corner of my eye and jumped back, tripping over the couch.

"Sweet Betty White's lady balls! Orthus, what the fuck is wrong with you? You scared the hell out of me."

His eyes grew wide. "Sweet *who?*"

I flapped a dismissive hand at him. "Never mind. Were you eavesdropping again?"

He didn't even have the good grace to look guilty. He just stared at me with those impenetrable dark eyes that seemed to see into my soul. "Yes." He tilted his head at me. "You have children?"

"Yeah, three. Which you know because your big hellhound ears were flapping where they didn't belong."

"Succubi?"

I shook my head. "No. Wolf shifters. It's a long

252

story. I'll tell you later. I didn't find out I was a succubi until I was already undead. Before that, children weren't really in the master plan." Mika McKellen, the girl I used to be, had no master plan. Fate had one, but not me.

"I was brought into existence in a time when you would have had five children and a husband by the time you were turned. I realize by today's standard, you would have been young."

I shrugged. I no longer mourned my mortal life. I was happy with the way things turned out. "It is what it is. I don't have any regrets." None I wanted to talk to a near perfect stranger about anyway.

Orthus cleared his throat. "I wanted to apologize for not telling you about the bond between Vali and I. It has been a part of me for so long, sometimes I forget that he hasn't always been a part of me. That once upon a time, we were two separate people. I didn't initially set out to deceive you."

I could understand that.

Orthus sucked in a deep breath. "And by the time I remembered, you'd agreed to help Vali, and I didn't want to ruin his chances at freedom by shackling you with an extra bond. I think Vali would be the hub between us, and it shouldn't strain you too much. If I could stay here, I would. Vali deserves a fresh start."

I tilted my head back and looked at the crumbling ornate ceiling. I was such a sucker for a self-sacrificing man with a tough exterior and a secret heart of gold. Honestly, it was my weakness. The Kryptonite to my Superman. The tendon to my Achilles. The Hitachi Wand to my vow of abstinence.

"You both do. I'm committed to helping Vali, but I want you to be happy too."

"Why?"

"The Member for the Fae would have you believe I'm a do-gooding Mary Sue with a savior complex, but really, I just have shitty boundaries and an inability to say no to a sad origin story."

A small smile curled his lips. "Did I tell you that I was dragged up from Hell and kept in a psycho witch's basement for a whole year?"

I shook my head, trying to straighten out my smile as I flopped down onto the couch and cradled my chin in my hand. "What a tragic backstory. Please, tell me more."

THIRTY

We had the ceremony on the roof of the brothel. The night was clear, the full moon swollen and bright as it hung on the horizon. We were all here, lining the edges of the space, the mood serious, as it should be. This was a huge step for us all.

As the sun fell below the horizon, Nico turned to me. "Are you ready?"

Uh, yep. As I was ever going to be. "I'm nervous. Is it weird that I'm nervous?"

X appeared with the rope, handing it to Nico. It was soft and supple—for some reason, I'd kind of expected it to be crunchy, with all the blood and 'coition demon release' coating it. "It's a change. It's okay to be nervous, Love."

Nico turned to Vali. "Are you ready also?"

Vali's face was an odd mix of hopefulness and trepidation. I understood the fear of the unknown. He hadn't traveled outside the walls of this city in centuries, and before that, he hadn't really left Europe. Now here I was, throwing him from his prison into the complete unknown.

He swallowed hard, casting a look over his shoulder at Orthus. He must have gained whatever strength he could from the hellhound, because when he turned back to me, there was determination in his eyes. "Yes."

X clapped his hands together. "Let's do this. The night has already started."

I reached out and gripped Vali's hand in mine. His fingers were long and strong as they threaded through my own. I gave his palm a reassuring squeeze and then nodded to Nico. Nico started chanting words I didn't understand, his fingers deftly winding the ropes around our clasped hands in a row of infinity-shaped knots, looping partially up our wrists also.

His words got louder until with a final tug on the knots, he cinched us together, bound hand in hand. Stepping away, he looked between Vali and I. "How do you feel?"

"Is this the wrong time to say I need to pee?" I joked. Well, mostly joked.

Vali laughed, his fingers flexing in mine. "Thank you. I can never repay what you're doing for us."

I choked down the lump of emotion in my throat, waving my free hand like it meant nothing to eternally tie myself to someone I hadn't known two weeks ago. "We're setting each other free."

At some point, someone must have decided that this should be a celebration rather than the clinical joining that I'd imagined, because X appeared with beer, stroopwafels, some kind of croquettes, and fries. So many silver trays of fries, with all sorts of amazing things loaded on top.

Why did no one tell me the Netherlands was the holy land of loaded fries?

My right hand was bound to Vali's left, which kind of made eating a bit weird, but it was okay. I was frie-dextrous. I could eat them without hands if I had to.

Tex strummed Orthus's guitar as we ate and chatted like I wasn't literally and figuratively tied to the man beside me. It wasn't set in stone yet—we still needed to kiss for that to happen—but I could feel the beginnings of a bond in my chest. Just a shadow right now, a small niggle in the space usually only occupied by Brody and Tex.

As the party continued, we just sat together as a group, feeling out this fledgling thing we'd created. There were large reclining sun loungers, and I sat on the one beside Vali, our hands resting on my armrest between us.

"Do you feel it too?" I asked softly, and he nodded.

He gave me a half-smile, his eyes on the bulbous moon overhead. "Yes, though if it was my first time having a bond, I'm not sure I'd recognize the sensation. Feels a little like indigestion."

I mean, he wasn't wrong.

"When did you bond with Orthus?"

Vali frowned, his eyes moving to the hellhound, who was chatting with X. "Just after I was cursed. He was still partially feral from being tortured for so long, and I was starving. We weren't in the best frames of mind to make such an irreversible, life-long decision, but it is what it is."

Apparently, impulsive bonds weren't a new thing for the incubus.

I dropped my voice lower. "You were lovers?"

His face was solemn as he nodded. "Yes. For a long time. First out of necessity, and then out of loneliness. Later out of love and mutual admiration. It is hard not to love the only constant figure in your life, whether it's healthy or not."

"But you aren't any longer?"

Vali shook his head. "No, not for a long time. Not since he fell in love with Tineke and married her. He is a faithful hound," he said with a huffed laugh. "And not since her death. He's wedded to the ghost of her, but that's okay. I was no longer starving, and it's his companionship that I need, not his body."

It was a nice body, though.

Vali raised an eyebrow at me. Shit, I'd said that out loud.

"So he's still in love with his wife? She was mortal?"

He nodded, his eyes turning sad. "She was really something. Beautiful. Confident. Liberated, in a time when women had no rights. She accepted Orthus like they were made to be together, and she didn't even blink when he came with baggage. She accepted me like I was hers as well, though we didn't have that kind of relationship. She was just a friend in a time when I had none. I loved her for that. You would have liked her."

He sounded wistful, and I squeezed his hand once more in mine. "I'm sure I would have. What did she die of?"

"Old age. Wasn't quite the same level of old as it is now, but well past the life expectancy for women in the eighteenth century. It broke his heart, and mine. He hasn't let anyone in since, but I can hardly blame him. We've made our enemies, and there has been no time for friends, let alone lovers."

I scoff. "Surely there can't be that many people chasing down the Night Demon that you couldn't ask the nice barista down the street out for coffee and a casual blow job."

A laugh burst almost violently past Vali's lips,

shaking his shoulders. "I guess not. I'll try and do better."

I gave him a tight smile, ignoring the way my chest tightened at the idea of him getting a blow job from a random person. The bond must be kicking in already. I took a long draw from my beer bottle and pushed down the feeling. My arm was starting to go a little numb from being at an odd angle for a long time, so I shifted my shoulders around to get some relief.

"Why do they call you The Night Demon? I mean, it's a badass title, and I'd keep it if I were you, but I was convinced you were going to be a sleep paralysis demon with pincers and an abyss instead of a face."

Vali snorted. "As fearsome as that would be, I'm afraid the truth is a lot more depressing and a little amusing."

"Do tell." I started to turn on my side, but my arm blocked me, and I huffed. Obviously, there was a reason being bound like this was part of the ritual. If I couldn't deal with being tied to him for a few hours, I probably shouldn't commit myself to him for all freaking eternity.

"Uncomfortable?" His eyes ran searchingly over my face, though what he was hoping to find was beyond me.

"Dead arm." I wiggled my fingers against his. "I'll just shift around to find a better position, while you tell me the story of how you became a legend."

Vali chewed his lower lip. "You could always come over here and lie beside me. I promise to be a gentleman, and your arm won't hurt if it isn't stretched out like that."

I looked over at him under my lashes, and gave myself a harsh pep talk. The time to be shy was gone. I wanted to be friends with Vali. He deserved a family who loved him, and we could be that.

Sitting up, I shuffled over to his chair. He scooched toward the other armrest to make a sliver of room for me on the lounger, but I would still be sitting half on him. Using his other hand, Vali grabbed my hip, rolling me to the side until my head was on his chest and our joined arms were resting between us.

"More comfortable?"

Uh, yeah, sure, as long as I didn't think about how good he smelled or the pounding of his heart or the warm scent of his blood. If I didn't think about the hard lines of his body or remember the look of unfiltered lust on his face from the other night. *Totally* comfortable.

Instead of saying all that, I just murmured, "Yes, thank you. Now tell me about the legend of the Night Demon." I needed a distraction from the fact that my hand was on his very defined abs.

Vali breathed in deeply. "I guess it started around the time Tineke came along. I no longer had Orthus to supplement my needs, so I had to feed more often. You have to remember that most people feel more allure toward me than you do. You're impervious to my incubus powers."

I didn't feel very impervious right now; the deep rumble of his voice against my cheek was doing things for me. Instead, I just nodded with what I hoped was a sage expression on my face.

"By then, Amsterdam was a booming port, and I couldn't walk through the market square without women and men whispering their addresses in my ear, or suggesting when their spouses would be away. Honestly, it was insane. I wasn't one to turn down the opportunity to feed, so I snuck into bedrooms under the darkness of night, made love to wives and daughters, to peasants and grand ladies alike. Shifters, humans, vampires, you name it. But never witches."

Guess he'd learned his lesson about the witches the hard way.

I nudged him with my shoulder. "They should have called you the Horndog. Way more apt."

"What can I say? It's in my nature." He cleared his throat. "The first time I got busted by a human husband, I managed to jump from the second-story window. The second time, Orthus had to move me through the shadows. Rumors started flying around that I was a demon, attacking women in the night, inflicting atrocities on them that made them writhe in pain." He gave a small, satisfied smirk. "They were writhing all right, but it wasn't in pain. But I guess if you'd never given your wife an orgasm, her O face might look like pain."

Facts. I was fairly sure my orgasm face looked like someone was waxing my butthole.

"The incubi had long since died out, and no one made the connection, instead assuming I was hellspawn, and honestly, I let them think that. Disreputable newspapers printed the story of hysterical women who claimed to be debauched by the Night Demon. Some I'd actually slept with, but many not. And thus, the legend of the Night Demon was born."

The warmth of his body and the belly full of beer and fries was making me sleepy. "That's really cool. You're like the Oprah of Orgasms."

"Who?"

"Never mind," I said groggily, and when his fingers started to run through my hair, I let myself drift off to sleep.

THIRTY-ONE

I was shaken awake sometime in the early morning. The moon was still up, and the dawn hadn't yet broken. I'd been having a great dream where Vali had cupcakes instead of nipples, and every time I licked off all the buttercream, they extruded more. It was like a never-ending fountain of frosting.

That was kinda weird now that I thought about it.

I was still pressed to Vali's chest, and he was tense. "What's wrong?" My body was alert, straining to hear for threats past the thundering of his heart.

I looked over at Tex and Orthus standing beside us. Orthus dropped into a low crouch. "The vampires are here."

I frowned. "I know. You invited us to stay."

He shook his head and looked at me like I was stupid. I was still half asleep, okay? "No, the ones you pissed off by crushing the jaw of their beloved progeny, and defanging him."

Oh. Whoops. Was it weird I'd forgotten about that? Life had been hectic in the last week.

"Nico will talk to them."

It was Tex's turn to crouch down, whispering, "They aren't here to talk, Raine. They've surrounded the building. Orthus says they are fitted out for war."

Geez, people were so touchy about a little bone grinding. The guy was lucky he still had a damn head. If it had been Lucius who got there first and not Nico, the guy wouldn't have a heart in his chest anymore.

"They started it," I told Vali, like the fact we'd come to town and crushed a vampire's jaw was completely justified.

I mean, could we have handled it differently? Probably. But honestly, vampires only knew one language, and it was power. It was an insult that Nico couldn't have let stand, no matter how much I'd hated the violent nature of it.

"They aren't here because they're worried we hurt their precious baby vamp. They're here because we hurt their pride," I grumbled, sitting up.

Orthus paced to the edge of the rooftop, looking down at the dark streets. Even the brothels had closed for the night. "I can't shadow walk with the two of you," he growled out, frustration evident in his tone. "We'll have to undo the binding."

Vali hissed out a breath. "No. We're so fucking close, Orthus. So close to being free. There has to be another way."

Walker appeared at the steps to the roof, moving swiftly toward us. "We run. I've called the pilot; he's waiting at the airport. We just have to evade them until the sun rises, you complete the ritual, and then we can be gone from this fucking town."

It sounded like a plan to me. I nodded, getting to my feet and pulling Vali up behind me. "You need to get your stuff. We can't come back." My heart broke for these guys. "I'm sorry. This is not how I wanted it to be."

Vali's hand stroked down my red hair. "This is how it always is."

I wanted to stomp my foot and shout, "Not anymore!" but it would be a lie. Soon. Soon they'd be safe and secure.

It was Orthus who answered. "We've packed the things we value most in preparation for your quick departure. Everything else is replaceable."

I nodded, but I still felt bad. "Maybe we can get someone to come and pack everything else up and ship it?" I didn't want them to leave their entire life behind in Amsterdam.

Orthus shrugged. "They're just things, succubus."

We moved off the roof and into the house itself. X and Judge were missing, but Brody stood at the base of the stairs, a rucksack strapped across his body. "I've got the basics. Everything else can be replaced."

I smiled at him appreciatively. Nico walked over, looking haunted. "I'm sorry I brought this upon us, today of all days."

I frowned. Yeah, the timing was odd. Why would they have waited until the full moon to come for us like this? Unless they *knew* about the bond and Vali... We'd been outed.

"Doesn't matter, Nico. I don't think this is a coincidence. We need to split up." In a giant group, we would be way too easy to pick off.

Nico nodded his agreement. "Yes. Walker, Tex and Brody, take the stuff and move back to the plane as fast as you can. Make sure the pilot is there and ready to taxi down the runway as soon as the doors close behind us," he said softly, his voice pitched low enough that people outside the room wouldn't be able to hear. "Buddy and Rio, X and Judge, escort Vali and Raine to the plane. Two on her, two in the distance. Remember, we can't leave until sunrise, so don't go straight there—we don't want a showdown on the tarmac. I assume you'll be with them too?" he asked Orthus, who nodded tightly.

Nico looked at his twin, at the man who was slowly losing himself back to the madness after his brief stint as Mr. Rogers. "Lucius and I will take out the trash."

Lucius's grin was every bit the blood-soaked madman I knew and loved. "Can't wait."

I looked at them both. "Don't attack unless they come at you first. I don't want this political bullshit to follow us home." I stepped toward Nico, leaving my bound arm behind me so we had some privacy. "Don't do anything reckless. I need us all to make it home," I whispered, and his eyes softened.

"Reckless, no. But Raine, you don't come for my family and expect to live a long life. I don't care who the hell they think they are." He kissed me hard, a claiming kiss. "Let's go. Lucius and I will go... distract them." He looked at Walker, Brody and Tex. "You first. Don't stop for anyone or anything." Then he kissed my head. "You go in the opposite direction. The long way around, okay? If we aren't there by sunrise, leave without us and we'll make it back on our own."

I slapped him on the chest. "If you think I'm leaving the country without you, you don't know me *at all*."

Lucius stepped up and kissed me too. "If it comes to it, cut the bindings. We can try again. You're worth more to me than he is." He looked at Vali. "No offense."

Vali let out a bitter laugh. "None taken."

Then Nico and Lucius disappeared out of the room so fast, even my supernatural eyes failed to keep up. We waited until we heard screams before we moved.

Orthus's eyes were wide. "I probably should have

predicted that. I'll check the coast is clear for you guys from the shadows," he said, stepping into the darkened corner and disappearing. So damn cool.

"Be safe," I whispered as I hugged each of the others. They disappeared out the back door, and my heart pounded at the separation from my guys. I hated not knowing if they'd make it back to me safe.

X drew two large daggers from sheaths on his torso, holding them loosely in both hands. "I won't let anything happen to you, Red. Bring your boy toy, and we'll turn him back into a frog by the end of the night."

Judge stroked his fingers down my spine reassuringly, then gently pushed me in the direction of the door. He had a gun in his other hand, though I had no idea where it had come from. I could sense the weak echo of Vali's bond, his tenuous grip on hope, and I flexed my fingers through his.

"Two hours until dawn. We've got this," I whispered.

"I don't want to get my hopes up." The shadows around us swirled, and Vali nodded. "Orthus is back."

There was something reassuring about the darkness. As a vampire, I lived in it now. I couldn't stand in the sun for too long without turning into a lobster, so I found beauty in the shadows of the night.

Hopefully, one day, the shadows found beauty in me too.

Vali was fast, but he wasn't vampire-fast. We

slowed our pace so he could keep up, but against a band of vampires, we might as well have been moving in slow motion. We took erratic turns, criss-crossing through side streets, trying to get as lost as possible. I tugged Vali along, and I wondered if he'd get mad if I just picked him up one-armed and carried him fire-man-style to the plane. I mean, it still wouldn't be fast, but it had to be faster than this.

We worked our way in the direction of the airport, one eye on the eastern horizon. Still dark. "Dammit. What time is sunrise today?"

"7:18."

I swore silently under my breath. Why hadn't we come in the middle of winter? Shortest bonding of the year.

As it was, we had just over an hour to go. It was too long. I knew it in my gut that it was too long.

In a dank little alley, on the other side of the city from where we needed to be, I was proven right. Twelve vampires moved out of the darkness, circling us like sharks. Vali gripped my hand, pulling me behind him. When I tried to tug him back beside me, he held firm. "Immortal, remember?"

I still hated it. What if he wasn't mortal anymore? What if I accidentally spat on him and it counted as a kiss and then he died?

Okay, that was pretty far-fetched, but you know what else was far-fetched? Getting kidnapped off a highway and getting turned into a vampire, then left in a ditch, while your maker—who was the town doctor and also your friend—passive-aggressively tormented you.

So excuse me if I tended to prepare for the most ridiculous scenarios.

Francois stepped out of the shadows. He raised his hand to signal the attack, but I yelled, "Wait!"

And he did. Go figure.

"Don't you have any demands? Any long and poignant—if a little deranged—soliloquies? You're kind of ruining the moment…" I blustered, trying to buy time.

Francois wasn't buying it. "I don't want anything from you but your death. The Night Demon is just an added benefit."

I looked over my shoulder at Vali. "What did you do to piss off the leader of the vampires?"

"Fucked his consort. She said he had a lot of power but a tiny dick. I was doing a public service."

I sighed. "I guess negotiation is off the table then."

As if to prove me right, the vampires attacked en masse.

THIRTY-TWO

You know when you go to the zoo, and you're in time for the lion feeding, and you watch these sorta lazy looking animals wake up, stretch, and then between one step and the next turn into giant killing machines?

That was what it was like when Judge and X really let go. Once a duo of assassins, they now moved together effortlessly, swirling around both Vali and I like a tornado of death. Judge's shout of, "Protect Raine," could barely be heard over the screams and gunshots as they moved like death personified.

Then the hellhound arrived.

Francois made a face as Orthus morphed out of the shadows, already transformed, his teeth snapping on both his heads, and fangs dripping with slobber—or maybe it was hellfire. His body was huge, easily the size of a rhinoceros, and the hide was similar, like tough-looking leather.

Honestly, it was impressive as hell, and I wondered if he'd let me pet him in this form one day. Think of all the ear scratches you could get if you had two heads, right?

Orthus backed right up until he was in front of us, his huge body circling, partially blocking me from the carnage of the vampires clashing. When X whooped, and a head rolled beneath Vali's feet, I knew that Lucius had arrived.

Was it weird that I associated decapitated heads with Lucius? Not if you knew him.

"Just leave, Francois. You aren't going to achieve anything but a decimated nest if you continue. Protect those who remain," came Nico's reasonable voice.

Lucius spat. "You're sending fledglings in as fodder in the hopes that, what? They get a lucky shot? Either fight yourself, or concede, you cowardly piece of shit."

The sun was lightening the horizon. We were almost there. Almost there.

Vali pressed close to my body, stooping down until he was close to my ear. "Get on Orthus's back. We'll make a run for it."

I didn't want to run. I wanted to hold my ground with this asshole.

Lucius looked over his shoulder. "Go, Raine. I'm about to end this for good."

Well, that sounded ominous. Buddy and Rio melted back toward us, standing either side of Orthus. Vali climbed onto his back, then dragged me up over the hellhound's shoulders like I was some kind of conquered beast of burden. But sitting two astride was impossible when we were fucking attached by the wrist.

Orthus didn't wait for me to get settled, bursting into action, running faster than I could have imagined. There was hardly anyone around, mostly just early morning commuters, and I doubted they'd be able to see the blur of the huge beast in their midst. They'd feel the gust of displaced air though; they'd feel that adrenaline boost that indicated their hindbrain knew they'd almost died, but wouldn't understand why.

Vali picked me up, and I settled my legs around his waist so that I could cling tightly to his body. Riding a hellhound backwards was not my favorite thing ever.

0/10 would recommend.

Vali was holding on for both of us, and that made my inner control freak absolutely flip out. I saw vampires running behind us, Buddy and Rio at our sides, but unfamiliar vampires behind them.

X darted out of a side street, took a running leap and sliced off one of the attacking vamp's heads like something out of an action movie. But the dumbass vamps just kept coming, kept pouring out of the darkness.

How many damn fledglings did this city have?

One tried to circle us, but got caught up in Orthus's jaws. He tossed it to the side, and Buddy leapt out, shoving a sword through his chest. The guy would heal, but it would take awhile. Except for the decapitated vampires, most of them would survive, but I intended to be long gone by the time they were back on their feet. It wasn't my fault that their leader had thrown them at us like they meant nothing. I tried not to feel guilty about this, but failed.

I clung to Vali as I looked around for the guys. Judge appeared, nailing a vamp in the face. Eesh, that was going to be hard to heal back to normal. I saw X again, fighting with another one of the vampires in the middle of the road. Thankfully, there were no cars around, though a human wouldn't have been able to see it at the speed they were moving. Small favors.

Because no matter how big our problems seemed right now, if a human got evidence of our existence, we were all fucked.

I reached out for Brody and Tex, and breathed a sigh of relief that they were fine. There was worry in the bond, but mostly for me. They'd made it to the plane then, thank god.

Beside the shifter bonds was something else now. Something weak and new, but still there.

Vali.

I mentally poked at it, making him startle. "Sorry, just checking," I shouted.

"We're almost there," he yelled over the rushing of the wind. Orthus dodged left down a street with no lights behind a bunch of large warehouses. He stopped dead, and shifted back to human even as I was still on his back. It was only Vali's arms around my waist that stopped me from landing on my ass.

Orthus was naked. And hung. Blood smeared over his body, and holy shit, I couldn't take my eyes off him. Orthus's nose twitched, and he raised an eyebrow.

"Goddammit, Vali. Turn it off. Now's not the time."

Vali stroked a hand down my spine. "Babe, my powers don't affect you at all. What you're feeling is compliments of your own libido, not mine," he teased, and my face flushed red.

Orthus disappeared into the shadows and returned fully clothed. Handy. "I couldn't approach the plane in my shifted form. Let's go. We're almost there."

He took off between the warehouses. We were definitely in an industrial district, and as a large fence appeared in front of us, I realized we'd made it to the airport. "Yes," I breathed. We headed to a private runway off to the side of the main airport. It was still too early for commercial flights, and I huffed a sigh of relief. I could see the lights of our plane in the distance, more visible as the sky turned pink.

Someone picked me up from behind, Vali too, and I let out a scream. "Just me, Rainy Day. We need to be out of here sooner than expected," Judge yelled over the sound of the rushing wind.

We were in front of the plane before I could blink. He dropped us down, and I spun as much as I could, looking for my guys. X wasn't far behind us, and he tossed the body of a vampire back over the fence of the airport.

"Nico? Lucius?" I asked, my heart in my throat.

"They'll be here, Sugar. Let's see if your bonding worked, hey?"

I looked at my watch. 7:16. Fingers crossed the weather man was being generous with the sunrise time. The sky was pink as I launched myself at Vali. I pulled his face down to mine and kissed him hard.

It was a claiming kiss, because I wanted the bond to have no doubts that this was what we wanted. I wanted to free this man, for him to be with me for as long as he wanted. Vali kissed me back, our twined hands pressed between our bodies and his free hand coming around to rest on my spine, pulling me as close as possible.

I felt nothing but the fledgling bond in my chest and the same rush of power I'd gotten from kissing him the other night. Nothing that felt like a bond.

Shit, had we done it wrong? After all this, had we failed?

I might have whimpered against Vali's lips. I'd expected more.

He pulled back, gazing down at me sadly. "It's okay, Raine Baxter. We'll try again another time. But you need to go. You're not safe here." His fingers stroked down my face. "Go home and try to be happy. You have so much love in your life, and I thank you for giving me this moment of hope. I'd thought I'd lost it so many centuries ago, but you've ignited it in me once more." He brushed my cheek, and I realized I was crying.

I'd failed these two. I looked at the bindings on our wrist. "It's not over. Take your pants off. I'll bite you, we'll have sex—we'll form the bond that way." He'd be tied closer to me, but I couldn't take the sadness he was feeling.

Vali laughed, but it was a tragic sound. He turned my head to the side, and I saw the vampires beginning to pool at the fence of the airport. Lucius, Nico, X and Judge were chopping them down as they climbed over, but they were getting forced back.

"There's no time, Raine. But the fact you tried has meant more to me, to us, than you could ever understand."

"No. *No.* We didn't come all this way to fail," I growled.

Orthus's hand was on my wrist. "It's over,

succubus. Cut the binds and I'll shadow-walk him to safety." His face was hard, but his eyes were sad.

"No!" I yelled, and grabbed Vali's face.

One more kiss.

One more try. I couldn't leave without knowing I'd tried.

His face shadowed by the rising sun, I kissed him once more, and prayed to anyone I thought would listen. I held him to my lips, more brand than caress, and cursed the witch who had trapped him by greed and death. I kissed him and declared to the world that he was *mine,* that no one was taking him from me.

Not a long-dead witch.

Not a narcissistic vampire.

Not the goddamn sunrise.

As the morning sun singed my skin, a new bond burst into my chest, like fireworks inside a bottle. The succubus inside me sang as if she'd been freed too. As the bond took hold, I smiled even as I fell to the ground, Vali falling with me, and I passed the hell out.

Good night, Amsterdam. It'd been a real bitch knowing you.

THIRTY-THREE

I woke up on the plane. Panic hit me hard, and I tried to bolt upright. But I was trapped in someone's arms and given that the rope was still around my wrist, I knew whose.

"It's all okay, baby," Tex said from somewhere in the cabin, and I twisted around to find him. He was in the seat across from me, and a small part of me unclenched at his soothing voice.

"Where is everyone? Are they okay? Nico and Lucius? Did they make it back? Buddy and Rio?"

Even though their literal job was protecting me, I felt responsible for the lives of my bodyguards. They hadn't known what they were signing up for when they'd volunteered as my security detail.

A hand reached up and gripped my thigh. A blood-splattered Lucius was lying in the aisle beside me. "We are fine, my consort. I wanted to hold you, but even unconscious, the incubus refused to release his hold on you." I searched his face for jealousy, but what I saw was an oddly clear expression. "This works. Though we might need to pay the pilot more. And the cleaning crew."

Looking around, I realized almost everyone was coated in blood. The seats were stained crimson, and it had been brushed over the walls and along the floor.

In case of emergency, follow the bloody footprints to your nearest exit.

The only person missing was Judge. I didn't even have to voice my question because Walker answered. He was beside Tex, facing me. "Judge won Rock-Paper-Scissors to get the shower first."

Lucius made a rude noise, and I stroked my hand over his. There were slowly healing cuts all up and down his arms, from fangs and swords and who the fuck knew what else. His blond hair was tinged red. His eyes were bright, and I could see dried blood around his mouth.

"Are you doing all right?" It was hard to know if this G-rated version of Lucius was still okay with the gratuitous violence.

He gave me a lopsided grin that was full of fang. "I am more than all right. I am delirious with satisfaction. The only thing that could top a morning for sanctioned bloodletting is if you let me crawl between your thighs and tongue-fuck you like this."

I really, really wanted to make his dreams come true, but I didn't particularly want the blood of some random vampire all up in my cooch. "I love you Lucius Flett, but hard pass." He pouted, and I reached down to stroke a clean patch of his face. "Next massacre, I promise."

The hand around my waist flexed, and I looked over my shoulder at the still sleeping form of Vali.

"Why is he still asleep?"

It was Orthus who answered. "The bonding, and the breaking of the curse, took a lot out of him. He's alive, though."

I shuddered, because he could have just died on the spot. Bonding could have broken his immortality curse, and he could have crumbled to dust in my arms. I was one hundred percent certain that would have scarred me for life, so his warm, hard body beneath mine was reassuring in ways I wasn't ready to describe.

"His immortality?" I tried to look over my shoulder so I could see Orthus, but I was trapped tight against Vali.

"I don't know, succubus. We will have to see when he wakes."

I rolled my eyes, and my bondmate laughed softly, probably feeling my irritation through the bond. I tilted my head back as much as I could, and caught a glimpse of Orthus's face.

"We're tied together forever now, so I think that means you have to start calling me Raine," I told him. I felt the bonds in my chest; Brody's reassuring power was there, soothing my wild emotions, and Tex's loving glow was instantly recognizable. The giant supernova that was Vali was right there too, and I poked at it. It sucked me in, filling me with power, like it couldn't wait to be friends forever.

But just on the other side of that, a softening to its bright edges, was Orthus. He wasn't bonded to me, per se, but I could see him there. Check on him. Push reassurance through Vali and into him.

I liked it.

"Raine," he said, without his usual edge of quiet disdain, tasting the word.

"You can also call me 'Mistress' if you want, but only if you're naked and strapped to a wall."

Orthus made a choking sound, and X barked out a laugh. "You wish, Red."

I didn't, really. I liked giving up control in the bedroom too much, but it was worth the joke just to screw with Orthus.

I rested my head back on Vali's chest, exhaustion pulling at my limbs again. Just a little more sleep, cuddled against his warmth, and then I'd go back to being Raine, Badass Bitch.

I breathed in deeply, letting the comforting scent of the incubus wrap around me. I wasn't sure why he smelled like ocean sunshine, but I liked it. His arms tightened around me again, and my eyes closed, our bound hands clutched against my chest.

I WOKE to Brody pushing a blood bag at me. "Eat, Rainey. You haven't had anything in a couple of days, and I'd really hate you to test your new bond's immortality the hard way."

Brody's voice was soft and soothing, and it made me purr. Which was when I realized that I had my mouth pressed against the throat of Vali, his delicious pulse beating quickly against my lips.

Whoops.

I pulled away and looked up into those sea-green eyes. So pretty. I cleared my throat. "You're awake," I murmured, like I was going to win a Mensa award. He nodded, gesturing to the blood bag. I uncapped it and held it to my lips, feeling a little self-conscious about it. "Pretend it's merlot," I said softly.

"I've been around a long time, and seen a lot of vampires drinking blood. I'm not squeamish. Enjoy your meal."

I drank it down quickly, not wanting to prolong the weirdness. When the bag was empty, Brody produced another one. "Thank you, Alpha," I whispered, and his hand reached up to stroke my hair.

"Anytime." He breathed out a long, shuddering breath. "I hated you being in danger and not being there to protect you."

I nodded, knowing it would've gone against every instinct a shapeshifter had for his mate. If he'd been less powerful, less in control, he probably would have fought with Nico about the order. But he'd been exactly where I needed him to be for my own piece of mind, so I couldn't apologize for it.

"I'll make it up to you, I promise." Brody rubbed at his chest, and I frowned. "Can you feel him too?"

He nodded. "Just the echo of him, but uh, I don't have your resistance to the incubus vibes."

I frowned. "What does that mean?"

It was Tex that answered. "It means we've both been hard as a rock since you bonded with him, and that's even after Judge jacked me off in the shower. Twice."

I gritted my teeth with a wince. I hadn't thought about that.

Vali tensed beneath me. "My apologies. Let me try to..." He screwed up his face, and I could almost feel him dimming inside me, the power no longer pulsing out of the bond. I guess the magical equivalent to Viagra would've been annoying for my mates all the time.

Both Tex and Brody heaved a sigh of relief, so I knew that was better. I looked down at Brody's jeans, at the painful push of his dick against the zipper.

"Thank you. I'll just go take care of this," he said, waving his hand at his general crotch area.

"I mean, I can...?" I was never one to let a good hard-on go to waste. The fact that I was a succubus made so much sense.

"Next time, Rainey." He laughed at my disappointed pout. "Baby, when we get home, I'm taking you to the hot springs and fucking you until neither one of us can walk and Tex has to come and fish us out like the Little Mermaid."

The sound of Tex's laugh washed over me like a soft blanket, warm and comforting in a way that would be hard to describe to anyone else.

Vali jerked, and I turned to face him. His face was pulled into a perplexed frown.

"What?"

"Apologies, Raine. I... The emotion that went through you when you were talking to your mates isn't one I'm used to feeling." He sucked in a breath. "It's nice."

"It's love. You've been alive so long—I'm sure you must have fallen in love once?"

Vali frowned again, as if he was searching his memory, but he shook his head. "No. I felt the echoes of Orthus's love, and his pain when she died.

But I don't believe I've ever felt the sensation that just passed through the three of you. To feel the emotion reciprocated viscerally." He shook his head again. "How do you not just spend all day having sex?"

The snort that burst out of me echoed around the room. "Not going to lie—there was a time we didn't do much else but have sex. A lot."

"Honestly, I thought my dick was going to fall off," Tex teased. He wasn't wrong. It had been wild.

"But that burning passion kinda simmers into a fire that will keep you warm forever, and you appreciate that just as much as fucking on every surface in the house."

Brody's hand cupped my cheek as he leaned in to kiss me. "Not that we don't do that too."

I gave him a saucy grin. "A lot." He stood up with a wink, shifting his dick around until it was comfortable. "Why are you delivering blood and not the hostess?" I asked him, as I looked around the plane cabin for the elusive employee.

"She's hiding in the cockpit with the pilots. Apparently, the fact that all the vampires turned up blood-soaked freaked her out."

Understandable. We were probably going to have to give her a substantial bonus too.

Judge was asleep beside Walker in one of the seats, and Lucius was passed out in the aisle, but thankfully clean. I could see X and Orthus talking further up the aisle of the plane. "Nico?"

"Asleep in the bedroom," Brody murmured. "Now you're okay, I might join him. The last couple of weeks have been a lot."

That was no joke. "Thank you for coming with me, Brody."

He reached down, stroking his fingertips along my jaw. "As if I could be anywhere else, Rainey. I just want to be wherever you are, no matter how much of a trouble magnet you are."

I didn't even deny it anymore. Trouble and I, we were besties.

Lifting my arm, I gave Vali a soft look. "Time to get out of these, don't you think?" He nodded, and we set about undoing the intricate system of knots. "Ready to be free?"

His hands picked at the final knot, but his eyes never left mine. As the ropes loosened and slipped to the floor, he smiled, and it was so radiant, my chest felt like it would burst.

"I'm already free."

THIRTY-FOUR

The plane landed in Vancouver and unloaded us immediately. I had a tiny inkling that the pilot really wanted us off his damn plane as soon as supernaturally possible, regardless of the fact I was a Convocation Member and deserved some kind of respect.

Honestly, I didn't care. You could hardly blame the guy.

Once we'd taxied to a stop, Buddy went out first to meet the rest of my security detail. They were probably glad they hadn't drawn the short straw and been stuck in Europe with me, being chased down by rabid vampires, watching as I got sucked into Hell shadows.

The crisp Canadian air was like a balm. I thanked Wayne Gretsky's left nut that we were back. My untraumatized bodyguards hustled us into SUVs to drive us back to Fox Falls, and bless them, none of them even blinked an eyelid at the scarred and bitter hellhound, or the handsome incubus.

My driver did shift around uncomfortably, though. I slid my eyes over to Vali. "We are gonna have to work on you toning that down. Otherwise, there's going to be a lot of impromptu orgies, and while I'm normally down for that, there are just some people I don't want to see having sex."

I loved Bert and Beatrice, but just... no.

"I'll try. It's stronger now we've bonded."

Yeah, I'd noticed. Even my own power had increased, and I'd caught myself flexing it when thanking the pilot. I didn't even mean to. We'd both have to work harder at keeping it under control.

"Tell me about where we are going," Orthus rumbled.

Dammit, that deep, guttural voice was killing me. X, who was sitting in front of me, looked over his shoulder with a grin. Yeah, he could smell how much Orthus affected me. The man could smell my desire like a shark could smell blood in the water.

I pushed my attraction down. God knows I already had enough dick to start my own weiner stand—I didn't need any more.

I cleared my throat. "Fox Falls is a former mining town that we've repurposed into a haven for rare supernaturals who don't have the benefit of large social groups. When there's only one or two left in the world, it makes it hard to be safe from people who want to use you. Many of our people have come from being collected like they're objects and not living beings." I couldn't keep the disgust out of my voice. "The town is warded heavily against people with ill intent, and there are enough rare, yet powerful supernaturals that they could probably hold their own until me and the guys got there."

I didn't mention that technically the guys—my guys—only protected them out of love for me. If, say, vampires attacked Fox Falls, they'd be committing treason against their own species and would be summarily executed. However, that had never happened, and I kept my fingers crossed that it never would. Titus had a tight hold on the vampire leadership, as did Alexander on the shifters, so anyone else could attack at will, and we'd be perfectly sanctioned to defend the town.

I looked at Orthus. He was strong; I could feel that. He'd gone head-to-head with Lucius and won. Where did he stand in the Convocation hierarchy? Was he a shifter? He did turn from a hellhound into a man. Or was he a rare supernatural, and therefore under my purview?

Why hadn't I ever considered this before?

Hell. I had a sneaking suspicion that with his

immunity to both Vali and myself, he might be stronger than us both.

That was a problem for later. I had enough on my mind right now, and most of it involved my bed. But first, I had to get these two settled in Fox Falls. If I immersed Vali straight up, maybe he'd get attached to his people and be enthusiastic about taking over my job.

I shook my head. This whole thing now felt so much bigger than getting another supe to take my place on the Convocation. It had changed my whole life, and those of my mates. Not to mention Vali and Orthus.

They looked out at the landscape, so different to what their home had been for so long. When we finally made it to the wild, forested area around Nîso, Brody looked over at Orthus. "Do you want to run?"

Orthus's head snapped toward Brody, his eyes wide. "What?"

"My Pack owns all this land. Do you want to shift and run? I'll run with you. I might have to shift to my cheetah form to keep up, but I'll try."

Orthus shook his head. "It's the middle of the day —that won't be a problem?"

Brody grinned. "I'm the Alpha of the North Western Packs. There's no one to offend but me. Rainey is in charge of Fox Falls, and Nico runs Dark River. This is our own little slice of heaven; I promise you're safe to run here. Just... don't eat anyone who pops out without checking first."

Orthus's lips parted, but he nodded. I told my driver to stop, and Brody and Orthus jumped out.

"I want to run too. I love beating the Snack Pack in a foot race," X added, climbing out after him.

I shook my head at him as magic tingled around Brody, and he shifted into a sleek, beautiful cheetah, but bigger. I honestly wondered if he'd be able to keep up with the hellhound. Even if he couldn't, Brody wasn't the kind of guy to get all bent out of shape about it. He knew his worth, and it wasn't measured by having to come first every time.

Orthus looked around the deserted landscape, filled with trees and rocks and wildlife, but no people. He seemed to take a shaky breath before he transformed. Once again, my brain struggled to make sense of the two-headed beast in front of me.

X sauntered around, rolling his shoulders. "Ready?" He looked at Brody. "See you at the finish line, wankers."

Then he was running, with Brody sprinting after him, his speed phenomenal. Orthus's heads looked around, one gazing back toward the car, and one looking at the two running supernaturals. Finally, he started to run, making up the distance in seconds.

"Shit, he's fast," my driver muttered, and I had to agree.

Vali chuckled. "Lots of shit to run from in Hell. You're fast or you're dead. A deader kind of dead, anyway."

I had so many questions about Orthus, but I'd mined Vali enough for answers that I should probably be getting from the source. Now I had Orthus on my home soil, me and the hound were going to have a long talk.

The driver started the car again, pulling back out onto the road, the other SUV well ahead of us now. Walker, Nico, Tex and Judge were all returning to Dark River to make sure the place hadn't burned down in our absence, and Brody would return to Fox Falls with me, then head up to Nîso to check that everything had run okay under Bobby's short reign. Lucius was running all the way from the airport, needing to burn off some of the frenetic energy that still seemed to consume him after this morning's battle.

"How many people are under your protection at the moment?" Vali asked.

Shit. I should know that. There had been 269 before the Manix, and now? Who knew. They were a secretive bunch.

"There are 133 in Fox Falls, and 136 out in the greater community that I know of. There are also the Manix, who we only recently discovered weren't extinct, and their total numbers are unknown."

He gasped. "There are still Manix? I thought they'd died out over a century ago."

I smiled, thinking about that weird race of creatures who looked like Mother Nature's leftovers, but could tear a vampire's skull from its body. You didn't fuck with them, despite the fact they looked like they'd been collaged together by a drunk man.

"Surprise! Incubi and succubi were extinct too, yet here we are."

Vali screwed up his nose. "Perhaps. But we aren't exactly the purest examples of our species, and it's more by coincidence than design."

I shrugged. "You never know. If your mortality is back on track, maybe that means you can make little baby incubi." I didn't mention that the idea of him having babies with others sat wrong with me, because I wasn't about to hamper his new-found life.

"They would eventually breed out with humans, so what is the point? It's... not something I want."

I bobbed my head sagely, hiding my happiness that he wasn't going to go out and impregnate a million women to repopulate the world with incubi. "Do you still feel immortal?"

He chewed his lip. Why were they so plump? "I don't know. Stab me."

I reared back, even though I couldn't go far in the car. "*Excuse* me?"

"Stab me. Hey, driver, do you have a knife?"

My driver, Johnson, looked at me like he was about to get fired. "Uh, I can't give you a knife, sir."

Vali raised an eyebrow at him. "Well, you're not giving it to me. You're giving it to Raine."

"Do it, Johnson. It'll be fine." Johnson passed the knife back to me, still looking at us both warily. "Now, is this SUV ours, or is it rented?"

"Ours, ma'am."

Oh good. Wouldn't want to mess up a rental plane *and* a rental car all in one day.

Vali was gazing at me expectantly. "Okay, go for it. Stab me in the thigh."

I looked at him like he was crazy. "Can't I just cut you a little or something?"

He shook his head. "No, I'm still supernatural. I'd heal a little cut in no time. Go for it, Red," he said, using X's nickname.

I gritted my teeth, closed my eyes, and stabbed him in the meaty part of his thigh.

"Argh!" he yelled. "You *stabbed* me!"

My eyes flew open. "You told me..." His grinning face greeted me. "Not funny, butthead."

Vali threw his head back and laughed, like he didn't have a dagger sticking out of his leg. "What kind of vampire closes their eyes at a little blood?"

Ugh, I wished he hadn't mentioned the blood part, because it really did smell delicious. "What kind of person laughs with a dagger sticking out of their leg?"

I quipped back, poking out my tongue. "We're pacifists, remember? Plus, there's a difference between drinking blood and stabbing someone."

I didn't like hurting people at all. Sometimes, like in Amsterdam, I saw the necessity for it, and I would do it in defense of myself or others. But it wasn't something I ever enjoyed.

I usually left that to my mates. Hypocritical? Probably.

My gaze stayed trained on Vali's thigh, and before my eyes, his leg healed. Faster than even a vampire would heal. I tried not to let my mouth salivate at the blood pooling around the wound.

"Guess the immortality is intact."

I didn't have to ask why that made him sad. Because in the wise words of Queen, who wants to live forever?

CHAPTER
THIRTY-FIVE

When the car pulled up in Fox Falls, the hellhound stuck a single head in the door before I could even get out.

"Woah, Fido, get your drool off the leather seats." If a dog face could say *go fuck yourself*, his did.

Vali laughed, pushing against Orthus's head. "It's fine. Just testing my mortality. Still unkillable." He didn't sound enthused about that, but it was okay. I was going to love this sad, yet somehow sexy incubus and his bad-tempered Hell puppy, whether they liked it or not.

Orthus morphed back into a human. "You couldn't wait until you arrived, where I could help if things went badly? What if you'd been mortal and hit a damn artery?"

Oh, shit. Good point.

I flushed, and pointed at Vali. "He told me to!"

X threw some pants at Orthus, though not without giving him an appreciative once-over. Orthus pulled on his pants, wiggling a little to get the jeans over his butt, because damn, it was fucking juicy.

Vali snorted a laugh, and I slapped his chest. "Shut up," I hissed.

The incubus held up both hands innocently. "I don't even know what you're talking about." He looked lighter again, the heaviness of the conversation finally dissipating. It was like every step away from Amsterdam was changing him into someone happier, and my soul felt lighter to see it.

I climbed from the SUV, realizing there was a bit of a crowd. Granted, Orthus had just given his new home a bit of an eyeful, but supernaturals didn't really view nudity the way humans did. Didn't mean we couldn't appreciate a good dick when we saw it, though.

Venny, the elderly leader of Fox Falls, had both eyebrows raised until they nearly touched her wispy hairline. She waggled them at me, lit a tiny flame on her fingertip, then licked it to put it out with a hiss.

I gave her a mock frown, clearing my throat. "Venny, this is Vali and Orthus. They'll be staying here for now."

She ran her eyes over them appraisingly. "Which one of them is your replacement?"

I froze. I hadn't discussed wanting to step down

with the people of Fox Falls yet. I'd wanted to wait until I had a good option for replacement.

Venny just rolled her eyes. "I'm old, Raine, not stupid. You've hated this for years, now you disappear to Europe on a secret mission? Doesn't take a rocket scientist."

I winced. "I would have told you."

Venny patted me gently on the shoulder. "We want you to be happy, Raine. You know that." She eyed Vali and Orthus up and down. "But we won't follow just anyone. No one wants to be a prisoner again." It had taken years to unwrap all the trauma they'd suffered at the hands of the Collector, and some of them were still suffering now.

"You know I wouldn't allow it either. No one is taking my seat until I'm one hundred percent certain they'll protect you with their life." I grabbed Vali's hand, pulling him forward. I sent some reassurance through his bond, and he smiled at Venny. "Vali is an incubus. He's immortal, and his background makes me think he'd be understanding of our people." Because if he took the mantle, he'd be my leader too. "Orthus is his bond-mate. A hellhound. He's protected Vali for a long time."

I didn't want to make any promises on their behalf, but I silently willed them to make a good impression. Venny held a lot of sway with the Town

Council, and her approval would help, even if it was tentative.

Vali held out a hand, and I could feel him tamp his power right down. "It's a pleasure to meet you, ma'am. I know what it's like to have no choices, so I wouldn't ever inflict that on you. I'm new to the country, but I promise that I'll do my very best." He looked over at Orthus. "And he's a hellhound. Protecting is what he does best. It's his nature."

That was true. Since I'd met him, he'd never shown any aggression outside of protecting Vali, and later me. As soon as Vali decided I wasn't a threat, any aggression toward us disappeared.

I appraised the hellhound in a new light. Noticed how even now, his body was a little in front of Vali's, his eyes drifting around the surrounding buildings for threats, his body tense. I moved closer to him, and put my hand in his reassuringly. There was no threat here to Vali. In fact, he was more powerful than most townspeople by a long shot.

"I saw him shift. He doesn't fall under Alexander's purview?"

"Who?" Orthus growled, and I waved a hand.

"We'll talk about it later." I gave him a reassuring smile. I didn't want to mention the dragon right now and scare them right back to Europe. "Venny, do we still have that little house down by the falls available?"

There was a rundown little cottage which looked

out over the waterfalls that Fox Falls was named after. It was way too far out for most of the inhabitants, who liked to be together in town, and although Venny had never said it outright, I suspected she might have been keeping it for me. It needed a lot of work, but these two needed something to help them settle. I couldn't throw them straight at the Convocation yet. They needed to feel their freedom first.

Venny seemed to know what I was thinking, because warm appreciation lit her eyes. "It is. We never got around to fixing it up. We were waiting for some water-based supernaturals who'd enjoy being close to the river, but so far I'm the only person with an elemental power. It's open if you want to check it out now, and I'll send Yuki down later with the keys and some essentials you'll need in the meantime."

I hugged the woman who took all the responsibility I offloaded onto her, and always stepped up. "Thanks, Venny. You're an absolute treasure."

She grinned. "Go on with you."

Brody had just finished talking with Justin, a swamp monster with a penchant for engineering. He'd done most of the structural refurbishments on the town's buildings, from restoring homes to ensuring that none of the main street buildings were about to fall down on people's heads.

Brody shook his hand, before walking over to me. He kissed me softly, first my cheek and then my lips. "I have to return to Nîso, but I'll be back on Friday morning for breakfast at the diner."

I hugged him tight. "I miss you already."

It was a running joke we had, like I couldn't be in his arms in fifteen minutes if I wanted to. But he needed to be Alpha, and I had to be a Convocation Member, and sometimes that fifteen-minute difference felt like a fifteen-hour trek.

"Love you, Rainey." With that, he shifted into a wolf form and trotted away.

I watched him until he was out of sight, then turned back to Orthus and Vali, as well as X, who'd reappeared with a giant pastry the baker in town had made just for him. Somehow, he'd convinced the guy to start making Cornish pasties, and X gorged on at least four every time we came to town.

"Ready, Love? I saved you a pasty, but got hungry between the bakery and here."

I raised an eyebrow. "It's like twenty feet away."

"A long twenty feet, Red. So long." He grinned, and I resisted the urge to jump in his arms and wrap my body around his. Honestly, so much of my life was spent trying not to maul my life partners these days.

I pinched his nipple in retaliation, but instead of shying away, he moaned loudly. And awkwardly.

"Oh *baby*."

"Stop it," I hissed, my cheeks going as red as my

hair when several people turned to look. "God, I hate you sometimes."

He booped my nose. "No you don't, liar. So, what are we doing?"

I started walking, telling X about our plans for the house near the falls. He walked silently, and when I looked back over my shoulder, he was eating another pasty.

"*Seriously?* You're supposed to love me, and instead, you're hiding your pasties from me like a squirrel!"

"Squirrels can only wish they had these nuts." He grabbed his balls, giving me a bashful grin. "Sorry, Love. But you and pasties are kind of on the same level for my devotion. Please, never make me choose."

Honestly, the shit I put up with.

It was a ten-minute walk from the center of town to reach the driveway of Falls House. Overgrown, it was kind of ominous, but also pretty. We were coming into fall, so all the large trees were turning a fiery red. The road out here was rough, filled with potholes, and I made a note to get the Town Council to bring out a load of gravel. I'd have to get the guys some kind of transportation too.

Finally, the driveway spread out, and sitting in the clearing was Falls House. On the plus side, it still had all its windows. But the door hung off the side a little, and the front steps were missing. Plus, there were a few rotting planks on the porch. The roof was good though, so that was something.

"I know it looks rough, but it's mostly cosmetic. The place is all yours, if you want it. If it's too much work, you can—"

"It's fine," Orthus grunted, and I looked over at his impenetrable features. I tried to see what he was seeing. Was it the water wheel that didn't turn anymore? They didn't really need it for electricity, not when we would put solar on the roof. Did he see the peeling paint and broken roof tiles, and the shit-ton of work it would need to take this building back to its original glory?

Or did he see what I did? A haven, sitting on the banks of a slow-flowing river, backdropped by the falls? It had stolen my breath, and had been the only place that ever made me consider moving out of Dark River.

I shifted from foot to foot. "We have lumber and any building materials you'll need back in town, and we'll help you out if you want help. If it's too hard, we can put you somewhere else until we get renovation work done..."

Vali turned to me, a huge grin on his face. He stepped close and wrapped his arms around my waist, spinning me in a circle. "This is perfect. *Perfect.*" He kissed me quickly, a hard peck basically, then he was striding to the front door.

I looked over at Orthus to see one side of his mouth tilted in a smile at Vali's enthusiasm. He looked back at me. "Thank you."

I didn't think he meant for the house.

I swallowed the lump in my throat. "Anytime."

CHAPTER
THIRTY-SIX

X had run back to town and grabbed a couple of tools we'd need to make the place habit-able. Orthus had gone to check out the old woodpile—which, thankfully, was dry—and had gotten a fire started. The chimney definitely needed cleaning, but that could be a chore for tomorrow.

I'd zipped around at super speed, wiping dust off things, starting at the top and working my way down. There was a little bit of furniture in here, but it was all at least fifty years old and most of the fabrics had not fared well. But the scarred wooden table was perfect, as were the little hand-carved stools. Vali and Orthus had moved the rotting old couch out of the building while X fixed the door.

Eventually, the place was empty but livable, and I was exhausted. By the time Yuki, a tiny kitsune, arrived with keys and essentials, I was almost re-dead on my feet.

I gave Yuki a quick side hug as I met her at the door. "How are you doing, Yukes? How's school?"

Yuki was doing a college course online, and loving it. She'd missed college as a teenager because she'd been locked in some psycho's basement.

She grinned at me, and gave me a shrug. "Good. I'm enjoying my language class, because my TA is cute and he gets annoyed that I keep correcting his Japanese."

I squeezed her one more time. "Troublemaker. Keep up the good grades, though. Beatrice says if you pass all your classes, she'll bake you one of those black bottom pies you enjoy so much to celebrate."

Yuki's eyes lit up. She'd missed so much, and in some ways, she was still innocent to the world—well, at least to the non-evil parts. She'd had way too much experience in the darker aspects.

I tugged her into the house. When Vali turned, Yuki gasped.

Yeah, I understood the reaction. I still sucked in a breath every time his beauty caught me unaware. But there, in the light of the setting sun, he looked almost angelic.

"Yuki, this is my new bondmate, Vali."

Vali gave her a soft smile. "It's a pleasure to meet you, Yuki."

Hearing Vali say the word *pleasure* made something zip along my nerve endings. I pushed the sensation down, and turned to look for Orthus.

However, I was distracted by X as he bounded in and picked up Yuki. "Baby Yukumber!" He spun her around, then sat her back down as she grumbled. "Did you grow a millimeter?"

Yuki gave him a sour look, but she was especially short. She barely made it to five feet. X had pulled Yuki out of that hellhole she'd lived in, and now they had a bond. He looked at her the way he looked at our kids. He was protective, and watching her grow into someone confident and self-assured made him happy.

"How Raine puts up with your ass is a mystery," she huffed. "Want me to drown him in the falls?"

I laughed, and grinned at X. "Nah, I'm kind of attached to him now. Plus, he can hold his breath for a really long time." Like, forever.

She gave him another mock glare, but ruined it with a smirk. "I could try." X pretended to be heartbroken, making her laugh. "Venny sent down two mattresses and some linens, as well as basic food. Nothing perishable until we find a fridge though, sorry," she said to Vali, looking slightly flushed.

Then Orthus walked in, and her jaw dropped. Her body went tense with fear, and I reached out to rub her back. "Yuki, this is Orthus. He's Vali's bondmate and protector."

Orthus nodded his head in greeting, then he looked up, his nose twitching. "Kitsune? I didn't think there were many of you left."

Yuki shook her head, still terrified. I looked between Orthus and Yuki worriedly. Orthus gave her a reassuring smile, which I hadn't even known was an expression in his arsenal until now.

I curled an arm around Yuki's shoulder. "Deep breaths, Yuki. Remember when I brought you here and swore that nothing would ever hurt you? I meant that with my whole heart. Orthus would chew off his own hind leg rather than hurt you. Breathe. I promise he's a good guy—the best kind of guy. I trust him with my life and yours."

Orthus gave me a weighty look, and I wished I knew what was going on behind his eyes. His gaze ran over my face, like he was searching for deceit in my words. He shook his head and looked back at Yuki. "The little demon fox is responding to the nature of a bigger demon threat," he told me. "I'm a hellhound. I mean you no harm, Yuki. On my honor."

"You're a hellhound?" she breathed. "My grand-mother spoke of your kind, but the same way you spoke of, like... the Devil. It wasn't like you'd ever run into one on the street or anything, unless you were bad."

He gave her a sad, lopsided smile. "Not far off. There are no other hellhounds who walk the earth. I am an anomaly." I must have looked confused. "Kitsune are a type of demon dog too. We are their version of the boogeyman. We're related in the same way chickens and velociraptors are related." There was no doubting who the chicken was in that analogy. "I'll go and get the things from the truck."

X offered to help, and as soon as they were both out of the house, Yuki let out a gasping breath. "You know, Raine, you collect the most interesting mates."

I choked on my own saliva. "Orthus isn't my mate. He's Vali's protector."

Yuki snorted, tapping her nose. "Can't lie to the nose, vampire. You want him. X wants him. Vali wants him." She shook her head. "I don't get it, because his energy just makes me want to pee myself in fear, but given your other mates, I'm fairly sure that's just your type now."

I made a shushing noise, as Vali raised an eyebrow at me. Flushing pink, I turned away, but I didn't miss the heat in his eyes. For the hundredth time, I told myself he was an incubus—heat in his eyes was just his default.

Orthus and X returned, and I pasted a pleasant smile on my face. They hefted the two mattresses to the bedrooms easily. Luckily, the heavy wooden frames in there had survived the decades of disuse well. Whoever had lived here at one point must've been both bored and quite the craftsman, because there were intricate carvings covering those too.

It made me wonder who would spend hours creating this beautiful furniture, and then just abandon it to time? The mine had dried up fairly quickly, so this place had been deserted within five years of opening.

There was still a large hole in the ground, but it had filled with water long ago. Justin the swamp monster had totally claimed it as his domain; though he was a nice guy, so he always offered to share. Did anyone else want to go down into a contaminated tube of blackness and death? No. But it was the thought that counted.

I went outside and grabbed some of the groceries, stacking them on the counter so Vali and Orthus could put them where they'd like them. I wanted them to make this place a home, and that meant getting to choose what went where. I shifted another box of towels to the linen press, as well as a box of crockery.

I remembered when I was starting out—still Mika McKellen, newly turned vampire—and Angeline had dropped off a box of stuff just like this for me. The ingredients for a new life.

The old wound of what happened way back when I was first turned ached in my chest. Most of the time it didn't even cross my mind anymore, but sometimes when I was standing at the door of The Immortal

Cupcake, or in a moment like this, I remembered the betrayal of my friends, the pain I'd felt for my family and for myself.

Some pain never truly went away, no matter how happy you were. That was the real trick of trauma. You could be happy and still laden down with barely healed wounds. They weren't mutually exclusive. You didn't have to forget your pain in order to be content.

Occasionally, I'd stalk my younger brother on social media just to see how they were doing. He'd gotten married to a girl in his twenties, and they'd just had their third kid. They'd called the first girl Mika, and I'd cried for days. Pictures of my mom, her hair gray and her face lined, holding baby Mika in her arms, had shattered my heart all over again. I'd repeated to myself that she looked happy now. She looked like my death didn't haunt her anymore.

It was a lie. If I looked closely at that photo, I still saw the pain in her eyes. So I stopped looking closely and enjoyed the surface level of their happy human lives. I knew one day, I would see that my parents had died, and I would crumble all over again.

A hand settled on my back, and I sucked in a deep and unnecessary breath. Plastering a smile on my face, I expected Vali, but instead it was Orthus.

"Your sadness burns my nose." He sounded really put out about it. I went to step away, to put a little distance between us, but his fingers gripped my shirt, holding me still.

"Sorry," I said roughly, smiling through it. Vali was over his shoulder, and I knew I couldn't hide my sadness from him. He had a direct link to my emotions now, a burning ball in my chest that would always know when I was happy or sad, angry or horny. Maybe not with quite as much clarity as my mates, but close.

Already, I could feel Tex and Brody pushing reassurance down my matebonds, because they not only knew I was distressed, but they knew me well enough to be able to label the type of pain I was feeling. They knew it was sad memories and not anything more pressing. Time could do that with your bonds. They weren't static things; they grew and evolved as we traveled through the years together.

Vali shook his head as he stepped forward, wrapping me in his arms. I always forgot just how huge he was. His arms encompassed me, swallowing me up. He didn't say anything—no false platitudes or questions, just warmth. I soaked it in, pushing away the sad thoughts, thinking of nothing but the steady thump of his heart on my cheek.

And Orthus's hand remained on my back.

CHAPTER
THIRTY-SEVEN

I slumped back in the booth of Bert and Beatrice's Diner with a contented sigh. I'd just eaten my weight in jelly donuts, and Walker held me on his lap, patting my distended stomach.

"I think you're gonna give birth to a litter of donut holes."

I rubbed my stomach, mainly so I didn't vomit. "Will you still love them like they're your own?" I whispered.

He leaned down, kissing me softly and licking stray sugar from the corner of my lips. "I'll even let you call one Walker Jr."

I honked out a laugh, making my stomach clench, and all the food inside it roll. "Don't make me laugh or I'll puke. Why did Bert have to make them so good? He knows I have no self-control."

Resting his chin on my head, Walker snorted. "No one made you eat twenty-five jelly donuts, Raine. You've got no one to blame but yourself when you're hugging the throne later."

I probably couldn't even look at another donut again.

It was so freaking good to be home. I'd missed my people. We were in a booth because Brody still wasn't back from Nîso, and Nico was dealing with a new resident of Dark River. Judge shook his head at me from the other side of the table, coffee in hand. Only Tex had joined me in my donut debauchery.

"How are your dirty Dutchmen settling in?" X asked, and I screwed up my nose.

"We are hard-passing that nickname," I warned him. "But they're good. We're slowly getting them set up, and Venny has been awesome. Soon enough, I'll be able to announce them to the Convocation."

"Uh-huh. And when are you going to announce that you want to bounce on their D's all the way to Hell and back?"

I froze in surprise, my eyes moving around the table, trying to see if anyone was as outraged by the concept as I was. "I do not."

X made a game show buzzer noise. "Buh-bowwwn. Wrong. You do too. We all know it. Trust me when I say the incubus *definitely* knows it. And whenever you're not looking, Orthus gazes at you like you're the finest rib-eye to ever come out of the abattoir."

I shook my head at his words. At best, Orthus tolerated me, though I knew he was grateful for me breaking the curse. They both were. "It's just happiness that they aren't stuck in Amsterdam anymore."

Lucius leaned back. "I was once locked in an iron coffin for a decade. I didn't look at my rescuers like I wanted to pleasure them until they couldn't breathe."

Judge laughed. "That's because it was Titus, and if you *had* looked at him like that, he probably would have stuffed you right back in again."

Lucius shrugged. "You know what I mean. What the hellhound and incubus feel for Raine isn't gratitude. And she desires them, which is also painfully obvious to anyone with a nose."

"Have you all been discussing this in the group chat? You seem surprisingly on the same page."

Walker's arms tightened around my waist, but not too tight, like he knew I was one quick squeeze away from exploding. "We want whatever makes you happy, Sweetheart. You haven't seen yourself from the outside since you bonded with the incubus. You're glowing." He paused, considering his next words, because if anyone thought before they acted, it was Walker. "It's almost like there was something missing inside you, or a craving we couldn't quite fulfill, and he plugged it up with a single kiss."

X snorted. "It was a hell of a kiss, though."

I mean, he wasn't telling me anything I didn't know. It had been a hell of a kiss. It had been a knock-out, literally.

I threw my hands up. "I'm happy with you guys." I softened my tone. "You're the best thing that ever happened to me. I don't want to cheapen two decades of love and commitment by picking up the first eligible bachelor who comes along. You aren't interchangeable. You can't be happy with sharing?" I asked Lucius, who just shrugged.

"It would be... nice to give you some room to breathe from my craziness. Selfishly, I wouldn't mind if fucking the incubus gave me clarity, so I wasn't forced to follow you around like a lovesick fool."

I froze again, my heart pounding in my chest. If I cured Lucius, would he even stay?

He reached out and stroked a thumb over my lip. "Don't fret, Raine Baxter. Our agreement might have begun as one of convenience, but I find that over time, even the madman loves you. I have no doubt that when I'm saner, I will still be just as besotted with you as the rest of these fools."

His words didn't chase away all the worry. Would I selfishly try and hang on to Lucius, even if the madness fully receded? I was too ashamed to admit out loud that a small part of me found satisfaction in how dependent Lucius was on me.

Eternity was a long time, and part of me continued to wait for the day that the guys were no longer content sharing me. That they'd had enough. Except for Brody and Tex—who had literally bound their souls to mine—my other lovers only stayed because they were happy. If the day came that they were unhappy, they could leave me... like if I started collecting harem members like a football team lineup rather than a family.

"Raine..." Tex's voice was soft, because he could feel my anxiety, but I shut down the bond.

"It's fine. I'll think about it, okay? We'll get everyone's agreement before I even approach the idea, because it does affect everyone." I turned to Lucius. "I would never stop you from feeding on Vali, as long as you got his consent. I want you to feel better." I cleared my throat quickly. "Want to take bets on how pissed Aquarius is going to be that the new Convocation Member is also tied to me too?"

Judge laughed, and the conversation moved on, but I couldn't shake the unsettled feeling in my chest.

CHAPTER

THIRTY-EIGHT

I didn't return to Fox Falls for a week, though I was close enough that I could feel Vali through the bond. He felt content, and apparently my sex life kept him sufficiently full, even from twenty miles away.

Well, at least until today, when an odd note of discontent brushed through my chest. It was gone as quickly as it appeared, but still, I decided it was time to visit them and see how they were doing. I was doing a shitty job of acclimatizing them to their new community, and it wasn't because I was running away like a chickenshit.

Really, I wasn't.

Plus, Titus had called and wanted me to come in for a talk, which even I knew was code for getting reamed out about the bullshit that had happened in

Amsterdam. So I needed Vali to get on board a little faster so I could offer him up as a suitable replacement, and everyone could just casually forget about my screwups.

I knocked on the door of Falls House, admiring the fact that it was once again straight and on its hinges. No one answered, so I walked around the porch to the back of the house.

My footsteps stuttered as I looked down at a pair of jeans strewn across the boards. Then another pair. Then a shirt, some socks, a pair of boxer shorts.

By the time I made it to the back door, I was already expecting to see the two men in the creek, splashing around and laughing.

Naked.

They looked so fucking handsome in the fiery orange of dusk. Orthus dived beneath the water, but it was so clear that he wasn't hidden at all. I could see every line of his back, the tight globes of his ass.

I watched as he took hold of Vali's ankle and dragged him below the water, dunking him quickly until he came up sputtering. I laughed at Vali's outrage, and something in the bond must have alerted him to the fact I was here, because he spun in the water with a smile.

"Raine!"

He was so happy to see me. I felt like an asshole for staying away for so long. I lifted a hand and waved back, just in time for Orthus to break the surface of the water. His eyes seemed to find me immediately, or maybe it was his nose.

I pointed to the depths of the river, somewhere in the vicinity of his penis. "If you aren't careful, a bigmouth bass is gonna bite off your dick, thinking it's a worm."

Vali's mouth dropped open, his eyes going wide as he searched the water like he was looking for jaws. Orthus just raised an eyebrow. "It's one way to catch a fish."

"Masochist," I teased, and he gave me a slow grin that set my insides on fire. Holy hell, that smile was a weapon. Part of me wanted to tell him to put it away for the safety of the general population, and for my ovaries. And maybe something significantly higher in my body and way more vulnerable.

"Maybe. Are you getting in?"

I looked down at my jeans and long-sleeved base-ball shirt. "Maybe next time? I'm not really dressed for a swim."

Vali laughed. "You're a succubus. Take your clothes off and get in the damn water. If you see my cock, I promise it's normally bigger, but this cold water makes it want to run and hide."

Mentally instructing myself not to think of his cock, I pulled off my shirt and jeans, leaving on my underwear. I didn't wear a bra anymore unless I was going for a run, because eternity was just too short for bras.

I tried to channel my inner sex kitten as I walked down the rough-hewn stone steps. I'd talked with all my guys, and they all seemed to be of the opinion that it was just a matter of time until I woke up and realized I wanted these two. As I stood beside the water wheel, watching them splash and play, I pushed away the guilt and uncertainty, and let myself just *feel*.

There was an attraction—that was obvious to everyone with eyes, and as Lucius said, a nose. But more than that, I liked seeing Vali happy and carefree. God, he'd been so miserable and without hope when I'd met him, and now he was splashing around and playing in the water.

Orthus watched him with a happiness that came from being responsible for someone else, and seeing that person finally content. It was like you'd fulfilled your purpose and the satisfaction you got from that was indescribable.

In short, their joy made me happy too, and I wasn't going to second-guess it anymore. I wasn't going to feel like I was betraying the rest of my family, because as Nico said when we'd discussed it, the well from which I drew my love was infinite and always full. X had chimed in that the "well" he loved was eight inches deep and fit him perfectly.

Yes, he was talking about my vagina.

"Are you getting in, or just going to keep staring?" Orthus asked, his eyes challenging.

I climbed into the water, and it was cold. I had a lower core temperature than anything living, so it must be truly freezing for these two. "Holy hell, how are you guys still swimming around in this? It's cold as balls."

Vali laughed. "You get used to it. You just have to move around more."

The creek was deceptively deep, the clarity of the water making it only look a few feet when it was significantly more. I swam a little further out, holding myself against the soft, swirling current. Flipping onto my back, I used my hands to beat against the current to keep me in one place. The cool evening breeze brushed over my exposed nipples, making them painfully hard.

This was nice. Why hadn't I ever tried swimming in the falls? Normally, I wasn't in town for fun; I was here solving some kind of crisis or dropping off a new resident, and then I'd rush home to the people I loved.

The stars were starting to come out as the dusk turned from pink to deep purples. "This is nice," I murmured to the guys, though I couldn't see them without tilting my head back. Their laughter had now stopped, so I dropped my feet and turned in the water. Their eyes were serious, all the mirth gone.

"I'm sorry. Is this too awkward? Do you want me to get out?"

"Raine..." Vali breathed, and I noticed his chest heaving. "I know I have no right to ask this, and you have to promise that if this is inappropriate you'll forget about it, but could I kiss you right now?"

My breath whooshed from my lungs. This was it. The moment of truth. Decision time. "I..." I sucked in a deep breath, pushing away all my other worries and recriminations. I just let myself feel. "Yes. *Please.*"

He was in front of me in the blink of an eye, his arms sweeping around me, and the current pulled us a little further down the river. He kicked us a little closer to the bank where the water wasn't so quick, allowing him to put his feet down a little. He wrapped an arm around my waist, pulling me tightly to his chest, my achingly hard nipples brushing against his pecs, making me stifle a moan.

"I've wanted to do this a thousand times. It's been torture..." He dropped his lips to mine, and the world exploded behind my eyes. The connection between us was electric, like putting your finger in a powerpoint, except the electricity went straight to your clit.

I moaned as his tongue slipped past my teeth to tangle with my own, and my hands went to his shoulders, gripping him tightly. His hands slipped down from my waist to the top swell of my ass, before going further down to cup my cheeks with a groan. "I've dreamed about having this ass in my hands. Your curves..."

I wasn't sure how long we kissed for, but soon, I felt the water around us shift, and my eyes opened to see Orthus heading to the stone steps. My hand whipped out and grabbed him.

"Wait," I breathed, and his eyes went wide. "Don't go."

His eyes flew from me and back to Vali. They did that a few more times, and I felt Vali's chuckle against my chest. His hands on my hips flipped me around, until my back was to his chest and I was facing Orthus.

I reached out a hand. "If you want—I mean, I want, but you don't have to if you don't want to..."

Ugh.

Vali was shaking with laughter behind me now. Clearly, I was a failure at being a sex kitten. Some of those succubus genes were buried real deep.

I was beginning to feel awkward under that dark gaze, his eyes searching my face. Fuck, maybe the guys had been wrong. Maybe it wasn't desire he felt at all, just simple appreciation like I'd thought.

Dammit, had I just made this super weird forever?

"Gah, I've totally misread this. Just forget—"

Orthus cut me off, launching toward me and covering my mouth with his. I was glad I didn't need to breathe, because I gasped as he kissed me hard, possessively. His teeth tugged at my bottom lip, and I felt Vali groan against my ear. Orthus didn't say anything as he pulled his mouth away and sank further into the water, taking my nipple between his teeth.

"Holy fucking hellhound," I breathed as my whole body jolted against the assault of his mouth on my breast. I buried my hands in his short black hair.

Vali decided to make his move, his lips running across my shoulders and nape, his hands moving from my waist down over my hips. "If you want to stop, just say the word."

Orthus's teeth scraped across one of my nipples, making me curl closer. "For the sweet love of Baby Yoda, *do not stop*," I gasped out.

Vali turned my face to his, and for the first time, I could see the demon in him, because the look on his face was pure devil. "You heard her, O. This is our chance."

The chance for what? I didn't know, and at that point, I didn't care.

Orthus's hands moved to my thighs, and he lifted me until I was floating on my back again. My nipples ached, making even the breeze against them feel good. One of Vali's arms slid under my neck, keeping me out of the water, and the other hand came up to stroke a finger over my collarbone and down between my breasts, making goosebumps rise across my skin.

"Do you know how beautiful you looked floating in the water a few moments ago? My cock ached with a need I haven't felt in so, so long. I wanted to be buried inside you, your body warming me even as the water is cold around us." He groaned. "Even just the thought makes my dick throb."

I was distracted from answering by Orthus's fingers hooking under the waistband of my panties and dragging them down my legs, tossing them onto the bank. Then he hesitated.

I lifted my foot, rubbing it against his side. "Are you sure? I don't want you to feel..." Obligated? Overwhelmed by the sex pheromones that I knew Vali and I were throwing off together?

Orthus caught my foot and lifted it over his shoulder. Then the other one went over his other shoulder. "I've wanted to do this since you stood in that dressing room, staring at my cock, and telling me you didn't want to fuck me." He kissed my inner thigh. "So fucking pretty, all perfection begging for my hands, looking at me like you wanted me to fuck you against the wall, but your words were all prim and proper." He groaned, biting hard on the soft fleshy part of my thigh. "God, I wanted you. A vampire of all fucking things, and I wanted you so damn bad."

His tongue darted out to trace the seam of my pussy, and I moaned, throwing my head back and meeting Vali's hooded eyes. He leaned down and kissed me again, even as Orthus continued, his tongue flicking over my clit.

"Sitting up in my room as your mates fucked you in the BDSM dungeon, the scent of your fucking stinging my nose and making my cock so goddamn hard, I couldn't jack off fast enough to get any relief." His tongue flicked and swirled, and I writhed in their arms. Vali's mouth moved down so he could suck my nipple hard between his lips, and I arched. Somehow, they were swirling at the same time, and it was doing shit to me. Good shit. *Oh my god, I'm going to come* type shit.

Cupping my ass, Orthus continued his slow tongue-lashing of my core as I moaned and squirmed in his hands. "Oh shit, oh shit, *oh shit,* I'm going to come…"

"Do it, Raine. Come for us." Vali pulled back and tweaked my nipple with just the right amount of pressure, and I folded in half like a cheap card table. My legs locked around Orthus's head, and he continued to lick me through my orgasm.

When my legs finally unclamped, Vali's hands dragged me through the water until I was wrapped around him, my legs around his waist and my arms around his neck. His hard cock was pressed tightly pussy, begging for entrance.

"Raine." He breathed my name like it was a prayer. "The taste of your pleasure…" He trailed off and shuddered beneath my hands. "What do you want, baby? Do you want to go back inside? We can stop here, or we can go further." His voice was strained, and honestly, no one had *asked* me if I wanted to go past third base since I was a freshman in college. It was kinda sweet.

"Vali, if you don't put your cock in me right now, I might go mad," I purred back. I took a quick moment to check in with my bonds, and sensed nothing but lust and contentment coming back at me. Wherever the guys were, they were getting the echoes of both my pleasure and Vali's. I felt high, but it must be just as bad for them. At least all the guys would know.

Vali groaned as he lifted my thigh and put it higher on his hip, his long, hard cock notching against my core. "You're everything I'd hoped for, Raine Baxter. Everything."

Then he pushed inside me and... I wasn't ready. I mean, physically, I was primed. If I'd gotten any wetter, we would have caused a flood on Fox River. No, I wasn't ready for the emotional orgasm I got from Vali.

Dumb term, but nothing else I could think of would explain the burst of bright, hot emotion that flooded my chest when he settled inside me. It was like two parts of a whole finally being reunited. Like a B-grade movie where the preppy archaeologist finally returned the keystone to the weird Incan pyramid hole or something. Lights burst forth, terrible CGI sparkles fluttered in my vision, and I came.

Hard.

Holy shit.

Vali had his face buried in my neck, his breaths just whispered curses. "Oh god... I didn't know. I didn't know," he chanted. "Too good."

How could anyone know this? He began to move,

and it was almost too much. Too much pleasure. Too much *everything*.

Vali must have felt the same, because he sent a pained look over my shoulder to Orthus. "O, do something," he gritted out, like he was in pain.

Orthus, bless his heart, delivered. He moved close to my body, his dick pressed to my lower back. His hand slid down my spine and down the seam of my ass. "This?" he whispered in my ear as a finger played with my tight hole. "Do you like this?"

I moaned out a "Yes," as I willed Vali to move. I needed *something*, even as the pleasure continued to wash over me.

"Can you take my cock?"

I nodded again. Look, I had seven mates and a lack of respect for my body's limitations. Of course I'd done anal. Several hundred times by now. The joy of being part succubus was that my body was made for taking dick. It was self-lubricating in both holes, happily adjusted to any size dick, and took multiple orgasms like a champ.

"Pull out, Vali," Orthus ordered, and Vali whined, but pulled out of me. I whined too, because it was like being stolen out of the sunshine. But then Orthus was filling me back up, his groan fluttering across my nape. "Fuck, you feel like fire." He pumped inside me a couple of times, and I didn't know if I whimpered or moaned, but it was a pathetic, needy sound.

Then he pulled out again, slipping the head of his cock along my taint and then slowly into my ass. The stretch and the burn cut through the insane cloud of euphoria, but he stayed still until I adjusted to the huge size of him.

Then Vali slid back inside my core, and my body relaxed around them both like I was drunk. High on cock. Smoking the blue vein.

They moved, and it was as if someone had thrown a toaster in the river, the way my body shook. They took it in turns, one sliding in and then the other, and I didn't know what else to do but hold on. I clutched Vali's shoulders, like I'd wash away without him.

I had my face buried so tightly against his chest that I'd probably leave a bruise. I was huffing out breaths I didn't actually need, but I was on fire. I whimpered and moaned, the sensations too much to formulate actual words, as I came over and over again.

"Fuck," Orthus grunted in my ear. "I'm going to fucking come. Vali," he groaned. "Make her orgasm." His teeth nipped my lobe, and my whole body shook. "I want to fill you with my seed while you're clenching around us, stuffed full of our cock." He flexed until he was balls deep inside me, and his wish was my command.

I came and came, and when Vali angled himself back and hit another place inside me, I continued to come until both guys were shouting their own releases into the now pitch-black dark.

We panted into the night, my body trembling, but not from cold. Vali pulled out first, kissing me hard, and there was a whole dictionary of unspoken words in the touch of his lips to mine. Orthus slid out slowly, and I whimpered. I felt so empty and achy.

"It's okay, baby. The night is still young," Vali whispered against my wet cheeks. From the river or from tears, I didn't know. We stood in the water a little longer, Vali's gentle fingers moving between my legs, helping the water clean me up a little.

Then Orthus scooped me into his arms and moved toward the rough steps that would lead us back to the house. When we reached the porch, he froze. Looking down, I saw why.

Lying on the deck was Lucius, flat on his back, his hand on his cock. He turned his head toward us, lips tilted up into a slight smile. "Didn't want to interrupt," he said softly, his eyes oddly wide and his expression slack.

I wiggled a little, and Orthus set me on the ground. I moved toward my lover, his cum soaking into the bottom of his shirt where he'd come on his abs and got a little more distance than he was counting on.

I stroked my hand over his face. "Are you okay?"

"Raine Baxter, I love you so fucking much." His eyes were completely clear of his madness. It was almost like talking to Nico. "I am better than okay. Fuck," he breathed. "That was something else." He looked down along his body. "I'm still hard. Quick, Raine, ask me to murder someone for you."

I frowned. "Anyone?" Huh, how far had my life come that I didn't even really have a hit list. You had to be careful having one of those around people who would, you know, actually hit someone. "Francois?" That vampire fuck was going down.

The self-satisfied smile on Lucius's face made me narrow my eyes. "Too late on that one, my consort. But even if it hadn't been, I have no urge to rend him limb from limb. I don't have an urge to bathe in anyone's blood. I kind of want to buy you *flowers*."

I resisted the urge to say *no, I don't like this at all*. That would be unfair and kind of cruel. I just had to get to know clear-headed Lucius.

"Do you know what I have the urge to do?" He rolled onto his stomach and then climbed onto his hands and knees, crawling toward me until he was kneeling at my feet. "I want to make love to you without biting you. I want to make love to you because I *want* to, not because I *need* to," he breathed. He tugged at my calf muscle until I lifted my foot and put it on his thigh, then he leaned forward and licked up my inner thigh, catching all the juices that were still leaking from me. As he licked, he looked up into my eyes.

I moaned. Vali moaned. Even Orthus watched the most vicious, deadly vampire in history lick cum from my thighs with heat in his eyes.

Something unclenched in my chest. Lucius still wanted me, and we'd deal with the rest as it came.

We all had sex twice more. Once on the porch, Vali sucking Orthus's dick and me riding Lucius, and then again in front of the fireplace, and I wasn't sure who fucked who then, because it was a mass of limbs and tongues and bodies.

And Lucius didn't drink from me once. He kissed me, and Vali, and even nipped at Orthus, but he didn't drink. Now he was passed out on the floor, his head pillowed on his arm, completely unfazed by his nudity or the fact he was surrounded by two other predators. The sleep of a man without voices in his head.

I shook my head in disbelief. An arm tightened around me, and I looked over my shoulder at Vali. "Believe it or not, I didn't come over to seduce you."

My skin pebbled as he huffed a laugh into my still

damp hair. It must be a wild mess. "It's nice to be seduced. I think it's the first time ever. Feels kind of nice to know someone desires me organically."

Orthus, who was lying in front of me, grunted. "I desired you organically."

"You don't count. I was your only option for about seventy years, and you know, proximity grows desire."

Orthus huffed. "No. I wanted you because you were kind and empathetic. Plus your ass was like a fucking peach, and I wanted to take a bite out of it."

It really was a nice ass. Perfectly proportioned, like it had been sculpted by a master craftsman, it was tight, hard, and honestly, I was going to sink my fangs into it one day too. Soon.

Orthus's nose twitched, and his eyelids grew heavy with desire. Oh, I knew that expression. "You best tell us what you came over for, Pebbles. Otherwise, it's going to have to wait another hour."

I didn't need to ask what we were going to do in that hour. His heavy cock lying against his stomach told its own story.

"I wanted to know how you were settling in, mostly. But also, I've been called to meet with Titus, the Convocation Member for the vampires, and it would be good if I could present you. Might take the edge off the fact we decimated an entire nest leaving Amsterdam."

Vali's thumb rubbed circles on my hip. "Want to use me as a human shield?"

"Hardly human, but no. Titus is a good guy. He helps me when I need to navigate things, and it would be nice if he met you first. Plus, he's nestmates with the Member for the witches and the Member for shifters, and if we could do this all outside of an official meeting of the Convocation, it would be beneficial, I think."

Orthus was tense. "That's a lot of powerful people," he growled softly. Was it weird that it made me want to climb onto his face?

No? Just me?

I shrugged. "They're powerful people you'll have to meet sooner or later... That is, if you still want to go ahead with your side of the agreement." The words tasted like ash on my tongue, but it was the right thing to do. "You mean more to me than a means to an end. If you don't want to take over my position, it won't change anything between us."

I'd go on being a miserable bitch every time I was called on to do something responsible, like an actual grown-up. But I wouldn't force anyone to do anything, especially not Vali. If anyone deserved to be free, and enjoy their freedom, it was him.

He held me closer, and I sighed at the warmth of him. "We had an agreement, *schatje,* and I won't go back on my word."

"*Schatje?*"

Orthus rolled his eyes. "It means 'little treasure' in Dutch. You're such a sap."

I raised an eyebrow at him. "Do I want to know why you called me Pebbles?"

He grinned, his hand reaching out to cover Vali's and then moving it up until they both cupped my breast. "In the water, your nipples were so hard, they were like little pebbles."

Vali's chest shook behind me. "Well, isn't that just the sweetest thing." He didn't even try to hide his sarcasm.

I rolled onto my back so I could see them both. "I know you stick to your word, but I want you to be happy. Not just free, and not just satisfied, but actually happy. Even if it means I have to stay on the Convocation for a little longer. Eventually, someone will come along and it's not as if my life is hard, exactly. It's just not what I imagined. Not what I'm good at."

Vali's hand slid up my body to rest on my sternum. "What makes you think I'll be better?"

It was a good question, one that I'd been thinking about for a week. Maybe the answer was a small part of the reason that I'd taken this step with him, with them.

"You went back to get Orthus, even when he was a stranger. Even when you knew it was dangerous. You buried the dead humans, even though it was time-consuming and emotionally scarring for you."

He frowned against the memories. "Anyone would have done that. It's asking for disease to leave them exposed in the streets."

I grabbed his hand and threaded my fingers through his. "Yes, but you dug individual graves when a mass one would have been better, easier. You took the time to lay them all to rest as individuals, like each of their lives mattered. That says something about you." He went to interrupt again, and I turned slightly, placing a finger over his lips. "It's the fact that you let Orthus go when he met his wife, even though you loved him, because you wanted what was best for him. It's the fact that you protected the women of the Red Light District against a serial killer, even though no one would ever know it was you."

Vali's eyes went wide, and I gave him a soft smile. "Yeah, I did the math. But it's more than that. You stood at the foot of that plane, with freedom in sight, and instead of bonding me with meaningless sex, you let me go. You didn't want to lock me into a lifelong commitment; instead, you were willing to give up your happiness for someone else's freedom. Again." I reached up and cupped his cheek. "That's why I know that our people will be safe with you. That you're strong enough to carry their burdens for them when they're too weak or pushed down to carry them for themselves any longer."

He leaned forward and kissed me softly, a barely there butterfly of a kiss. "Introduce me to your friends on the Convocation. I'm ready to begin to make a difference."

I reached back and grabbed Orthus's arm, pulling him closer to my body until he was fully wrapped around me. Tucking my nose against Vali's chest, and with my foot on Lucius's hip, I let myself drift off to sleep knowing that this was the beginning of something big, something important.

THE FIRST STEP before introducing Vali and Orthus to the Convocation was introducing them to Dark River. Honestly, that might be even more terrifying. I messaged the guys and told them what was happening, and they all promised to be there, a united front. No one would whisper about ill feelings among the group over the new guys—none of that.

Normally, I would go to the diner, but I wanted Vali and Orthus to see The Immortal Cupcake. To fall in love with Dark River through that place, the way I had.

As we climbed out of my SUV, Orthus huffed out a

rushed breath. "This place is surreal. I thought Fox Falls was cookie cutter, but this..."

Everyone was setting up for the Fall Festival, which was basically just a good excuse for us to make mulled wine that was more blood than booze, and for X to win the pie-eating contest for the fifteenth year in a row. Marcy from above the hardware store also did artistically carved pumpkins, and there were other quirky little games that the town enjoyed. Sometimes, it was just trivial little things, but it broke up the year and made everyone happy. We had one for every season.

So as I looked at the town square with its fairy lights, carefully mowed lawns, and little striped tents that will eventually hold food and games, I could imagine how it looked to an outsider. Like a story book, or the town at the beginning of a horror movie. They were oddly similar.

"It looks like it can't be real, right?"

Vali shook his head. "The vampires don't even try to hide their abilities here?"

I shook my head. We all zipped around at super speed, running around even though it was nearly five a.m.

Anyone stumbling into town usually got freaked out enough that they left straight away, but that was because when a human arrived, everyone would stand on the sides of the road and watch the car go past without blinking.

Hence the horror movie theme.

That had been Tex's idea, and I was pretty sure he still giggled every time someone tore out of town after our best rendition of *Children of the Corn*.

I gripped both Orthus and Vali's hands, dragging them toward the front of the store. "Welcome to my favorite place in the world." Well, my favorite place that didn't involve naked bodies. "The Immortal Cupcake."

The little bell jingling over the door had the townspeople inside looking up, their smiling greetings in my direction morphing into something like curiosity. I didn't stop to introduce them yet; that would come. And by that, I mean the first three people who saw Vali and Orthus would spread the word right through town and half the population would soon be in to see them like a sideshow.

Honestly, Nico and I had spent most of the morning making extra cupcakes to cover the influx of people "just stopping by for one of those cupcakes" and definitely not to gaze at the two men who sat at my table.

"Wow," Vali breathed, and I grinned. It really was wow.

I'd made The Immortal Cupcake my own. It had been nearly two decades, and while it still had touches of Angeline, it was just as much mine now as it had been hers. It had taken me a long time to get to this point, but I'd grown a lot in that time.

Walker had helped by having sex with me on almost every surface in the place. Don't worry, I wiped everything down with extra-strong disinfectant afterwards. Luckily, we didn't get health code inspectors.

"So this is the main cafe. We do mostly sandwiches, bread and cupcakes. Anything else you can get from the diner. I'll take you there next time." Baby steps. I led them through the cafe to the bookstore. "This is where I fell in love." I'd upgraded the projector last year, and now the quality of films we showed was almost as good as a cinema. "We have movie, cocktail and cupcake nights."

I looked over at Orthus, but he wasn't looking around the bookstore, he was looking at me. "You love it." It wasn't a question.

I sighed happily. "I do."

I couldn't interpret the look on his face, but it was something positive. "It's nice."

I'd been so focused on Vali, on setting him free and installing him as the Convocation Member, that I'd never asked Orthus what he wanted. I'd fix that. Everyone deserved to find a purpose in life, something that made them as happy as this store made me.

Stroking my hand down Vali's spine softly to get his attention, I tilted my head at the table that ran right along the wall of the cafe. It was our table. Enough space for all my family. "Wanna taste my cupcakes?"

Vali wandered off toward the table, and Orthus moved past me, his hand brushing across my breasts in what might have been an accidental touch if he didn't lean close and say, "I thought I already had, Pebbles."

Oh boy.

I followed behind them to the table, smiling and saying hello to people I knew, dodging their questions and quizzical looks. Along the wall were all my guys, Walker striding in the door just as I walked past. I stopped and turned into his arms.

"Hey baby, I missed you," he said against my hair, picking me up and walking me back toward the tables.

I squeezed him tightly. "Missed you too. Come over tonight?"

His hands slid down to squeeze my ass. "Try and stop me." He put me back on my feet, and I took my seat in the middle between Judge and X.

Brody was talking to Orthus, and Nico was chatting to Vali about Fox Falls. They'd all accepted them so easily, and a part of me kept wondering if it was too easy.

Judge turned to me, his brows pulled low. "What's wrong?"

I smiled brightly. "Nothing."

"Don't lie to me, Rainy Day. I know you better than that."

I sighed, pushing my hair out of my face. "I keep thinking this is too easy. I keep thinking that one day you're going to feel like this is too much and..."—I choked down the lump in my throat—"you'll leave, find someone who can focus solely on you. Make you happier than I can."

Judge huffed a noise, dragging me into his lap so he could talk softly into my ear. "Raine fucking Baxter, listen to me. If there is one thing I'm certain about, it's that you're it for me. I wandered for a century, Sugar. Nothing felt right, until *you*. I'm not going anywhere. X? A thousand percent besotted by you. Lucius is Lucius, and despite the fact he talked to me about *baseball* yesterday, he still wants you. You can see it in his eyes every time he looks at you. Both he and Nico are now enamored with you, and if you think they haven't been with every type of woman to ever exist, you're crazy." His eyes slid to Walker, who'd joined the conversation with Vali and Nico about Fox Falls. "That Sheriff didn't know how to love before you. He is a stubborn fucking fool, but he bent for you. He *loves* you. He's not going anywhere either.

"You're stuck with us, Rainy Day. All of us. None of us are hurting for love or attention, because you're unselfish perfection. You don't demand to be the center of our world. We love each other as much as you. Instead of one person to share our joy and hardships with, you've given us an entire network of love and support. You've created something special. Two more, or twenty more—it isn't going to change how we feel about you."

My Drifter. My heart.

I let out a shuddering breath, and gave him a tremulous smile. "I love you."

"Love you too, Sugar. Always."

FORTY-ONE

I was nervous. Was it weird to be nervous? What was the worst that could happen—they might say no? I'd be disappointed, but it was hard to be sad about it, given my relationship with Orthus and Vali. Even if it didn't work, this budding thing between us meant something. It was special.

We were meeting Titus and Alexander at a restaurant in Edmonton. The place was owned by shifters, so we got a private room and were able to talk freely. Miranda and Wilde had planned to come too, but apparently they'd been called to some witch emergency in New Mexico.

I sat in the restaurant with Lucius and Nico on my left, and Vali and Orthus on my right. Tex was with me too, at Alexander's request. "It's been too long since I saw my grandson. Bring him with you," had been the surly dragon's exact demand.

What Alexander wanted, Alexander got. Unless you were Tex. He often told him no, and I was sure that was half the reason Alexander loved his grandson so much—he wasn't awed by his power or reputation. To Tex, the man was just his loving grandfather, and sometimes he called him on his bullshit.

Yeah, better Tex than me. Alexander still scared the shit out of me, even after all these years.

The private dining area was upstairs in the restaurant, and from the flurry of voices downstairs, I was going to go out on a limb and say the others had arrived.

They were part of the strongest inter-race family group in history, consisting of three Convocation Members and a powerful witch, so they were basically celebrity gods in our world. Gossip about them spread like wildfire through the community, most of it not true. People held them in awed esteem, and anyone who was prejudiced about the idea of them all being a Pack kept it to themselves. You didn't fuck with those four.

Finally, the hostess showed them into our private dining room, and I got to my feet with a smile. They nodded at me, and I did a respectful bow back. Once the hostess left, I went around and kissed them on the cheek. All-powerful Convocation Members they were, but they were still family.

Titus smiled. "Raine. You look well."

I gave him a crooked grin, trying not to look at Vali and Orthus. I didn't want to give away that we'd bonded. Well, not just yet. I was going to drop that bomb gently.

I should have known better. "You added them to your harem already?" Alexander said, throwing his arms up in the air. "Aurelius and Stuart are going to have kittens about this." That made him grin. He liked needling the other Convocation Members; it kept him entertained. An entertained dragon was the best thing for the whole world.

He grabbed Tex and pulled him into a tight hug. "Kid, it's good to see you. Is that gray hair?" he teased, which made Tex elbow him in the stomach. But when Alexander met my eyes over his head, I saw the same fear in his eyes that I felt in my soul.

Tex was aging.

"Sit down. This place has amazing pizza. Dough so soft, it's like eating a cloud," Alexander said with a rumble.

Titus tilted his head at me. "Are you going to introduce us to your friends?"

I shook the extraneous thoughts from my head. "I'm sorry. Guys, this is Vali, an incubus, and his protector, Orthus. A hellhound."

Well, that got their attention. The silence in the room was loaded.

"You wanna come again with those introductions? Wilde didn't mention a hellhound," Alexander muttered.

Vali stood, holding out his hand. "Valor Vervloet. My friends call me Vali. The last incubus—well, that I'm aware of, anyway."

I tried to keep the surprise from my face that Vali was a nickname.There was still so much I didn't know about these guys, but I'd thought I had a handle on their names at least.

There was plenty of time. I wasn't worried, as long as the two men in front of me didn't catch on that I hadn't even asked his name before I put him forward as a potential Convocation Member. Realistically, it was probably proof of my ineptitude.

Orthus stood and offered his hand too. "Just Orthus. Hellhound."

Alexander shook his hand, and something tense passed between them. "Shifter?"

"Only in a very basic sense."

"Under my purview?" Yeah, this one was tough. Alexander was big and scary, and nearly eternal but not quite. The way Alexander had explained it to me once was that eventually dragons just went to sleep, but only after thousands of years. They were immortal the same way that vampires were immortal. It depended on the person and the choices they made.

But Ortheus was a hellhound and was legitimately, *actually* immortal. As was Vali now. It created a quandary, that's for sure.

Orthus shook his head. "No. I talked it over with the Alpha, and he suggests I would fall under Vali and Raine's classing, rather than yours. I'm the only one of my species on earth, and I am not physically mortal."

Alexander made a low noise in his throat, which may have been an agreement, or not. Then he shrugged. "Works for me. I don't particularly want to fight a multi-headed creature from Hell."

"Don't think you can win?" Lucius teased.

Titus turned to look at him, a curious expression on his face, but Alexander answered. "I could always eat him and we could lead together, Jonah and the Whale style."

Orthus raised a brow. "Not a good idea. Hell creatures are spicy. Not worth the indigestion."

Alexander laughed, and the tension between them dissipated. We stared at the menus as the waitress snuck into the room like we were all strapped with explosives, taking our order with shaky hands and leaving again as quickly as possible.

I told them a little about what had happened in Amsterdam, and Titus's jaw clenched at the mention of the attack by Francois. But Alexander was furious at the fact that someone had attacked Tex so blatantly. It wasn't common knowledge, their blood connection, but that was by Tex's choice and not Alexander's. If the dragon had his way, he'd declare it to the entire world so no one would ever harm a hair on Tex's head.

Tex had argued that no one would really want to, unless they already knew they could hurt Alexander by doing so. It was a convoluted circle where Alexander wanted to protect his grandson, and Tex wanted to be free.

Loving people was complicated, no matter what kind of love it was. Its complexity was what made it so satisfying when you reached that moment of happiness. You'd worked hard, overcome the things that threatened to break the tenuous connection. You'd struggled—now love was your reward.

We were having coffee after the meal when Titus finally snapped. "What is *wrong* with you?" he asked Lucius, his body tense. "There is something off, but I can't..." Lucius smiled, and Titus flinched back like he'd been struck.

"Nothing is wrong, brother," Lucius said, leaning forward further, but Titus moved away, the heavy sound of his chair scraping on the floorboards unnerving.

Nico stood, standing between his brothers. I felt like it wasn't a new move, though it was probably the first time because Lucius was being *too nice*.

Nico looked imploringly at his older brother. "It is okay, Titus. It's..." He struggled to explain the Mr. Hyde version of Lucius who was currently sitting at the table. "He's Lucius. From before."

I reached out and threaded my fingers through Lucius's, reassuring him. I hadn't reacted much better, this I knew. But it was hard to fall in love with one man, and then have another take his place. Clear-headed Lucius was thoughtful. He was funny. He was still absolutely filthy in bed and fucked me senseless, but that crazed desperation that was almost scary at times was gone.

It would take some getting used to this dichoto-mous creature, but I loved him enough that it didn't matter. He was still the man I'd fallen in love with. And despite not being a madman anymore, he was still a little bloodthirsty, which I somehow found reassuring.

The other day we'd been watching a news spot about a shooter walking into a shopping mall in Calgary, and Lucius had disappeared in an instant. Later reports said that the man had killed three, and wounded countless others before being found dead in an accessibility toilet on the third floor, from apparent self-inflicted knife wounds to the jugular.

When Lucius had returned later, speckled in blood, he'd just smiled. I was the only person who could find the smile of their blood-splattered lover to be a reassuring expression, rather than creepy as hell.

I'd asked him about it, and he'd merely shrugged. "I'm still me. But instead of the urge to kill controlling me, I control it. I find that I get quite a lot of satisfaction being the hero instead of the villain."

Then he'd fucked me into the mattress like it was his only mission in life.

Lucius's fingers squeezing mine brought me back to the present. I cleared my throat. "I don't want you to freak out—"

Alexander huffed. "Too late."

I ignored him. "But we discovered something that happens when Vali and I, uh, combine essences. The elements of my release that affect the ennui madness are multiplied by an unknown amount until it almost cures it altogether."

Titus looked at his brother as if he was seeing a ghost. Lucius's hand clamped almost painfully tight around mine as he stared at his older brother, the man who'd turned him and started him down the path to become the bloodsoaked Mad King, the boogeyman of vampirekind. I knew Titus carried an intense amount of guilt about that; Nico had told me as much.

Swallowing hard, Lucius gave him a smile that wobbled a little at the corners with sadness. "I'm so sorry, brother."

Titus shook his head furiously, stepping back until

he was out the door and down the stairs faster than my eyes could follow.

Alexander watched him go, the line of his mouth tense. Dragging his gaze back to Lucius, he nodded. "Give him time. But it's good to have you back, old friend."

Lucius sucked in a long breath through his nose, slumping in his chair. "It's good to be back. I just didn't think it would be this hard."

"A millennia is a long time to be someone, Lucius. It'll take time for people to forget. Some people might never. But the people who matter most to you want you to be well," Alexander said firmly, before clapping his hands and getting to his feet. "Well, looks like I'm picking up the bill. See you three next week."

"The Convocation acknowledges the presence of Raine Baxter, Member for Endangered Preternatural Species."

I raised my hand as the Voice droned out my title. "Present."

The barely stifled huffs around the table entertained me no end. No point letting them forget that I annoyed the shit out of them before my big reveal. The Voice, Aquarius, looked like he wanted to strangle me with his bare hands.

Hell, maybe I'd miss this after all.

"The Member for EPS has called this meeting, so perhaps we could get on with it," Aurelius said with a sneer.

"Hey, I came when you wanted to get your dumb breeding law passed, so zip it with the drama."

"*Member Baxter*," the Voice exclaimed indignantly, and I rolled my eyes so far back into my head, I almost saw the past.

"Fine. You will all be happy to know that I've found my replacement. Hooray. Happy days." I grabbed the cake box beside me and flipped it open. The three-layer chocolate cake said *Happy Retirement (and good fucking riddance)* in baby blue piped letters across the top. "It's got French meringue buttercream. It'll make you buttercream in your pants."

Alexander boomed out a laugh, and the Voice continued to look horrified. I grinned, completely unapologetic. Hell, I might've even been a tad more extra than usual.

"At the last Convocation meeting, you said if I could find a replacement who was as strong, or stronger than me, then you would be willing to consider them for my position as Member of Endangered Preternatural Species. You guys are in luck; he'll complete the sausage fest because he has a dick." A nice one at that. "Gentlemen and Aurelius..."—the Fae leader growled at the inference—"may I present, all the way from Europe, the Night Demon."

We'd agreed that Vali would enter in his full incubus form, his wings held high and wide, his tail whipping behind him. Was it weird that I really, really wanted to fuck him in this form? Like, *really*.

Vali's eyes slid to me as he picked up the lust in our

bond. I could see them dancing with desire, but the rest of his face was shut down tight in a fierce expression. Goddamn, he was hot.

The Voice gasped. "An incubus? I thought they were extinct."

I did jazz hands, with a stupid, smug grin on my face. "Surprise! They aren't. *And* he's a pure-blood incubus with immortality to boot."

Aurelius looked between us. "You've bonded with him?"

Fuck, how did he know that? I hated the Fae princeling with his holier-than-thou attitude, but he was powerful and he did tend to just *know* things. I thought he might have a touch of the sight.

Aquarius narrowed his eyes. "It is the opinion of the Voice that this new candidate isn't as strong as the current Member for Endangered Preternatural Species."

Wilde threw his hands in the air. "Are you *serious* right now, Aquarius? You've been trying to get rid of her for two damn decades, and now you're putting up a fight about it?"

I stared at Aquarius like he'd grown two heads. "This is *clearly* the best candidate for the job. He has fucking wings like harpoons. He could make you all strip off and have an orgy, and you'd thank him at the end." I waved my hand in the direction of Vali. "I have vampirism and a bad attitude. And you don't think he's a better option than me?"

Vali placed a reassuring hand on my shoulder, squeezing tightly. "It is an honor to meet you all. Perhaps I can answer any questions that might assure you of my ability to undertake this role?"

Aurelius leaned back in his seat, and I just *knew* I wasn't going to like the next thing to come out of his mouth. "I'm sure we all have many questions for you, incubus, but that isn't how we settle these kinds of questions here. There's only one way to settle a question of competency. Voice, I request a Supremacy Battle to the death."

Whoop, there it was.

I glared at the fucking Member for the Fae. "Just so you know, I hate you."

He smirked back. "Duly noted."

Turns out, no one had to die. If neither party wanted to battle to the death, then they could just battle until one conceded. Stepping foot into the arena and saying "I concede" didn't count either—I'd asked.

Despite everyone's protests, Supremacy Battles were mandatory. Accepting the call for the battle was one of the primary powers of the Voice, and didn't need the consensus of a Convocation vote.

I really hated politics.

Apparently, it had to be undertaken immediately to prevent the parties from engaging in any under-handed tactics like power boosts or whatever, and I wanted to throat-punch Aquarius. Fucking douchenozzle. He'd been almost gleeful as he'd called for the meeting to shift to the damn underground arena we had for this purpose. Apparently, every Convocation office had one, just in case.

"This is so dumb. I don't want to fight you," I muttered to Vali as we sat off to the side while everyone got settled. Orthus was busy pacing back and forth in front of us, his face folded into a frown.

Vali frowned. "If you think I'm going to lay a single hand on you, then you don't know me at all. You're bonded to me. It would be like hurting myself, but worse."

This right here was what I hated about politics. It was like a sinkhole of outdated traditions that you couldn't escape, even if you tried.

"It'll be fine, Vali. I just need you to bang me up a little. Think of it like rough sex. Wild foreplay." He gave me an unimpressed look, and I shrugged. "I have five vampire consorts. A bit of blood during sex means a good time."

Orthus growled. "Not helpful."

Yeah, Orthus wasn't taking this well. He'd almost gotten his head chopped off when we told him, because he'd immediately launched himself at Aquarius. It was only Alexander's firm hand on his arm, pulling him down the hall, that had stopped him from getting a treason charge.

"Stop stressing so much. He just has to throw a few hits in, and I'll run around and look impressive, and then after an appropriate amount of time, I'll concede. Easy-peasy."

I definitely didn't feel that laidback about this, and it wasn't going to be that easy at all, but an enraged hellhound helped no one.

"Let's get this done," someone called, and I turned to see a grumpy-looking Alexander perched on his damn throne. He wasn't impressed about this either, nor was Titus. Who knew what the fuck impressed Wilde? Fresh eye of newt maybe? But his lips were a tight line, so I was going to pretend he was outraged on my behalf.

They were eyeing Vali like this might have been his plan all along, and I totally got it. They didn't know him, but there definitely would've been easier ways to whack me than this. Honestly, if this really had been a grand scheme to have me killed and to usurp my place, I'd probably be impressed by his commitment.

I stood, stretching, then walked over and hugged Orthus. "It's going to be okay. But *do not interfere*. Do you hear me?" He wouldn't meet my eyes, so I gripped his chin and dragged his face to mine. "I can get banged around a little, and then we can all go home tonight, have wild celebratory sex and maybe some cake, and wake up happy tomorrow." I stroked a thumb over his sharp cheekbone. "Or you can do something stupid, get yourself thrown into Convocation prison and probably executed—or whatever they do to immortals—and Vali and I can mourn you forever. Do you need to ask which ending we'd prefer?"

A huge breath fanned over my face, and he dragged me to his body, holding me tight. He just kept holding me, and I wondered if I'd have to wiggle out of his arms. Finally, he let me go and grabbed Vali, dragging him into his arms too. He whispered something in his ear, and Vali nodded.

I looked at Alexander, then flicked my eyes to Orthus. I hoped he could read my expression as I mentally begged him to stop Orthus from doing anything stupid. Our relationship might be new, but I knew one thing about Orthus: he found it hard to stand by when people were being hurt or suffering. It was one of the things I really admired about him.

But I swore on the Ghost of Heath Ledger that I would kick his ass if I had to start a fight with the entire Convocation to save him.

Vali and I stood in the middle of the arena, and I lifted my chin, glaring at the men sitting in the seats above us. "Are you not entertained?!" I shouted in my best Australian accent. They looked down at me blankly, though Vali chuckled beside me. "Really? Come on, you guys. Gladiator? No?" I huffed. Honestly, there was no hope for these people. "Let's get on with it."

The Voice stood. "For the seat of Endangered Preternatural Species, may the Battle of Supremacy begin."

I turned to face Vali. "Just like rough sex. Winner gets to give the loser oral for the rest of the month."

"But you want me to win."

I grinned at him. "I want us all to win."

I launched myself at him, and instead of dodging, he caught me around my waist and kissed me. His wings came around me as he dropped us to the ground.

"This is not how you fight," I growled against his throat.

"Bite me," he whispered back, so I did. Not a vicious kind of bite you'd use in a fight, but the kind you used on a lover. The only person who'd instantly have known the difference was Titus. Doing what he asked, I sank my fangs into Vali's throat, and he made a moaning noise that immediately made me wet.

"I've got an idea—it has the potential to blow up in all our faces, but go with it, okay?" He said the whole sentence in a moan, and I felt his dick hardening against my thigh. Hopefully, they just thought he was moaning in pain. Rolling me onto my back, he grinned down at me. "Let's show them why coition demons were really feared so long ago."

With that, his wings went wide, and his tail whipped around to hold my wrists above my head. Oh. Okay then. That was flipping fire.

"Ready?" I felt the bond in my chest flare at his question. "They'll not underestimate us again." Then he swooped down and kissed me.

Even I felt the mushroom cloud of lust that burst from our embrace. I strained my power, molding it to my will. I wanted to use it to incapacitate the Convocation, to bring them to their knees with delirious pleasure. I wanted them to want my pleasure more than their next breath. It was so intense, my skin felt like it was alive with electricity.

My body rolled against Vali's, and energy seemed to crackle in the air around us. My hands ran over his straining shoulders as he climbed to his feet, his hands still gripping me tightly. Power roared in my ears, and Vali's wings glowed with it.

I was just sensation at this point. The taste of Vali's lips on mine.

The feel of his hard body between my thighs.

The sound of our combined moans.

We were feral with power, clothes divested, hands roaming. It wasn't until someone gripped the back of Vali's blond hair and yanked his mouth away from mine that sense trickled back into my brain.

I saw Orthus, gritting his teeth beside us. "Control... it," he growled, his skin rippling, his face a mask of pleasure and pain.

Vali's hands dropped me, only his tail wrapped around my wrists keeping me upright until I got my legs to work. I looked around the room, and my stomach sank.

We might have fucked up.

CHAPTER
FORTY-THREE

How to know you've fucked up, maybe just a little.

Sign number one: the Voice was on the floor with his hands down his pants and, I shit you not, cum in his eyebrows. I mean, the guy must have had some serious backlog to create that much pressure.

Sign number two: an enraged Convocation leader was giving you resting witch face. Wilde was going to kick my ass for months about this.

Sign number three, and this one was probably the worst: the Convocation Member for the Fae was giving it to the Convocation Member for the Djinn, and they were not stopping.

Oh. Shit.

The thing about my power was that the pleasure was compulsive, but it couldn't make you do things that you didn't already want to do. It wasn't a gross, violent power. You'd definitely try and jerk off—in fact, you wouldn't want to do anything *but* jerk off. However, my power wouldn't make you force someone, or compel you to submit to someone you didn't already desire with great need.

But if before, my power had been a gentle shove in the direction of one's desires, then Vali and I together were like a battering ram.

"I concede?" I said, but not nearly as forcefully as I'd like.

Alexander's skin was rippling with scales—black, green, blue—and he was breathing hard through his nose.

Eek, we were so dead.

I immediately tamped down the rest of my power, and I felt Vali rein in his too. But the Djinn and Fae politicians kept going. Damn, this was gonna be awkward.

The Voice sat up, tucking away his weird little wrinkled dick and wiping cum off his face with the sleeve of his robe. The silence in the room was intense.

At least until someone started clapping.

All eyes flicked to the other side of the room, and I sucked in a sharp breath. Vali went dead still, like a rabbit in the beam of a spotlight. I didn't know what to do. What to say.

Lucifer was here, and he had the biggest grin on his face.

"Holy home, I'm so glad I chose today's meeting to come to. A little birdie told me you might need my support to have a quorum in your favor, but I didn't expect a show."

The Fae and the Djinn finally jerked apart, and I averted my eyes. I kind of felt a little guilty, even though they had tried to make me fight my lover to the death.

Lucifer was leaning back on his throne, which somehow just seemed too small for him, his legs propped over one of the arms like he was in front of his television and not watching the most powerful supernaturals in the world go at it like bunnies. He seemed completely unaffected.

"You're right, Raine Baxter, last of the succubi. Your powers have no effect on me. You're born of the original sin, and am I not the King of Sinners?"

He'd read my mind. Holy fuck.

Lucifer's eyes turned to the man beside me. "Vali. It is good to see you out of your shackles."

Vali actually smiled at the King of Hell. If I didn't have the bond, I wouldn't even know how shit scared he was. "It is good to be free."

"I didn't think you'd be tying yourself to a different lodestone so soon," Lucifer said flatly, his eyes sliding to the Convocation Members beside him.

"I would have agreed to anything to be free, sir, and now I'd do just about anything for another reason." Vali's hand tensed in mine, and I squeezed it reassuringly.

"Ah, I see. Some bindings set you free in their own way," Lucius replied softly. "Orthus!"

Orthus was fighting the change. "My lord."

Lucifer waved a hand. "Stop it. We aren't in Hell now. Call me Luc." He put both feet back on the floor and leaned forward, elbows on thighs, his chin resting on his steepled fingers. "I'm so glad I caught you today, and not just because it's amusing to watch the Fae and the Djinn avoid eye contact like they didn't just enjoy carnal relations."

My eyes flew to Aurelius and Stuart. They both looked embarrassed and so fucking angry that I knew there'd be retribution for this.

Orthus cleared his throat, drawing everyone's eyes back in our direction, including Lucifer's. So fucking brave, this one. "It's good to see you too, Luc."

"Now you've absolved your debt to the incubus, I wanted to offer you your place back in the Elysian Fields. I know your family misses you. I'm extremely upset you were ever summoned. Such a gap in our security," he muttered to himself. Then he looked at Wilde. "If your kind ever tries it again, I *will* decimate your entire species."

Wilde had giant balls of steel, because he just shrugged. Shrugged! "No one has been that stupid since."

Luc nodded. "Keep it that way."

My eyes went to Orthus, and he was frozen in place. Was he considering leaving us? Did he want to go home?

Would I beg him to stay?

I wanted to. I wanted to get down on my knees and tell him that Vali and I could make him happy, but Vali's hand on my arm stilled me. His eyes were filled with unshed tears as he watched the side of Orthus's face, clearly struggling with the decision. I didn't even know he had a family, one that he'd clearly been stolen from several hundred years ago.

I willed him to look at me, just so I could read his face.

I couldn't even feel the faint shadow of Orthus in my bond with Vali, so I knew one of them had shut it down. Was it Vali, trying not to sway Orthus with his pain? And he *was* in pain. Or was it Orthus, hiding his thoughts from us because he really wanted to go home?

The uncertainty was like an elephant on my chest.

Finally, he looked over at us, and what I saw in his eyes stole the oxygen from my lungs.

Love.

"Thank you, sir, but my heart is here now. Please, give my love to my family. Tell them I'm happy."

When Lucifer smiled, it was a disconcerting expression that made you want to cower in your seat. "Will do. Or at least, I'll get Ace to do it. She's much better at sentimental things." His head whipped to the side, and he stared at the Djinn Member. Stuart looked like he was about to pee himself under the glare of the literal Devil's scrutiny. "You are going to want to stop that thought right there."

Stuart hadn't even said anything. Lucifer's ability to read your thoughts was... terrifying.

Luc jumped down into the arena, and when he landed, he had wings. Enormous, pitch-black wings, so dark they sucked the light out of the room in a way that made my insides feel wrong. He strolled around me and Vali, and I locked my knees to keep from shaking.

"Orthus is one of mine, and if you must categorize him, he would fall under the Deity purview. He is eternal. *You* are not." His eyes were back on Stuart. "Any plans you have of running your little Supremacy Battle to pit him against the dragon ends here."

I glared at Stuart. That fucking piece of *shit*. Orthus

let out an impressive growl that was only eclipsed by the actual smoke coming from Alexander's nose.

Oh yeah, Stuart was going to remember this.

Lucifer stopped in front of us. "Do you know you were originally my creations? There are still more of your kind in Hell, but you are the last of your kind on earth." He gave me a lopsided smile. "I think even Ace would like you, and she hates the succubi. It would be a shame for the earthly plane to lose the last two of my creations. Such a pretty matching pair."

He looked back up at the dais around the arena. "These two are under my protection. They are my creations, and I would be *extremely* displeased if anything were to happen to them as a result of today's battle, which *you* insisted upon. As my consort would say, one doesn't shit in the nest and then complain that it stinks." Lucifer grinned like a man in love, and honestly, it was disconcerting as hell. What kind of woman could make the Devil smile like that?

The question became irrelevant as Lucifer stretched his wings, and with it, his power. It was barely contained in his earthly body, and I began to whimper, falling to my knees, Vali and Orthus bracketing my body.

"You have power because I allow it. You rule because I choose not to. If anyone would like to Battle for Supremacy now, please, let them step forward."

No one moved. They might be pompous assholes most of the time, but they weren't fools.

"No? Well then, I've been gone from Hell too long. Until next time." Then he wrapped his wings around himself and disappeared, as if he'd never been here. I collapsed onto my back, heaving in deep breaths.

The silence in the arena was taut with unspoken fear and anger. "I move that Vali and Raine rule in the position together. They are a gemini pair, and therefore their vote will count only for one. If they can't agree, their vote is null," Wilde said loudly.

"Seconded," Alexander groaned out.

"I concur," Titus added, his chest heaving.

I... What? That was *not* what I wanted. But honestly... it was better than what I'd expected to happen after they suggested we fight to the freaking death. I heaved a sigh. I'd take it, and we'd figure out logistics later. "Agreed."

The scratchy sound of the Voice speaking echoed around the arenas walls. "Motion passed. Convocation dismissed."

Everyone disappeared at supernatural speed, leaving me and the guys still lying on the arena floor. "That was..." Vali started, but paused. Describing it was pointless.

"Fucking *reckless*," Orthus growled. "What the hell were you two thinking?"

I laughed, the hysterical kind of sound that only

came when your adrenaline crashed after something traumatic. "I was thinking with my lady balls."

Vali began laughing along with me, and soon, we were all hysterical on the floor.

Eventually, Orthus scooped me up off the ground and started walking toward the large entrance doors. "Let's get the fuck out of here."

I snuggled into his chest. "Let's go home."

EPILOGUE

"Stop pacing! You're making me tense," Tex teased, but it was easy for him to say. I'd been planning this night for months, and I wanted it to be perfect. The moon was full, and everyone was here in Dark River, at the main house. I had what I wanted to say planned, right down to the amount of breaths between words.

In short, I was nervous as hell.

"You don't have to be," Tex said soothingly, and I realized I was talking out loud. He stepped toward me, pulling me into his arms. "This is what you want, right?"

"Absolutely." There was no doubt in my mind that I was making the right decision.

"You feel amazing, you smell divine, and you're going to knock his socks off." He kissed my temple, careful not to ruin my makeup. "Let's go—everyone's here, and Judge cracked out the moonshine already."

Ugh, so we only had thirty minutes until someone was drunk off their ass. I wanted them all sober for this. I strode out onto the back deck of my little black cottage in my favorite town in the whole world. I looked out over the nine—freaking *nine!*—men who loved me and each other more than I could've ever hoped for.

The kids had been here all afternoon, getting to know Vali and Orthus, and although I didn't think they'd ever be as close to them as they were to the rest of the guys, they seemed to like each other. Carmen got on fabulously well with Orthus, especially once she'd found out he used to cage fight and they could bond over their shared pastime. I shuddered at the thought that my baby had been cage fighting fully grown supernaturals. As a teenager. The things that could have happened...

Enit seemed to sense something in Vali, so she'd spent the entire afternoon talking to him about her rescue work before heading home to her Pack.

Christopher had stomped around, looking somber, and there was something up with him. I saw Brody watching him out of the corner of his eye too, and when he gave me a nod, I knew he'd talk to him.

Once the kids all went home, the only people left were the ones who somehow co-shared my heart. That was the real beautiful thing about our polyamorous relationship. Not the sex—though that was amazing —or the shared streaming accounts, which was also cool. No, it was the amount of love, the sharing of responsibilities, being there to give each other a hand over hurdles... Those were the truly wonderful things about my life and the crazy relationships I'd found myself in.

This was unconventional, sure, but there was so much joy that it was hard to ever view it as a bad thing. Somehow, this little family became what everyone needed, helped soothe our demons, and bred happiness like rabbits under the full moon.

I cleared my throat, my eyes finding Vali's. He gave me a wink; he knew my plan and had given me his wholehearted approval. I sucked in a deep breath. "Guys! Listen up!"

Tex snickered from behind me. Okay, so not a romantic start, but I could come back from that.

"I, uh..." My eyes found Orthus's, and my brain went blank. There was nothing there but the white-hot buzz of nerves and desire and love. "I want to tell you something... *ask* you something."

"If you're gonna tell us you're pregnant, Red, I'm gonna have to ask for proof and someone should call the Vatican." Judge elbowed X in the ribs, and he mimed zipping his lips.

I stepped toward Orthus. "I know this is kind of

unconventional, but Orthus, I wanted to know... I mean, I was kind of hoping..." Fuck, I was bungling this so bad. Fuck, fuck. I stared up at the moon, like it had the words I wanted to say written across its pock-marked surface.

"Dammit, I'm screwing this up. But it's because I love you and I wanted tonight to be perfect, so I could ask you to bond with me, and we could look back on it in a hundred years' time and I could tell you how much it meant to me. I want to bond with you so you *know* I love you, and I know when you're happy, or when you're sad. That you can feel what I feel for you without needing the words. And I hope that you might love me too—or if you don't know, that you feel even a little bit of what I do—"

Lips pressing firmly against mine cut me off. Arms wrapped around my waist, and I knew just by the feel of those arms that it was Orthus. I'd know those lips with my eyes closed, surrounded by a hundred other people.

"I'd be honored to be your mate, Pebbles. I'd love to be in this Pack forever, as long as I can spend forever with you."

Relief whooshed out of me, and I kissed him again, elated. The guys cheered behind me, X catcalling us. I could feel Vali's joy, and the happiness that flowed down the bonds with my shifters.

When I pulled back, I looked around at my

vampire lovers, at their wide, happy smiles. Vali was the first to come over and hug us, but then one by one, they all came.

Surprisingly, Orthus's love language was touch, and he soaked up their embraces like a sponge—or like a man who'd been denied that touch from anyone but Vali for so long. Not that he didn't love Vali; I think even now, I probably still came second to the incubus. But I didn't mind. We had centuries to learn to love each other on that deep, visceral level.

Brody kissed my temple and slapped him on the back. "Welcome to the Pack, friend."

Tex hugged us both. "About damn time," he grumbled beneath his breath, but his face was cracked into a wide, beautiful smile.

Judge came up, shaking hands and kissing my cheek. "Welcome to the sausage factory, brother. One day you'll wake up smiling, and you won't know exactly why, but you'll know it has everything to do with Rainy Day here."

Gah, that sweet Southern bastard was going to make me cry.

Nico hugged us both. "It's where you're meant to be." No one even commented on the fact that he was wearing a shirt with X's face all over it. X had gotten it for him for Christmas because he was a dick like that, and I loved that Nico still wore it anyway.

Lucius planted a kiss on my lips and then a hard,

quick one on Orthus, which made me laugh. He didn't need words, my not-crazy-anymore lover.

X grinned, wrapping us both in his huge arms. "You know what this means, right?" I rolled my eyes, because I definitely knew what was coming. "Pack orgy! Gotta celebrate our boy O in the proper manner, in all our sweaty, naked glory." He looked Orthus up and down. "How do you feel about ropes?"

Orthus laughed. "Pretty good if I'm the one tying them."

X rubbed his chin. "I'm okay with that. With seven people to suspend from the roof now, it's hard fucking work. It's tough being the maestro, you know. I could use an extra set of hands."

Walker nudged him out of the way. "If you think you're tying me anywhere, you're out of your mind," he snarked at X, before smiling at me and Orthus. "I knew this day would come. I'm happy for both of you. I'm happy for all of us. Lord knows, we need an entire army to keep Raine out of trouble."

I frowned, shoving at his chest, although he didn't move an inch. He grinned, and I couldn't help but laugh. "I mean, you're not wrong, but try not to scare him away *before* we bond, yeah?" Orthus's arm tightened around me, and I panicked again. Shit, maybe it was too soon to talk about the actual act. "I mean, whenever you're ready. It doesn't have to be now. We can wait until whenever you like."

Orthus spun me in his arms, clutching me close. "I've waited long enough. I'm ready for my happily ever after now."

And that was how I ended up naked, on my back lawn, under the light of the full moon, with Orthus's teeth in my shoulder and his cock pounding into me, making me his. In that moment, as the bond snapped into place, I knew that I'd found my happily ever after too. In this place, in these men.

Who could ask for more?

ABOUT THE AUTHOR

Grace McGinty is eclectic. She has worked as a chocolatier, a librarian, a forensic accountant and finally a writer. Like her professional career, the genres she writes are also eclectic. She writes romance, reverse harem romance, fantasy, contemporary young adult and new adult books.

She lives in rural Australia with her crazy family, an entire menagerie of pets, and will one day be crushed by the giant piles of books that litter every room.

Head over to www.gracemcginty.com and join my mailing list for sneak previews into what I am working on and to stay up-to-date with new releases and giveaways!

Not ready for this to end?

Check out chapter one of Manix (Shadow Bred Series, Book One), available in ebook and paperback now!

INTERCONNECTED SERIES LIST AND SUGGESTED READING ORDER

ALL SERIES CAN BE READ STANDALONE

Hell's Redemption Trilogy

A deal between omnipotent forces puts a dying woman in the path of the Seven Deadly Sins. The only way she can save herself is to save them all.

Damnation MC Duet

What do you do when the Angels are the demons and the Four Horsemen are your protectors?

The Azar Nazemi Trilogy

Azar just wanted to hide from the supernatural world, helping humans with her djinn fire powers. However, when the two worlds collide in the deadliest way possible, only Azar can help save them all.

Dark River Days Series

What happens when you wake up Undead in a town filled with reformed Vampires and your murderer is a citizen who is willing to kill you permanently to keep you from talking?

Black Mountain Mates

Years ago, a knock at her window sent Isla running from her home and the boys she loved. But they never gave up on finding her, and when they do, they are never going to let her go again.

Eden Academy Series

Welcome to Eden. A safe haven for the preternatural, for the lost and for the hunted. An Academy where young supes can learn who they are and grow into their powers safely. Well... almost safely.

Shadow Bred Series

The Manix have been hiding for a century, and now they were nearly extinct. Their female Omegas were all but a myth, and even female Betas were rare. That is until an impossible scent on the wind gives the entire species hope.

MANIX : SHADOW BRED BOOK ONE

GATLIN

This parking lot smelled overwhelmingly of vomit and dried bodily fluids. How the outdoors, with all this fresh mountain air, could have such overwhelming scents was truly a miracle of nature. The crumbling building, lit only with flashing neon signs, sat in the center of a lot filled with pickup trucks. To the left of my group, a couple were fucking down a side alley and the male sounded like a boar with a hot poker up its ass.

I realized why it smelled so much like puke when I stepped into a small puddle of it, and it splashed up onto the laces of my boots. Humans were fucking disgusting sometimes. I lifted my hand to motion us forward and we walked into the club, which was devoid of security at the front door.

The establishment vibrated with too much bass,

like a tribal drumbeat, and it had whipped the crowd into a frenzy. The smell of sweat and lust permeated every corner, and we tightened our formation around Raiden.

The distressed scent of an unfamiliar Omega had me growling low under my breath, and the humans who lingered too close quickly moved away. Not because they could hear the growl, but because they could feel the coiled violence that rolled off my Pack.

Finlo stepped closer to me, leaning in to be heard over the ear-shattering noise of the music. "Are we sure this is the place? Perhaps Seven's nose is broken?" the other Alpha asked.

Seven scowled, baring his teeth at Finlo. Seven was a Beta, but he was a strong Beta. Too strong. It was a generally held belief that a strong Beta would resist orders and cause problems. And it was true, Seven did cause issues at times, especially when given orders. But our Pack weren't hardcore traditionalists when it came to hierarchies. I treated Seven the way I'd treat any other Alpha—hell, any other Manix—with respect and understanding. In return, Seven was grateful to even have a Pack, even if it was one filled with misfits. He was loyal and loved, and that was worth something too.

"My nose didn't lie. There is an Omega here, one that is close to heat."

Ellar hovered over Raiden, practically glued to his

side. "I trust Seven's tracking. His nose is his best trait. Goddess knows, it isn't his winning personality," he joked, making Raiden chuckle. Unlike Seven, the family's other Beta was like me. A half-blood Manix. He'd had no other choice than to join us, because no one else would muddy their bloodlines with a half-caste.

This was us. A tiny, ill-formed Pack, except for our one crowning jewel—our Omega.

One of the last male Omegas left, he'd chosen us to be his mates. When an Omega comes of age, he is allowed to choose which Pack he joins. No one had been more shocked than us when he'd chosen ours. Until Raiden, we'd been a rag-tag bunch of mutts on the outskirts of Manix society.

I looked over my shoulder at Raiden, whose soft expression met mine. Just a look from him shored up my resolve. Although our natural instincts wanted to protect and coddle Raiden, he was a warrior in his own right. Maybe that's why he picked us. He didn't want to be pampered and adored. He wanted to fight and fuck, which was wildly un-Omega like. Despite the fact that I *knew* he could defend himself against humans, my Alpha instincts insisted that he be protected at all times. He was the heart of our Pack after all.

I scanned the crowd, but the overwhelming conflicting scents muddled everything. "We'll split up.

Raiden will come with me. Trust Seven's nose," I warned Finlo.

Finlo was my childhood best friend, and had chosen to build a Pack with me rather than join one of the more prestigious warrior Packs more suited to his bloodlines. I owed him everything.

He nodded and split off, the two Betas following behind him. I tucked Raiden closer to me as we waded further into the club. There were stages dotted around the room, each lit up with a different color. Blue, red, purple. On each stage, a woman danced, spinning around a pole. I'd been born in human society, raised here until I was eleven, and I knew what a strip club was. But Raiden didn't, and his eyes almost bulged out of his head. He shook his head at me as he grinned.

"My sire was right, the only place you could take me is into the gutter," he teased.

Yeah, not everyone had been overjoyed that Raiden had chosen my Pack. I nudged his shoulder with mine, despite the fact that I wanted to reach out and place a kiss on his temple. "Admit it, you like being dirty down here in the gutter with me."

He laughed, reaching down to squeeze my hand as we parted the crowd. "Wouldn't be anywhere else."

We were getting a few weird looks, and that was another reason we needed to split up. Together, we seemed inhuman. Ridiculously tall and broad, we looked like the warrior race we'd once been, before we were killed off and forced to flee to the mountains of Montana, forever separate until we were slowly dying out for other reasons.

Manix. We were the real reason the word manic entered the English language. It was the way early humans described the rut, where we thirsted for blood or sex, and wreaked havoc. But now there were barely two thousand of us left. Of that, there were less than a hundred full-blooded female Manix. Only twenty-five Omegas, but none of those were female.

We were dying out at a rapid rate. Which is why when Seven said he'd scented an Omega female on the wind, we'd come on this wild goose chase. I was happy to chase a wild goose if it gave my Pack a chance at a real future.

I stayed at Raiden's back, my eyes trawling in front of us for threats. "Scent anything?" I asked, despite the fact it galled me. I was half-blood, the result of a Manix male and a human female. Mating with humans was frowned upon, and according to the Manix Legion, little better than lying with a beast. As a result, I was little better than an animal to the upper crust of Manix society.

I pushed down the residual rage I felt toward the Legion and searched the crowd. Raiden tilted his head, his pupils blowing out wide. "That way," he said softly, his feet taking him in the right direction before he'd even lifted his arm. If I'd had any doubt about

Seven's nose, it disappeared at that moment. I kept my hand on Raiden's belt as he moved through the crowd with single-minded focus. He might have been the smallest of us, but he was still over six feet in height, tall in comparison to a human.

He stopped in front of a small platform, bathed in blue light so it appeared like it was in the depths of the sea. Raiden's eyes went wide and his knees nearly buckled as he looked up at the girl on the stage. Finally, her scent permeated my duller senses.

And when I scented her? My dick went rock hard.

She danced in heels that had to be six inches high, her movements easy as her body swayed to the music. She kept her eyes closed, like she could block out the world if she just deprived herself of the sight of these salivating humans.

She was small, tiny in comparison to a Manix female. Her body curved sharply though, her figure like an hourglass of old. Given the overwhelming smell of lust that hung like a cloud around us, she had a body that men would bankrupt themselves to have just a touch.

Wearing basically nothing, her scent was like a caress, followed by a slap to the face. I could feel the Omega presence, scent her oncoming heat cycle. I cast a worried look at Raiden, whose whole body was taut with the urge to rut.

Breeding in Manix society had historically

occurred in one of two ways. A female could be impregnated by a single Manix male, and would usually give birth to a solitary offspring. Or, a female and male Omega could mate during a heat cycle, and the male Omega would draw the viable eggs into himself. Afterwards, the pack would lie together during the rut and all the eggs had a chance to be fertilized. It was animalistic, feral sex that would leave the entire Pack drained and weak.

This is why the heat in a female would send us all into an insane rut, but especially Raiden, as our Pack Omega.

I noticed my Packmates on the other side of the stage, also looking up at her like she was a gift from the Goddess. She was definitely the one, and I would make her ours. Raiden was all but shaking with need, and I moved him toward the back wall so we could watch her and be obscured by the shadows a little more.

Her hips swayed with exaggeration to the music. She hooked her leg around the shiny metal pole in the center of the stage, swinging in a slow loop, her left foot barely scraping along the floor. Her breasts were barely contained in a tiny little bikini which matched the barely-there thong that both covered her intimate flesh and attracted the gaze of the audience to it.

As I searched the crowd, watching the hungry eyes of the humans, smelling their lust and violence, my

Beast rose up in my chest. They were looking at what was mine, or at least, what would be mine. I looked at the red lever beside me, secure behind its safety glass from accidental knocks. The fire alarm.

Looking over at Finlo, I lifted my chin toward the girl. Finlo would know what to do. He nodded back, so I pushed through the safety glass and pressed the fire alarm. Within seconds, there was a loud whooping noise that blared across the music, the interior fire sprinklers opening the metaphorical heavens.

Panic ensued, and there was a mass exit for the door, people pushing and shoving as they nearly trampled others to make their escape from nothing. As people turned and fled, the girl jumped off the stage, but Finlo moved incredibly fast. He gathered her up into my arms and walked out the rear exit, the girl over his shoulder, Seven and Ellar at his back.

Raiden whined as he lost sight of the other Omega, and we moved with the tail end of the panicked exodus. The rest of our Pack would get her where we needed her to be. I would just take care of Raiden.

An Omega pair... Could we really be that lucky? Raiden whined low under his breath, his hand gripping mine. "She's close, Gat. So damn close. Maybe a week? It's making my skin itch."

Female Omegas had been the first thing to die out. There were no Omega pairs left. Back when they'd found out the Omega females were dying out, we'd tried the Omegas of different species, but while they might be hierarchically the same, they weren't physiologically similar enough for there to be an Omega bonding. That had led to an uprising against us by shifters, because the Manix of the past didn't exactly ask for the Omegas nicely, which drove us further into the Mountains, isolating us even more.

It had been a bleak time in our history. Because we weren't like shifters, or other supernaturals. We were different completely, an entirely different genus. That was why the girl we'd just pulled off the stage was such a miracle, a true gift from the Goddess.

She was going to save our Pack, and then maybe, our species. But first, we had to get her to like us.